"An exciting debut!"
—Susan Plunkett, 1999 RITA Award
finalist for *Heaven's Time*

I BELIEVE I CAN FLY

Carly watched as he searched her face, his eyes intense, mirroring her own passion. *He's a kindred spirit,* she realized with a jolt.

"Never in my life have I dreamt so vividly, milady," he said, using his expressive hands as he spoke. "Until the storm wakes me, I am sailing on the air, faster than any ship I have sailed. The clouds are but an arm's reach away. Aye, the stars, too. Yet, the sea is far, far below."

The flickering flame of the bedroom candle imbued his skin and hair with an amber glow, and his robe clung to the hard lines of his powerful body. She watched him in awe, drawn to his confidence and masculinity in a way that left her breathless.

For the first time in her life, Carly understood what it meant to experience desire, true desire. The feelings she'd had before now seemed childlike and insignificant in comparison.

"A wonderfully entertaining time travel full of excitement, danger and high seas romance. Set sail for a delightful, fast-paced adventure with talented new author Susan Grant."
—Patti Berg, *USA Today* bestselling author of *Wife for a Day*

ONCE A PIRATE

SUSAN GRANT

LOVE SPELL BOOKS NEW YORK CITY

LOVE SPELL®

February 2000

Published by

Dorchester Publishing Co., Inc.
276 Fifth Avenue
New York, NY 10001

ISBN 0-505-52364-7

*I dedicate this book to my children, Connor and Courtney.
Thank you, my loves, for giving my life meaning.*

*This book is the result of the encouragement and patience
of many wonderful people: Damaris Rowland, for believing
in me from the beginning; Susan Crosby, Caroline Fyffe,
and Theresa Ragan, for being friends, critique partners,
and so much more; Captain Wade Biggs, for your expert
and enthusiastic answers to my nineteenth-century sailing
questions; and Chris Keeslar . . . because undoubtedly
"You were right."*

ONCE A PIRATE

Chapter One

The storm lifted the F-18C fighter jet like a child's toy, plucking the aircraft from the clouds and tossing it about in the wind. Lieutenant Carly Callahan braced herself. In the space of a heartbeat, the single-seat jet plunged three hundred feet, and her stomach hit her ears.

Exhilaration blended with shock. "You call that turbulence?" Carly bumped the throttles forward and pulled back on the stick. "There. Kid stuff."

In answer, clouds engulfed the fighter and snuffed out the stars. Rain hissed past in fitful bursts. Carly returned her gaze to the radar display, where pinpoints of light marked the other jets in the VFA-60 squadron, the Jolly Rogers, as they flew toward the USS *Dwight D. Eisenhower*, almost twelve hundred miles off the coast of Spain. Ahead thunderstorms showed up as blurred splotches of yellow and red—if they showed up at all. She'd trust the radar in combat any day, but it sure as heck was a crummy way to choose the best route through the weather.

Nights like this over the Atlantic Ocean demanded stamina, patience, and precision—skills that came easily to her after five years as a navy pilot. But tonight, after only two hours aloft, she was worn out.

The flight surgeon had warned her about this.

And lectured her just last week on the physical consequences of emotional exhaustion. But in the end, the doc had surrendered to her cajoling and cleared her to fly.

The sea was the best medicine.

Mom was gone; Rick, too. For once, Carly looked forward to her mandatory six months of carrier duty. She planned to forget her troubles, lose herself in the busy days onboard the city-sized ship. There'd be plenty of company—male company. Good times . . . but no time to get close. Not what the doctor ordered, but exactly what she needed. It'd be a long time before she allowed a man close enough to hurt her again. The door to her heart was boarded shut. No solicitors.

Trespassers would be shot.

Lightning flashed nearby, painfully intense. Carly blinked away white spots and flickering black specks. Harmless static discharge fanned out over the cockpit window. Eerie and curious, the blue fingers of St. Elmo's fire crept toward her.

The radar display flickered.

"Don't do this to me," she muttered through clenched teeth, staring at the screen. Without radar to guide her, it would be impossible to avoid the thunderstorms. They could rip an airplane apart.

Procedure dictated that she radio her flight leader. Her finger hesitated over the mike button. She detested asking for help. Not because the men in her squadron would think less of her—they'd earned each other's respect years ago—but because she'd rather rely on herself. There was always less risk when you didn't depend on anyone else or expect others to keep their word, to follow through—

She gave her head a curt shake. "Jolly Roger One, this is Jolly Roger Four."

"Go ahead," crackled the voice in her headset.

"My radar's acting up. Are you painting anything on yours?"

A static-filled silence, then, "Stay on your heading. There's one mother of a boomer to the south. After that it's clear sailing."

Carly exhaled. "Roger. Thanks."

Incredulous, she watched her radar display dim, then go dark. She was flying blind. *This is not good, not good.*

"Jolly Roger One, this is Jolly Roger Four," she stated calmly.

A burst of static.

"Jolly Roger One, how do you read? I've lost radar, need headings."

A prolonged sizzle, then a few clicks.

"How do you read?" she persisted, urgency slipping into her tone. "This is Jolly Roger Four. Does anyone read?" She pounded the instrument panel with her gloved fist. St. Elmo's fire erupted into shards of light within the cockpit and streamed down her arm to her chest. Prickling and burning, it coursed through her. Every hair on her body stood on end.

Her fighter plowed into a raging wall of rain and hail. She fought the bucking jet, using everything she had to keep the wings level until she burst out of the

11

clouds into the stark, starry night. The silence was overwhelming. It should have been reassuring, but it wasn't. She listened to her ragged breathing and the pulse hammering in her ears. It was quiet.

Too quiet.

Crap. Both engines had flamed out.

She accomplished an emergency restart, moving the throttles to the OFF position and then forward. The balky turbofans did not respond. She eased the jet into a shallow descent and tried again. *Nada.*

Cold trickles of fear seeped into her. *No time to be scared.* "Mayday, mayday."

She got no reply. Carly attempted the sequence for the third time. *Start, start, start, please start.*

Fifteen thousand feet and dropping.

Dread pooled in her belly. Then anger. *This can't be happening. Why won't the buggers start!*

Eight thousand . . . seven thousand . . .

Start, start, start.

Fury dissolved into grim resignation. She prepared for ejection—stowing loose equipment, tightening her seat harnesses and oxygen mask, lowering her visor, mentally reviewing the ejection procedure, all while dealing with two engines that were deader than a week-old steak.

At least she wasn't loaded down with armament or missiles. One less thing to worry about when the jet went down.

That is, if she didn't break her neck on the way out. Punching out of a plane was a risky deed at the best of times. Tonight was not one of them.

One thousand . . . eight hundred . . .

She blinked perspiration out of her eyes and pressed her back into the seat. *Now!*

She blasted from the jet like a bullet from a gun. The acceleration punched the breath from her lungs.

She met the storm head on. Rain battered her helmet. Icy needles scoured her unprotected neck. The muscles in her back stretched to their agonizing limits. Tumbling, she clutched for a handhold but caught only fistfuls of wind. Then the parachute opened, jerking her upright seconds before she slammed into the sea.

Frigid water sheathed her in agony. Darkness, pressure. Her lungs burned as she fought the almost unbearable urge to inhale. She desperately pedaled her arms and legs, couldn't tell up from down.

Her panic rose like bile. *I don't want to die.*

Then her training kicked in. She forced herself to be still and let her buoyancy bring her to the surface.

She burst through the waves. Her life raft, straining on its tether behind her, inflated automatically with a screeching hiss. She quickly discarded anything that might puncture the raft when she climbed in—her sodden parachute, the notepad she'd forgotten was strapped to her thigh.

Her oxygen mask was filling rapidly with seawater. Gagging, she tore it off and tried to raise her rain-streaked visor. It was jammed. Her throat and nose were on fire. The wind shrieked, mocking her.

Man, if this wasn't hell, it was a good facsimile.

Gulping cold, rain-splattered air, treading water, she pulled off her helmet, then wished she hadn't. Rain pummeled her face, half-blinding her, and the frosty wind numbed her ears and cheeks. She groped behind her, clawing the tether into her hand. The ragged end fluttered in her fingers. No raft! Her stomach clenched with fear and frustration.

A piece of timber drifted by, then another. Wood?

13

This far from shore? Well, it beat treading water. She waited for the next one to roll by, then seized the cold, splintery hunk. Grateful for the chance to catch her breath, to gather her wits, she closed her eyes.

But several rhythmic nearby booms jolted her upright. Wind carried the odor of burning wood toward her from where two hulking forms pitched on the waves, ghostlike in the predawn dimness. A green-orange flash arced between them, rocking her insides with another resounding explosion.

Ships! Old-fashioned wooden ships, with tall masts and rolled-up sails. She blinked to focus. The smaller one listed at an impossible angle, its sails engulfed in flames.

She was hallucinating . . . or she'd landed in the middle of a B-rated, 1940s pirate movie.

Either way, your number's up, Callahan.

Swells pushed her closer. She heard shouts and screams. Male voices. A series of pops sounded suspiciously like gunshots.

Not the kind of rescuers she had in mind, but beggars couldn't be choosers. "Help!" she cried, waving one sluggish arm. A swell toppled her piece of wood. Somehow, she hung on. "Help! Please, I need help!" Her head slammed into a whirling chunk of flotsam. She fought an unnerving sensation of falling, but the black void rushed up to meet her and swallowed her whole.

Andrew Spencer froze, cocking his head. "Did you hear that, Cuddy? A cry."

"My ears ain't as good as yours," his first mate replied, following Andrew's gaze to the battered *Merryweather.* "From the water, you suppose?"

"Aye." Andrew shielded his eyes against the rain

and urgently scanned the swells. " 'Tis her. She's jumped ship. But I cannot see fifty paces."

Again he cursed the poor light. The *Merryweather* rolled to her side, her flames turning the swells the color of blood.

Blast its crew for attacking, giving him no choice but to return fire. Now his prize, Lady Amanda, had fallen into the sea. Bloody hell. If he were to kill an innocent, he would be no better than the duke.

"Please, I need help!"

Andrew swerved his gaze toward the faint, unmistakably female cry, his heart leaping. "There!" Just off the bow, a small body clung to one of the timbers rising and falling on the waves. "Have the men hold their fire, Mr. Egan," he said, wrenching off his boots.

"Hold fire!" Cuddy shouted. "Hold fire!"

Andrew tossed off his coat, his cravat, and his gloves. Then he sucked in a mighty breath and dove into the sea.

Surfacing, gasping from the cold, he grabbed hold of the timber. "I've got you, milady. 'Tis far too stormy a night for a swim." He wrapped one arm under her chin and drew her close. Weighed down by wet clothing, her limp body offered no resistance.

Dread shoved aside the triumph, the relief he had felt upon spying her from the deck. "Come on, stay with me!" He could not afford to lose her. Urgency drove him toward his ship with powerful one-armed strokes.

Breathing heavily from his dangerous ascent up the rope ladder, he allowed two men to haul him the last few feet to the deck.

Cuddy steadied him by gripping his shoulder. "Is she dead?"

Blinking seawater out of his eyes, Andrew scrutinized the pale, shivering girl in his arms. Blood trickled from a cut just above her right ear. As he scanned lower, expecting to see twisted, sodden skirts, he found trousers and boots. "No, she's alive," he said, admiring the soul who had thought to disguise her as a man. The stinging rain kept him from further inspection of her odd attire. "I'm bringing her inside straightaway. Keep watch for Paxton's other ship."

"Aye, aye, sir."

Andrew bellowed across the deck to his steward, "Mr. Gibbons! My quarters!"

"Aye, Cap'n!"

Andrew held Amanda close to his chest to shelter her from the curious stares of the crew. Some men snickered as he passed by. He could hardly blame them, considering her grotesque black boots and the odd-looking flag and snippets of fabric sewn to her short brown leather coat. Wherever had she obtained such garments?

He kicked open the door and strode through his makeshift study to the aft bedchamber. Gibbons's heavy footfalls sounded behind him as he gently settled Amanda on his bed. Andrew inspected her injuries, probing cautiously for broken limbs.

Gibbons's dark brows lifted. "I'll fetch clothing and blankets. Bandages?"

"Not necessary. There's a scrape and a small lump, nothing more, thank heaven. I'll need fresh water to clean the wounds." Andrew straightened, massaging the sore muscles on his forearm. "And I could use a brandy, if you would be so kind."

"Aye, Cap'n."

* * *

Something was tapping her cheek. Carly flicked her hand in the air as though shooing off a fly. "Go away."

"I think not, milady," rumbled a deep, rich voice.

Pain streaked across her scalp and lodged behind her right eye. She felt weak, nauseated, and her stomach lurched ominously. Moaning, she brought her fists to her forehead. Nightmarish scenes roared through her mind. The storm, the ejection. She'd fallen into the sea—

"God's teeth, woman. You had me worried."

Slowly, she lowered her hands and opened her eyes. A broad-shouldered man leaned over her, concern evident in his blue-eyed gaze. He must have pulled her from the ocean. Even with hair hanging over his forehead and water dribbling down his nose and chin, he was a hunk. Well, she thought, if you had to be rescued, it might as well be by Adonis himself.

"You saved me," she murmured. "Thank you."

"Are you back with us, then?"

She nodded, smiling. An English accent, too. Boy, this was getting better by the minute.

Cupping her chin with a callused hand, Adonis turned her head one way then the other, his expression of vague amusement transforming into a dark and calculating scowl. Sudden awareness of her vulnerability ignited her fear. "What's wrong?" she blurted.

He lowered his hand. "I'd imagined a different wife for Richard."

Richard? He couldn't possibly mean her ex-fiancé Rick Harwood, grade-A jerk.

"You're a little long in the tooth for the duke," he went on. "I was told you were fifteen, which, as it stands, is years older than his fancy." He shrugged indifferently. "No matter. You're an acquisition, a

17

pawn in his chess game. Once Richard acquires your fortune, your looks will mean little to him."

What fortune? What was he talking about? A queer edginess forced her mind back to survival. She gave the dimly lit, stuffy room a quick and thorough scan. There was an open door opposite the bed. It led to another shadowy cabin. A possible escape route, should she need one. The furnishings were antique— lanterns, a bolted-down brazier, and an old clock. The bed was attached to the ceiling with ropes, allowing it to swing as the ship rolled.

Everything resonated with an inexplicable familiarity. Which made sense. She'd seen similar pieces in the maritime picture books she compulsively collected.

"This ship is beautifully restored," she said, willing the anxiety from her voice. "Do you use it for charters? Or fishing, maybe?"

"Fishing?" Adonis crossed his muscular arms over his chest. He was looking at her as if she was from another planet.

Okay, so he wasn't the brightest crayon in the box, but he'd been heroic enough to rescue her, so she might as well try to get along. Offering a conciliatory smile, she held out her hand. "Lieutenant Carly Callahan. I don't believe I know your name."

He coughed out a laugh.

"Is something funny?"

"Aye."

Carly jerked the wool blanket taut with white-knuckled fists. Was it possible to go from gratitude to fear to exasperation in the space of two minutes? "Who are you?"

He inclined his head in a mocking bow. "Sir Andrew Spencer."

Bitterness left over from her dirt-poor childhood—and from the man who had so recently spurned her—coiled its fingers around her stomach. She'd bet Andrew Spencer was nothing more than a conceited, titled aristocrat playing war games on an antique boat.

"I trust you recognize the name?" he inquired crisply.

"No. I'm afraid I don't."

He snorted. "Mr. Gibbons!"

An enormous black man with a cottony mop of white hair emerged from the room next door, startling her.

"Have Jonesy secure the guns," Andrew said. "Then join Cuddy at the helm."

"Aye, Cap'n." Gibbons collected a wet towel and a bowl, then backed toward the door, nodding respectfully. "Good evening, Lady Amanda."

Carly blinked. "Who's Amanda?"

"I fear you have been knocked witless," Andrew said, chuckling.

"I may have been knocked out," she shot back, "but I'm not witless." Gingerly, she probed the matted hair above her right ear and winced. "And I'm not Amanda."

"I see. Then how do you suppose you came to be swimming in the middle of the ocean?"

Talk about witless. "My plane went down near your ship. You must have heard the crash." She pointed to the patches sewn on her flight jacket. "Look. Says right here—*Lieutenant C. Callahan. U.S. Navy pilot.*"

"I am in no mood for this child's play," he said, bringing his face close to hers.

She caught his scent—masculine, a hint of sweat, brandy, the sea. His unkempt brown hair curled around his collar, and she doubted he'd seen a razor in at least a week.

19

"Your time would be better spent pondering the seriousness of your situation, Lady Amanda."

She tore her gaze from the whiskers on his jaw and met his glare. His pupils were dilated, turning his disconcerting blue eyes into unyielding black orbs. Her heart skidded to a stop.

Oh, God, he was a drug runner. Or maybe he wanted to salvage the downed jet and sell the parts. One thing was certain: She wasn't going to stick around long enough to find out.

She shoved the blanket to her waist, pushed herself upright. He reached for her. She blocked him with her arm, and he grabbed her wrist.

"Taking your leave already?" he drawled.

Run! her senses screamed, but there was no way around him. *Okay, Carly, time to think your way out of this—and fast.* She swallowed, cleared her throat. "I'd like to use your radio to contact my carrier."

His scowl deepened. "Who is Ray Dio?"

"Radio," she repeated, as though to a child.

They looked at each other long and hard, then shook their heads in identical displays of bafflement. He released her wrist, but only after gaping at her wristwatch as though he'd never seen one before.

Several shouts echoed from the deck, reminding Carly of the sinking sailboat. "By the way, what happened to that other ship? Was there an explosion?"

"Not that I am aware of."

"Were there any survivors?"

"You."

She stared at him blankly—then she opened her mouth.

He held up one hand. "Enough! You will send me to an early grave with your ceaseless babble."

20

Andrew could not imagine what her father, Lord Paxton, had been thinking when he'd hired this girl's governess. The woman must have been an uneducated native of the colonies, no doubt; that would explain Amanda's odd accent. Jamming his fingers through his hair, he paced briskly, no small feat considering the narrow space between the bed and the wall. Blast her incomprehensible chatter! He reached for his decanter and filled his glass with brandy, pausing to contemplate the woman in his bunk, who was anything but fifteen. Hair the color of moonlight spilled from her braid, a few silvered strands sticking to her moist, flushed cheeks. Her fine-boned hands were clenched.

'Twas disconcerting, but he felt as though he knew her, although, to his knowledge, they had never met. "Milady," he said quietly, "when you are not reciting gibberish, you are quite an enchanting creature."

Her golden-brown eyes darkened with fury.

Andrew smiled and took a sip of brandy. After sighting the *Merryweather* off the coast of Spain, he'd dispatched two men to Malta on one of the longboats. By now, they were well on their way to London—and Richard—with the ransom note. It was long overdue, but the duke would pay. Aye, he would pay for the lives he had destroyed. Finally, Andrew had gained the upper hand, possessed what the duke so desperately wanted. Ah, how he looked forward to dangling the sweet bait all the way to Emerald Isle.

First, however, he must determine whether a second ship had accompanied her. If he could cripple another of Lord Paxton's vessels, it would further disgrace Richard, demonstrating that the cur was incapable of protecting his future father-in-law's interests. Sighing contentedly, Andrew nursed the pleasant thought.

The smell of wet wool reached his nostrils as he settled onto a chair and propped his rugged boots on the bed. "Now, *I* will ask the questions, milady."

In response, she folded her arms over her chest and thrust her chin in the air. He chuckled. It would not take long to whittle the chit down to size. Indeed, in a scant two minutes he'd have her bawling like a babe.

"Carly Ann Callahan, Lieutenant, 242-54-1879," she repeated calmly.

Andrew shot to his feet, nearly knocking the chair over. A muscle in his jaw twitched, but his hand was steady as he poured another brandy. He'd expected a spoiled but submissive young girl, not this stubborn woman who willfully stood up to him. No woman had ever dared defy him, not even the spoiled bitches of the *ton*.

They had been at this for over an hour, and she hadn't given him a snippet of useful information about her father's ship. When he informed her that she'd been kidnapped, she'd prattled on and on about strange laws, Warsaw conventions, and prisoners of war. By God, she'd insisted that she'd fallen into the sea from a flying machine!

"Just let me use the radio." She watched him expectantly. "And maybe I can help you find your friend's ship, okay?"

"Who the bloody hell is 'O.K.'?" She'd mentioned the initials a dozen times. For the life of him, Andrew could not recall an acquaintance of Richard's with those initials. "Oliver . . . Oscar . . ."

"I don't know who you're talking about." Her long lashes framed eyes that were wide and without guile.

Her innocent look. He detested it.

22

"Quiet!" This was maddening. Perhaps her head wound wasn't the cause. Perhaps she was daft—a family weakness. He recalled the gossip he'd heard years ago about her now-deceased mother's antics. After a sip of brandy, he resumed his inquiries with a tenuous grip on his composure. "Shall we try again? When did the other ship depart India for England? What is the name of the vessel? What goods do they have onboard?"

"Carly Ann Callahan—"

"Blast you, woman!" He slammed down his glass. He'd been too easy on the wench. It was time to switch tactics.

Strolling to her side, he lowered himself to his knees. He touched his fingertip to her temple, then traced the line of her jaw. She shuddered, but the two clenched fists in her lap indicated her resolve.

"As I've said, I'm holding you for ransom." His voice dropped lower. "Your intended, Richard, Duke of Westridge, will hunt you down. Oh, but we'll lead him a merry chase first."

"Look, you have the wrong woman. Let me go."

Undeterred, he lifted a lock of her damp hair, rubbed it between his fingers. "Oh, no, sweeting. Not when I am so close. So close . . ." He leaned closer, until he was certain she felt his breath against her chin. "You will bring Richard to me. He needs you to breed his heir. Are you looking forward to that, Lady Amanda?"

She stiffened, and a part of him wondered why. Until now, she had held up magnificently under his barrage. Perhaps there was something in her past, something she wished to hide. Delighted, he reloaded and fired the next salvo: "Spineless Richard. A little

23

boy masquerading as a man. Ah, my lady, do you long to see your belly swell with his child?"

She swallowed hard. Her gold-flecked eyes misted over as she pressed her palm to her stomach. For a long moment there was silence between them. Then, for the first time, she glanced away.

Andrew reared back. Bloody hell. What had he said? His chest ached with the vulnerability, the grief in her eyes. What had caused her such misery? And what made him want to take her into his arms and comfort her?

No! She was no different from the duke's well-bred companions who had ruined him, the flighty aristocrats who had turned their backs while Richard had destroyed the only two people Andrew had loved.

No, he would not waste his pity on Lady Amanda.

Shoving himself to his feet, Andrew raked the fingers of both hands through his hair. "Don these dry clothes and return to my bed. Do not move from it." Shaken by his reaction to her, he shouldered open the door to the forward cabin, then kicked it closed behind him. He shrugged off his soggy shirt, yanked on his greatcoat, and stormed outside to the deck.

"Cap'n'!" Andrew's cabin boy slid the last few feet down the rain-slick mast, landing deftly on his feet. "Mr. Gibbons told me all about it! Everything she said!" As was usually the case of late, Theo's declaration ended in a squeak. The lad cleared his throat and deepened his voice. "Conked in the head, she was. In all my days, sir, I've never heard stranger words."

"In *all* your days, Theodore?" Andrew repeated, amused.

"Aye, Cap'n." Hands clasped behind his back, Theo

24

mimicked Andrew's stance while attempting to keep up with his long strides.

"I've quite a few years on you, lad, but I agree wholeheartedly. 'Tis nonsense befitting the wards of Bedlam."

Carly sagged forward, seeking peace in the darkness of her palms. It hadn't been easy, but since returning to duty, she hadn't let her sorrow interfere with flying, nor had she allowed herself to dwell on her loss. But this man had nearly toppled her with mere words and a cold-hearted stare—eyes fraught with a bitter grief that echoed her own.

Hell, that was his problem, not hers. She threw off the scratchy blanket, staggered across the cabin, and cautiously opened the door to the adjacent room. He was gone. She stepped inside, memorizing as many details as she could. Paneling covered the walls and matched the antique furniture, which had to be reproductions, because the pieces were in mint condition. Burgundy curtains ran the length of one wall and half-covered a rack that contained silverware, glasses, and decanters. There was a desk, several armchairs, a quilted blue satin robe tossed over one of them, and a brass-trimmed trunk.

Adrenaline pumped through her veins as she lifted the weighty lid and rifled through the trunk's contents. It held clothing, period costumes of some kind. Slamming the lid shut, she turned her attention to the desk. A lamp and a half-smoked cigar sat next to a veritable mountain of leather-bound books. She bypassed the volume opened on the desk, *The Elements and Practice of Rigging, Seamanship, and Naval Tactics,* and peered inside the lamp illuminating the pages. Inside was a stubby, yellowish candle, not a lightbulb. Chewing on a fingernail, she glanced around the room. No plugs, no switches, no phone jacks. Not a single sign that the twenty-first century existed here.

Maybe the storm hadn't taken out the ship's generator.

Maybe there *was* no generator.

Dread crawled along her spine, chased by an eerie, ever-present sense of déjà vu. Fingertips trembling, she brushed the throbbing lump above her ear.

Could she be dreaming this? Reliving some past life?

Yeah, right. This isn't the twilight zone. This is real life, and you're in a heap of trouble.

She resumed her search of the desk, finding old-fashioned pens, a seal with a fancy crest, a pair of wire-rimmed spectacles, but no electronics, no portable telephone, and no radio transmitter. A worn black book sat next to a bottle of ink. The captain's log. She swished through the dog-eared pages, reading as she went. Most of the records centered on one man, the duke of Westridge, and more recently, a woman, Amanda Paxton—who Andrew thought *she* was! Carly dislodged a quaint *London Times* clipping announcing Lady Amanda's engagement to the duke of Westridge. The ensuing entries, meticulous notes, detailed plans to abduct the woman.

She nervously skimmed to the last page. January 23, 1821. Today's date, she realized belatedly, but almost two hundred years in the past, matching the time frame of the other entries.

Written on pages that looked . . . new.

Carly shuddered and shoved aside the log. *It's another fake antique.* She inhaled a calming breath, then opened the outside door and stepped down to the deck. The storm had passed, but the spray-laden wind was strong enough to push her backward. Eyes watering, she squinted at the early morning sky, praying that maybe, just maybe, there would be a helicopter circling, searchlights, anything. But only Venus hovered above the silvered horizon.

Swells slammed into the ship and spray slashed horizontally over the deck, whipping her hair across her eyes. She pushed the strands aside to find dozens of men leering and laughing at her. Scruffy and hard-eyed, they looked like a gang of bikers minus the Harleys.

"Get back to work, the lot of you!" Andrew shouted from where he stood, evidently not noticing that she was the focus of their attention. In quite a different tone, he addressed the silver-haired man standing next to him. "Let us get underway again, if you please, Mr. Egan."

The older man cupped his hands around his mouth and called out a series of rapid-fire instructions.

The ragtag group sprang into action. Men scurried up and down the swaying masts, yelling incomprehensible orders one after the other as they loosened the main sails. Like enormous sheets hung out to dry, the sails thundered in the wind, then billowed and stretched taut. Ropes uncoiled. More sails unfurled. The ship tilted to one side and the wind caught and lifted her like a graceful bird.

Awed, Carly grabbed the polished wooden railing with both hands. A sailor, no more than a boy, clam-

27

bered up the tallest mast. He tore down a tattered English flag and fastened another in its place. Unfurled, the black canvas snapped in the wind, a grinning white skull above two swords.

A pirate's flag.

A shiver of fear and dread raced along her spine. "God help me," she whispered, and made the sign of the cross.

Chapter Two

"Sail ho!" cried a sailor from a lookout high up the mast. He held an antiquated telescope to one eye. Another man in the rigging echoed his call.

Hope surged through Carly. A ship had been sighted—search and rescue, surely. But where?

"Beat to quarters!" shouted the man named Egan.

The Jolly Roger came down, but no flag went up in its place. The sailors rushed off in all directions. If their anxious expressions were any indication, whatever was approaching frightened them.

Pinpricks of frozen mist scoured her cheeks, hampering her ability to scan the horizon.

Her heart lurched. A majestic, old-fashioned wooden vessel glided past. Its sails were plumped with wind, and it flew an unfamiliar flag. The moisture in her eyes blurred the ship into a mystical, ethereal beauty. She blinked, and its sails were back, as clear and real as everything else around her. Raw fear punched her in the belly.

"She's run up her colors," someone shouted.

"Aye. And she's got no reason to lie."

Evidently, that dissolved the tension, and the sailors drifted away from their battle stations.

Hands trembling, Carly backed away from the railing, her thoughts a whirlpool of denial, disbelief, fear. One antique vessel was explainable; another was unthinkable.

She must have been hurt in the ejection, knocked senseless. She was in a coma and this was her sick nightmare. Perfectly understandable. There'd been so much stress lately. Any second she'd wake up in the hospital, her body bristling with IV tubes. She gave a quick little laugh.

"Damnation! What is she doing out here?" Bare-chested, his coat swirling, damp hair whipping around his face and neck, Andrew strode toward her.

Gritting her chattering teeth, Carly forced herself to keep eye contact with him as she'd done once with a stray dog she'd feared would turn vicious. Wrapped inside her F-18, she was equal to any male foe. Here, she was nothing but a small woman armed with her wits . . . and the Glock 26 handgun hidden in her thigh pocket.

"I don't know who you are, mister, or who you think I am," she said with a bravado that was slipping fast, "but you can't hold me prisoner."

"I cannot?" He fastened the buttons on his coat one by one. "Mr. Gibbons, return her to my quarters. And bolt the door."

The white-haired man grabbed her wrist.

Carly tried to yank her arm free. "I'm not going anywhere. Not until I use your radio."

"Take her," Andrew said in a dismissive tone as he walked away, "before I weary of her game and toss her overboard."

"That's against the Geneva Convention! Don't forget, I'm a naval aviator." Addressing Gibbons, she demanded, "That ship that just sailed by—whose was it?"

" 'Twas but a Dutch merchant." Gibbons gave her wrist a gentle tug. "Come now. You need to change into dry clothing or you'll catch your death."

She followed, mute and outwardly compliant, while her thoughts raced ahead at Mach three.

A bearded man sporting a glittering gold tooth hopped down from the rigging, blocking their path. "Where ya keepin' our precious cargo?"

"Cap'n's quarters." Gibbons added pointedly, "Cap'n's orders."

The man with the black beard licked his lips, eyeing her hungrily. "Wants her close by, does he? How close? She'll be worth nothin' to us unless he keeps her in original condition."

Carly recoiled. The man resembled a child's make-believe pirate, from the sword dangling at his hip to the red bandanna on his head. But instinct warned her that he was no storybook character; he radiated as much malice as he did the odor of cheap booze.

Gibbons shoved past, and she was more than happy to follow him into the quarters she'd just fled.

He pointed to a shirt, pants, and shoes on the bedside table. "The trunks with your gowns went down with the ship. Young Theo lent you these."

Silent, Carly shoved her hands into her pockets and

31

flexed her tingling fingers. She would not change out of her flight suit. She was a captured pilot. She'd stay dressed as she was, the way she was taught in prisoner-of-war training.

Mistaking her reluctance for repugnance, Gibbons apologized. " 'Tis the best we can do, milady. We're not accustomed to having ladies aboard the *Phoenix.*" The creases around his startling green eyes deepened. "No *proper* ladies, that is."

Gibbons struck her as fatherly and friendly. Maybe he'd help her—if she played things right. "The captain and I have had a small misunderstanding," she said. "I'm sure he wouldn't mind if I used your radio. It'll only take a minute."

"Have you a fever? Aye, but I knew you'd sicken, dressed the way you are." He covered her forehead with his huge cool, dry palm.

She jerked away. "Where's your phone?"

His expression of concern dissolved into pity. "Once we're underway, the cap'n will answer your questions. Sir Andrew's a clever one, all right."

His use of her captor's title pricked her hatred of the wealthy and their vanity. "Ah, yes. Mr. Aristocrat."

"Aye, he's a duke's son, all right. But the title he gained from the war, not blood."

She perked up. Any information might help the navy with Andrew's prosecution. "The Gulf War?"

Gibbons shook his head. "Not against your Jackson in the Gulf. Cap'n fought in the Atlantic, and not a battle lost. Get your rest now, milady. Good night."

Gibbons slid the bolt into place.

So much for answers that made sense.

Shaky from exhaustion, Carly yanked off her combat boots and sodden wool socks, placing them in front of the brazier to dry. Two feet away from the stove the heat dwindled into biting dampness, cold enough to see her breath as she paced barefoot over the planked floor.

She'd bailed out of a jet two hundred miles off the coast of Spain, only to be rescued by a mob of seafaring Hell's Angels. The bizarre interrogation by their eccentric, unpredictable, and incredibly good-looking captain was simply the icing on the cake. "This would be hilarious if it wasn't so pitiful," she muttered, pushing aside the curtains to peer outside. Distant lightning pulsed on the horizon, ribbons of blue sky twisting through the clouds. The weather was clearing, which meant she was running out of time.

Nobody could survive for long in these frigid waters. If search-and-rescue didn't find her soon, they'd figure she had drowned and would call off the search. She'd become another statistic, her entire life reduced to a measly paragraph in the newspapers: *Female aviator crashes in storm. Squadronmates mourn at memorial service. No surviving family. . . .*

The door in the adjacent room banged open. Frosty air swept into the cabin along with the sound of stomping booted feet. Her heart thudded anew. The last thing she wanted was another round of questions with Mr. Egomaniac.

Carly hunkered down by her bolted door, peeking through the space between the door and the frame. The sour odor of perspiration and dirty, wet wool seeped through the narrow opening. Soundlessly, she unsnapped her thigh pocket, opened the waterproof pouch, and touched her fingertips to the handgun.

"We lost plenty in the storm, Cap'n. But we hauled most of her dowry aboard."

Black Beard! It was the man from above who had asked where they were keeping her.

"Go on, Booth," Andrew prompted.

"We're rich men . . . for awhile," the pirate boasted. "Gold coins, jewels—thar's a sapphire the size of a robin's egg. We tossed the china into the sea but kept the silver."

"Continue."

"Thar's medicine, three crates of oranges—"

"How are our men, Mr. Egan?" Andrew interrupted.

The silver-haired man she guessed was the second-in-command spoke up. "A broken bone or two, bruises. As for the *Merryweather,* it was a small crew, under a dozen. All perished. If Lady Amanda hadn't fallen overboard, we'd have lost her, too."

Andrew's mouth thinned. "Not how I prefer to do business, Cuddy."

"Aye, I know."

There was silence for a moment.

"Did you see what they had her wearin'?" another man asked, cleverly redirecting his captain's wrath.

The men howled their laughter.

Carly's cheeks grew hot.

"Why,'tis the latest thing in Delhi," the man added.

The pirates laughed harder.

"She was raised there, wasn't she?"

"Nay," Cuddy said. "She was born in London, raised in the colonies. America. She accompanied her father and sister to India seven years ago."

Great. The others believed she was Lady Amanda, too.

"What I find perplexing is that I was told she was still a girl," Andrew stated, thoughtful. "The chit is easily twenty."

"A change of pace for the duke, I'd say."

All but Andrew laughed at Cuddy's remark. He rolled the handle of his dagger between his palms. "Keep an eye on her. She's incapable of obeying orders."

"I'll watch her," Cuddy offered. "She's a pretty thing."

Andrew frowned as he cleaned his fingernails with the knife. "I expected her to be dark-haired. She's fair."

There was a muffled remark and the men laughed.

"She's warmin' your sheets, sir?" *Booth again.* "Plannin' on havin' her, then? To see if the duke's gettin' his money's worth?"

"Bed the wench?" Andrew roared with laughter. Wiping his eyes, he said huskily, "Good God. She resembles a drowned cat. Perhaps she'll improve once dry."

Carly let out a positively feline hiss, but none of them seemed to have heard. The men rose, said their good nights. Then the door slammed and all was quiet. Andrew exhaled noisily, combed his fingers through his wavy brown hair, and unbuttoned his pants. She caught a glimpse of a lean, muscled torso before averting her eyes.

When she peeked through the crack again, Andrew was dressed in the blue robe. As though he hadn't a care in the world, he poured a drink from a crystal decanter and sat at his desk to read a book.

The gale continued to howl as the sea thundered against the sides of the ship. Daylight trickled through the curtains and a small dirty window opposite the bed.

Weak from fatigue, Carly crept back to the brazier, her arms heavy, her eyes throbbing. Gingerly, she

unzipped her jacket and flight suit, peeling off the protective rubber suit she wore underneath. She had no
choice. If she didn't strip to her underwear, the seawater would rub her skin, giving her sores.

She dragged the blanket off the bed and wrapped it
around her, scooting close to the dying coals in the
brazier.

A clock ticked softly, steadily.

A heartbeat.

Her throat tightened. The sorrow always caught up
to her when she was tired, and today was no exception.
Tenderly, she smoothed one palm over her stomach as
she curled onto her side, knees drawn to her chin.
Oddly, she no longer felt frightened, only alone, very
much alone.

"All hands ahoy!"

Shouts and bells woke her. Her eyes flew open. For
a moment, her cheek pressed to the cold wood floor,
she had no idea where she was. She stood too quickly.
Her vision narrowed, and she nearly passed out. "Oh,"
she moaned. Her throat was raw, her jaw and neck
bruised from the ejection.

More shouts coaxed her to the cloudy, salt-crusted
window. The sun was directly overhead. She must
have slept for hours.

She spied Andrew, and her pulse quickened. Broad
shoulders squared, back straight, he had the air of
someone comfortable with command. The crew
snapped to his every order as though they wanted to
please him. A natural leader. She'd been around long
enough to know that men like him were rare. For that,
she grudgingly respected him.

A chill draft washed over her bare skin, dousing her

with reality: She was dressed in lace underwear on an antique sailboat crewed by biker guys somewhere in the middle of the Atlantic Ocean.

"Oh, shoot." Hastily, she donned her flight suit, still damp and caked with salt. Her boots were worse. Cold and wet, the leather abraded her blistered toes. She tried the door. Locked.

She perched on the edge of the bed until Gibbons lumbered in a short while later. One green eye was clouded over. Cataracts? The other twinkled with good humor. "Good day, Lady Amanda," he cheerfully sang out. "Would you be hungry?"

Her stomach growled at the very suggestion. "Yes, I am. I'd like something to eat."

"I haven't decided whether I shall feed you or not."

She jerked her attention to the doorway. Andrew's imposing frame loomed there, blocking the outside light. Dressed in a blue cutaway coat worn over a vest and shirt with a stand-up collar, he was the image of a regal nineteenth-century sea captain. Though his face was impassive, his eyes glittered like blue ice.

Clasping his hands behind his back, he stepped into the cabin. "Do not feed her, Mr. Gibbons," Andrew said quietly. "I want her to learn what hunger feels like."

Incredulous, Carly glanced at Gibbons, desperate to gain some insight into this latest game. The man's attention was riveted on his captain, something akin to fatherly disappointment on his face.

Andrew circled her in a silent, unnerving inspection, his powerful thigh muscles flexing beneath pants tucked into knee-high boots. The leather creaked with each step he took. "You haven't known a day of hunger in your short, privileged life. And never will, I fear. Thus, I have taken it upon myself to treat you to the experience."

The old resentment roared to the surface. The last thing she needed were hunger lessons. Andrew, on the other hand, could use a few. She'd bet he'd never worried whether his school lunch would be his one meal of the day, a meal donated by his classmates' parents, choked down to the tune of their taunting chants.

She sucked in a steadying breath. "The international laws governing prisoners of war dictate that you supply me with food and water."

"Prisoner of war? Is that what you think you are?"

Squaring her shoulders, she nodded curtly.

Andrew drew back in surprise. He'd expected tears but had seen none, only a fleeting, haunted vulnerability, now gone. In its place was the unflinching resolve of a fighter facing impossible odds. A position he knew all too well.

A rush of tenderness and respect for Richard's betrothed caught him off-guard. Recoiling at the unaccustomed sensation, he snapped, "This is most disagreeable behavior, Lady Amanda. You are far too old to cry over milk and biscuits."

Before she could fire off another volley of nonsense, he turned to his steward. "I'll see you on the deck, Mr. Gibbons."

Andrew strolled from the cabin to the deck and headed toward the bow, port side. He'd give the chit an hour or two to ponder her empty belly before having Willoughby prepare her meal. Halfway to his destination, a voice interrupted his thoughts.

"Sir!"

Andrew halted, one brow raised in question. "Yes, Mr. Gibbons?"

" 'Tis not right to torture a high-born lady." Gibbons's voice carried clear across the deck. Andrew looked around to see who had heard.

"I—"

"The men will not stand for it," Gibbons went on. "She's a lady."

"Mr. Gibbons—"

"No man on this ship shall torture any soul, high-born lady or no," a voice said. It was Cuddy, who must have heard and come over to join the rather one-sided discussion. "Have you heard a man speak of doing so, Mr. Gibbons?"

"Aye." Gibbons removed his hat, bowed his head. "The cap'n. He refuses to feed Lady Amanda, though the lass is hungry."

Andrew rolled his eyes and rested his palm on the ivory hilt of his dagger.

Cuddy looked him over with a good deal of disbelief. "Now, where would Gibbons get such a notion, sir? That's *torture!*"

Before Andrew had the chance to reply, a whoop of delight interrupted him. Theo, the cabin boy, shimmied down a mast and landed lightly before them.

"Torture? Have you sighted Lord Paxton's other vessel?" the boy asked eagerly. "After we sink the ship, will we hang the men or feed them to the sharks?"

Andrew uttered a weary groan. "No one is to be hanged or tortured, Theodore."

Gibbons brightened. "Ah, I knew you would come

39

to your senses, sir." He inclined his head toward Theo. "Cap'n intended to torture Lady Amanda."

Theo's eyes opened wide.

"Wasn't going to give the lass any food," Cuddy chimed in.

Andrew gripped the handle of his dagger with a white-knuckled fist. "I am merely administering discipline, which the chit sorely lacks."

Gibbons brows drew together in anger. "The lady needs a meal more than she needs discipline."

"She has eaten today, has she not?" Cuddy inquired.

"She's a wee bit of a thing," Gibbons added. "She needs meat on her bones else she'll blow away with the trades."

The entire matter had sailed out of control. His sole intent had been to goad the wench.

Andrew sauntered to the railing. From there, he turned and faced his men. "She's too big for her breeches. A little hunger will do no more than whittle her down to size, so to speak."

Cuddy threw his head back and laughed.

Unappreciative of his friend's mirth, Andrew scowled. They'd served on the same ships, fought side by side, caroused and shared countless bottles of spirits. Their years together had given Cuddy the uncanny advantage of being able to read Andrew's thoughts. He wondered what his friend thought he knew.

Cuddy joined him, standing shoulder to shoulder against the railing. With his thumb, he bumped his tarpaulin hat back on his head and scratched his thatch of prematurely silvered hair. "Go on, feed her, Andrew," he said under his breath. "Why try to break her spirit? What will that gain you?"

Andrew had no answer. In the space of a single day,

the woman had driven him half mad. When he wasn't aching to shake sense into her daft little head, he was dying to kiss her soundly. "I can hardly wait to dump the infuriating wench in Richard's lap."

His steward, cabin boy, and first mate frowned at him.

Damnation. "Is this mutiny, then?"

Their expressions remained unchanged.

Andrew held up his hands in surrender. "Fetch some biscuits and salted beef from Willoughby and feed the woman, then." Eyes narrowed, he glared at each man in turn. "However, do not forget that she is our cargo. *Cargo,* gentlemen. With no more rights than the crates of oranges belowdecks. Do I have your complete understanding?"

"Aye-aye," the men chorused, aiming three crisp salutes in his direction. "Cargo."

Carly shoved aside the curtains covering the large window that faced the stern. A long, lonely ribbon of foam unfurled to the horizon, a horizon empty of ships . . . below an equally empty sky. She filled her lungs with sea air scented with wood smoke, exhaling with a groan. Nothing in her training had prepared her for this.

Instinct told her this was no ordinary imprisonment. It smacked of something personal, as though she'd stumbled into the middle of a long and bitter feud.

Between Andrew and someone else. *Not* her.

Gibbons trudged through the open door into the cabin and set a tray on the bedside table. "Milady, the cap'n wants you to eat."

At the sight of the biscuits and dried meat, her stomach clenched with hunger. "Nice of him not to starve me."

"That wasn't his intent."

She snorted. "Right." Anchoring a strip of jerky with her teeth, she tore off a piece and chewed angrily. It tasted as though it had come close to spoiling but had been rescued in time by a heavy dose of salt. Regardless, she was too hungry to question the origins of her first meal in twenty-four hours.

She perched stiffly on the edge of the bed and took another bite. Gibbons watched her, his expression pleasant. A cutlass hung from a leather strap worn over his blue-and-white-striped shirt. Wide-legged canvas trousers covered his boots.

"Question for you, Mr. Gibbons."

He nodded.

She cleared her throat. "Are you guys . . . pirates?"

"Aye, that's the way of it, milady."

She nearly choked. She'd been hoping for some other answer. *Any* other answer.

The big man's good eye gleamed. "Cap'n snatched the *Phoenix* from under their very noses. They've been chasing him for three years."

"Who has?"

"Why, the Royal Navy."

A groan escaped her. Of all the ships in the Atlantic, she'd hitched a ride on a stolen maritime museum. "Tell Adonis that people are looking for me, and the first port I see, I'm swimming."

Gibbons chuckled. "Is that what you call the cap'n?"

Oops, she thought, shrugging. *Shouldn't have let that slip.*

"Adonis? Have I heard correctly?" asked an all-too-familiar deep voice.

42

Chapter Three

Delight curled Andrew's expressive mouth. "Adonis. I rather like the sound of it. Shall I call you Aphrodite, then?" His gaze drifted over her body. "The goddess of love and beauty?"

To her dismay, her cheeks warmed. "Go to hell."

"Already been there." He swaggered toward her.

She scooted backward off the bed. A mistake, for now her back was to the wall. "I'm not Lady Amanda."

He simply sighed.

"I overheard you say she was dark-haired. See this?" She lifted her waist-length braid. "Exhibit A. And listen to my accent. Do I sound British?"

"I fear not, milady." The corners of his mouth twitched as he walked to where she stood. "You were raised in America. Virginia, I believe."

"But you said my family was British. They would have spoken the Queen's English, right?"

"The King's English, I trust you mean."

"Whatever."

"Perhaps the lack of nourishment has aggravated your head wound." He took another step forward. She took another step back. "I pray your abilities will return as you heal. Else it will be a long voyage for all of us, Lady Amanda."

"My name is Carly. Lieutenant Carly Callahan."

"A man's name."

"No," she shot back. "It's Irish."

His mouth twisted wryly. "Ah, a new story. I thought you considered yourself a Jonathan."

"A what?" she asked, flabbergasted.

"A Jonathan. An American."

"I *am* American."

"Colonist upstarts, the lot of them."

Carly refused to retreat anymore from the cool, patrician way he observed her. She'd seen that holier-than-thou look before. Well, this time she wasn't going to take it. This time she was going to fight back, the way she should have all those months ago when Rick betrayed her. "This is your idea of a game, isn't it? A rich boy playing on some one else's ship. Why? Wouldn't your daddy buy you your own boat?"

Eyes igniting with fury, Andrew slammed his powerful hands onto the wall to either side of her head. Terror raced along her spine and plunged into her belly. She fought the urge to bolt past him and out the open door. "I'm a lieutenant in the U.S. Navy. If you want to keep me against all rules in the civilized world, fine. But at least give me one radio call."

Raw emotion thrummed between them, profound and painful.

Bewildered, she paused to gather her wits before continuing. "How about it?" she coaxed as politely as she could stomach. "Just one radio call."

"You think I should take you to Ray Dio?"

"I do."

Andrew felt his first twitch of doubt when Amanda raised her brows in a silent plea. Had he made an error? Could he have taken the wrong woman?

No, he had simply put the characteristics of one sister on the other. Instead of the dark-haired, clear-headed younger one, Richard was to marry the older, fairer sister. The one with porridge for brains.

A perfect match.

The light from the window illuminated Amanda's pale skin, causing the shadow of her lashes to flicker over her unblinking brown eyes. Those infernal eyes! Andrew narrowed his own in defense and leaned closer until her rapid breaths stroked his chin. Fear sparked in her gaze, but to his amazement, the little waif straightened her shoulders and set her jaw. It was time to teach her a lesson.

"Because I am a reasonable man," he explained, expelling the words through gritted teeth, "I will help you find Ray Dio." Grabbing her wrist, he pulled her away from the wall, dragging her through both cabins and out onto the deck.

Pausing outside the door to his quarters, he bellowed, "Ray Dio! Where are you, lad?" He peered up and down the deck. "Front and center! I wish to have a word with you. The lady does as well."

Carly's hopes fizzled. He couldn't be serious.

After another moment of theatrical searching, Andrew assured her, "If he's onboard, we'll find him." Clamping his hand around her wrist, he jerked her forward.

Carly tripped over a coil of rope and bounced along the deck planks like an uncooperative two-year-old.

He halted, helping her to her feet with unexpected gentleness. "Now, shall we resume our stroll?"

She answered him with a scowl.

"Ah, very good."

He led her forward at a slower pace. All the sails were being used to harness the afternoon breeze. A British flag fluttered high above, contrasting with the sun-bleached white canvas.

They crossed a small bridge leading to another, wider deck and the tallest mast. Carly remembered enough from her military history classes at Annapolis to recognize this as a nineteenth-century warship, a ship armed to the gills and ready to do battle. Like sentries spaced along the length of the deck, massive cannons faced the sea. A man sat astride one, scrubbing it with a brush.

The premonition of catastrophe that had been seeping into her consciousness flooded her now. She took another look at the pungent-smelling crew, three-fourths of whom were dressed like Halloween pirates, and the others—including the captain—who were attired like characters from a Jane Austen novel. There were no T-shirts in sight, no logos, Coke cans, or even something as simple as a wristwatch.

She was scared out of her wits.

Oblivious, Andrew towed her along. The men stared. Others roared encouragement and offered vulgar suggestions. A group of sailors that included Black Beard held their ground as Andrew forced her past. She crossed her free arm over her chest, a paltry barrier against their brawny frames.

Black Beard cupped his hand over her buttocks. "Yer keepin' the cargo in fine shape, Cap'n."

"Hands off!" Carly cried out, whirling around.

Andrew slammed Black Beard against the side of the ship, practically lifting the heavier man off his feet. "Mr. Booth, if you so much as touch her again, I shall hang you from the yardarm. Is that clear?"

"Aye," Black Beard grumbled.

Andrew tugged her away from the silent, now respectful crowd. Speechless, she gave her unexpected protector's hand a grateful squeeze. No one had ever come to her rescue like that. She was used to fending for herself, and had considered herself stronger for it. She'd never wanted to rely on someone else. Now she wasn't so sure. Hell, she wasn't sure of *anything* anymore.

At the bow, Andrew released her and strolled to the mast head. On her belly, back arched, her arms lifted to either side, the lifesize carving of a nude woman soared over the waves as spray dribbled from her cold, unyielding breasts.

"Ah, Savannah, you are exquisite," he murmured, stroking a possessive, knowing hand over her wooden calf, his thumb moving in slow, lazy circles above her ankle before easing higher.

Higher . . .

Carly saw that strong, long-fingered hand gliding over her own bare flesh, caressing her with the same tender and confident erotic skill. Bewildered, she

47

shuddered and buried her fists in her pockets, struggling to stem a rush of heated, physical yearning that was both inappropriate and inexplicable.

Andrew tilted his head toward the carving as though sharing secrets with a lover. "If there were a Ray Dio onboard, you would know, wouldn't you, dear Savannah?" After a pause, he returned his haughty gaze to Carly. "Alas, there is no Ray Dio on the *Phoenix.*"

Rubbing her wrist, Carly refused to look at him. She hated that he'd made a fool of her, hated her attraction to him even more.

The ensuing silence was as dense as morning fog.

"Milady?"

Their gazes met, held.

"Have I hurt you?" he asked quietly.

The remorse melting his glacial blue eyes puzzled her. *Don't fall for it, Carly. He's no different than the rest.*

"You haven't hurt me," she stated. "And you've made your point."

"We will reach Emerald Isle in six weeks, where you will be returned to Westridge. Until then, you have my permission to be on the deck. However, do not bother myself or my crew with Ray Dio again." He watched her carefully. "Have I made myself clear?"

"Perfectly, Captain. When I escape, it'll be without your help."

His remorse chilled into indifference. Once more, his eyes bore the weight of the world. "You know where the galley is now. Find Mr. Willoughby and have him prepare you something to eat." Without waiting for a response, he strode back to the main deck, leaving Carly alone at the bow.

The wind whipped sheets of foam across the swells and filled the amber-hued sails, pushing the *Phoenix* inexorably southward. Farther away from whatever it was that had brought her here.

Wobbly from hunger and exhaustion, she slumped next to the masthead. "Woman to woman, Savannah, how about a little advice. I'm a soldier and a pilot, not Lady Amanda. I'm about as far from an heiress as you can get. I've fought for everything that's come my way." Carly swallowed hard, then whispered, "But how the hell do I fight *this?*"

Facing the horizon, Andrew raised his telescope to one eye and scrutinized the shimmering swells. It was the sunniest, warmest weather in the week since he'd taken Lady Amanda aboard. By the end of February, they'd be nearing the equator and far hotter days. The thought pleased him. He missed sleeping under the stars and longed to abandon the cramped hammock he'd hung in his study.

"Carly! How are you?" cried Theo from nearby.

"Good God," Andrew muttered. His musings had summoned the nightmare herself. With a spring in her step, she was clearly searching for someone. He prayed she didn't head in his direction.

She responded to Theo's greeting by curling her fingers against her palm and thrusting her thumb into the air. The boy returned it in kind. Andrew's heart sank. He was afraid of this. In the short time she'd been aboard, she'd managed to worm her way into even the hardest hearts of his crew. It was inevitable, he supposed. The freckles on her little nose and her pitiful, eccentric ravings were quite endearing. Thankfully, his men were profiteers at heart. Their ultimate interest would be in the profit that would come from handing her over to the duke, not in gaining the lady's favor.

"Good day, miss," Cuddy called out. "Fine weather, ain't it?"

Exasperated, Andrew drummed his fingers on the railing. At least *he'd* never have to worry about falling prey to her charms. She stubbornly refused to change out of her ridiculous attire, and the one-piece, body-hugging thing left little to the imagination. She was slender and small-breasted, with a nice round rump, not at all like the lush women he favored. Still, she was indeed a better sight than Cuddy or Gibbons.

"Captain Spencer?"

Blast. She was on her way over to him. He hardened his countenance into a scowl. "What is it?"

"I have a request," she said.

"Allow me to guess. Another search for, ah, Ray Dio?"

Despite his disdainful tone, Carly sensed Andrew's discomfort. If nothing else, the man had a conscience, and he didn't appear to savor the memory of her unhappiness through that ordeal any more than she did. "I'd like to take a bath."

"And you're asking for my assistance? I see. I suppose I can accommodate you." His eyes glittered wickedly. "Shall I scrub your back first, or perhaps somewhere a little harder to reach?"

She blinked away the sexy image his suggestion conjured. It was bad enough that after a lifetime of independence she had to rely on this man—a wealthy man, no less—for every basic need. Having to fight her attraction to him made the situation downright unpalatable. "I'm filthy. I want to wash my hair. I want to wash my clothes." She'd been wearing the same underwear for a week, and although she used a wash-basin morning and night to clean her hands and face, her hair was matted and barely recognizable. "By the way, I found a flea on me. I think it came from your bed."

"I do not have vermin in my bed!"

Several nearby sailors glanced Andrew's way, amused.

"The sheets were changed at the beginning of the voyage," he said in a whispered growl.

She raised her eyebrows. "Well?"

"Well what?"

She plunked her hands on her hips. He stared at her. She glared back. Why was it so difficult to have a conversation with this man? His riveting blue eyes were too damned distracting—that was part of the problem. And those dimples in his cheeks sure didn't help.

"I need a tub, hot water—" She counted briskly on her fingers as she spoke. "A bar of soap and a towel. Otherwise I'll grow so ripe, you won't want to live next door anymore."

"Ah, that is a concern," he said tiredly. "Get what you need in the galley—and in the future, don't burden me with the petty details of your toilette." He went back to playing with his antique telescope.

Carly tossed her braid over her shoulder and walked off. Theo trotted up beside her. "I'm going to the galley for hot water," she said. "Want to come along?"

"Aye." Grinning, Theo shoved a striped stocking cap back on his head, allowing his reddish-blond hair to spill forward. The weather-beaten bandanna knotted just above his collar was as grubby as the rest of him.

She patted the F-18 patch on her shoulder. "Later we'll find a comfortable spot and talk jets some more."

His blue eyes flashed with anticipation. "Aye, the flying machines!"

Theo was like every other thirteen-year-old boy she'd ever met: He loved hearing about fighter jets. Yet, unlike those teenagers, he showed no grasp of twenty-first-century culture or technology. She might as well add his all-encompassing ignorance to the list she was mentally compiling. Already, there were the dates in Andrew's log; the ancient *London Times* clippings that appeared new; the crew's assertions that it was 1821. Not to mention the utter absence of modern items on the *Phoenix*.

She shuddered—perhaps from her mounting fear, perhaps from a week's worth of restless nights.

Or perhaps from the noxious odors oozing under the galley door.

Inhaling one last breath of fresh sea air, she followed Theo into the cramped galley. Vials, tins, and jars were wedged onto crooked shelves, and a pile of bloody chicken feathers was stuck to the table underneath. A pot rattled atop a scarred, rusty stove, its contents overflowing in sizzling bursts. The boiling chicken—or what she assumed was a chicken—did little to mask the smell in the room, reminiscent of the odor of a backed-up garbage disposal.

The tall, gangly cook sat on a stool. It no longer surprised her to see him using a quill pen to scratch wavering trails of indecipherable numbers on the pages of his ledger. She'd come in several times since her capture, and the man was always working.

"Hello, Mr. Willoughby," Carly said.

His wizened features softened. "Lady Amanda."

"Miss Carly," Theo corrected.

"Ah, yes. Miss Carly." Willoughby rapped his knuckles on the side of his head. Then he selected several cylindrical tins from a wooden box. Reading the labels, he logged more figures into his book.

"Would you mind heating some water for my bath? Mr. Gibbons said he'd carry the buckets to my quarters."

Willoughby set a kettle of water on the flames. He gestured to his stool. " 'Twill be a while yet. Have a seat."

Carly watched him stir the contents of a huge copper pot. The hunk of dried, salted beef had been towed overboard in a net to wash out much of the salt. Then Willoughby had boiled it all afternoon. Now he reached into the water with a ladle and scooped up a glob of the lumpy yellowish fat floating on the surface. "Fresh skimmings, milady. Fetch yourself a biscuit."

Carly's stomach roiled. "You're kind, really, but no thanks."

"I won't hear of it, milady. Eat your fill while there's the chance." He slathered a thick layer of glistening fat atop a biscuit. "I'll be selling the lot by noon tomorrow."

"You go right ahead and serve yourself, Mr. Willoughby. Don't worry about me."

He made a tsking sound and ladled the remainder of the fat into a crock to cool and congeal.

The ever-hungry Theo plucked two biscuits out of a basket, handing one to Carly as Willoughby served them soup.

"If you won't take your skimmings," the cook said, "I want you to eat this. You're too thin."

53

"I don't know about that. I could live for a month off my thighs alone." Carly tapped her biscuit on the sideboard to dislodge any weevils. Hunger had almost deadened her aversion to the creatures that inhabited the bread onboard the ship, but smearing unadulterated, artery-clogging fat on her biscuit was a line she would not cross. The men, though, were more than happy to buy the coveted lumps of lard. Willoughby made a handsome profit selling it.

The curry-scented broth should have been tempting, but she didn't feel like eating. She propped her chin on her hand and pushed her spoon through the maze of turnips and bits of chicken.

Willoughby resumed his inventory of the tins. He lifted a lid and inhaled. "Ah, nutmeg. The booty from your ship is a cook's dream." He thrust the tin at her. "Smell."

She sniffed gingerly, then read the invoice attached to the box. BRITISH EAST INDIA COMPANY. SHIPPED AUGUST 1820.

Shaken, she dropped her spoon. It splashed into the pewter bowl. Vaguely disoriented, she let her eyes drift closed. The invoice was another brick in an insurmountable wall of evidence. Maybe the last brick.

In warfare as well as life, those who failed to adapt perished. If she wanted to survive this and return home, she had to accept the extraordinary possibility that she'd moved through time. There was the Bermuda Triangle, after all, and the Druids with their circles of stones. Plenty of people had mysteriously disappeared over the centuries. What if she had, too?

But what if this is some kind of purgatory, the place you go if you aren't quite good enough to go to Heaven?

With that, all the dirty laundry of her sad little past flitted before her eyes. There were the wild Friday nights at the officers' club. No doubt those had gotten her here. So did picking wimpy strawberries from the green plastic baskets at the supermarket and replacing them with the ripest, monster-sized berries. And she drove fifty-five in the thirty-five mile-per-hour zone each morning on the way to the base because she knew the cops never patrolled that street before six.

God was watching.

If she was truly deserving of Heaven, she wouldn't have felt compelled to lie about her rich father, saying he'd died before she was born. She would have been strong enough to admit that he'd dumped her white-trash mother after getting her pregnant. And had never once come to see their daughter.

A small, tired moan escaped her. "I should have known it would all come back to haunt me," she whispered, shoving away from the table.

Willoughby and Theo stared at her with that now familiar look of pity and regret. How could she explain her predicament when she didn't understand it herself?

Without saying good-bye she fled the galley and ran to Andrew's quarters. There had to be something she'd missed, something that would explain what had happened to her. A clue she hadn't seen.

She yanked open the door and stumbled to Andrew's desk, tipping over a stack of papers, which sent an ink bottle crashing to the floor. Shards of sticky glass crunched under her boots as she tore through Andrew's books. Keats, Sir Walter Scott, Shelley. Published: London, 1816. "No!" She threw the book against the wall.

Andrew appeared in the open doorway, an ashen-faced Theo behind him. "Run along, lad," Andrew said to the boy and closed the door.

Palms raised, as though soothing a wild animal, Andrew stepped toward her.

"What year is it?" she demanded.

" 'Tis 1821."

She crushed her hands into fists. She was a logical, reasonable person, a highly trained professional. Things like this didn't happen to people like her. She picked up an unlit candle and hurled it at him. "You're lying!"

He swerved out of the way. "I would not lie to you." He ducked as a copy of Sir Walter Scott's *Rob Roy* sailed over his head. " 'Tis 1821, five months since you left your home in India."

"No!" She clamped her hands over her ears. The vise she'd clamped around her self-control wrenched open. The control had gotten her through her mother's sickness and death, her fiancé's betrayal and the catastrophe that followed. But the added pressure of not knowing whether she'd see her home again proved too much.

A sob tore from her, and her face contorted. "Why has this happened to me? Why?"

Startled and dismayed by Amanda's tears, Andrew snatched her wrists. "Don't. Before long, you will be in England with your betrothed. The duke is anxious to marry, I'm told. You could have done far worse. Richard is neither fat nor old." Andrew could hardly believe that he was attempting to make the despicable wretch appear palatable, but he continued nonetheless. "In fact, the ladies find his appearance quite pleasing."

She searched his face, her dark lashes damp. "I'm not her. Don't you see? I don't belong here. You have to help me get home."

Home. To a union that would bring her nothing but misery. Richard's atrocities toward Andrew's family attested to that. Bile rose in Andrew's throat, and shame seeped into the hollow place inside him. Using Amanda to punish the duke made Andrew as much a monster as Richard.

Weeping now, Amanda tried to tug away. Awkwardly, Andrew drew her to his chest. She seemed to welcome the embrace, burying her face in the hollow between his shoulder and chest. As he held her, wrapping her petite frame in his strong one, her warm curves molded along the length of him, as though she were a piece that had always been missing.

"There, there," he whispered, patting her on the back as though this sort of thing came naturally. As though he had held her once before.

He pointedly ignored the disconcerting thought.

Murmuring soothing words and bits of phrases that made no sense at all, he stroked her hair, losing himself in the feel of her until the clock chimed, startling him from his trance. Her tears had stopped.

Good Lord! He was resting his chin on her head.

He propelled her back to arms' length. Her eyes mirrored his alarm. And for good reason—she was betrothed to another man. He had no right to hold her in this intimate way. Once before he had desired what wasn't his, and it had cost him all he'd loved. He would not make the same mistake twice.

"Have you recovered?" he inquired in a clipped tone.

She pushed away from him and backed toward the aft bedchamber. "I'd like to be alone for awhile," she said in a shaky voice.

He had reservations about leaving her. But what

harm would come to her in his quarters? "I'll have Mr. Gibbons bring your bath," he said and eased the door closed.

Mortified, Carly sagged against the wall. She knew better than to give in to her fear, her neediness. Yet, that was exactly what she had done. Thank goodness Andrew had wedged his icy contempt between them before she'd revealed how much his comfort meant to her, and how safe she'd felt in his arms.

Smudging moisture from her cheeks, she peered around the old-fashioned cabin. She loved technology, every gleaming, wondrous, timesaving marvel, and now she'd landed in a place devoid of it all. Good-bye electricity, computers, and microwaves. Not to mention showers, Tylenol, and tampons.

There had to be a way home.

An idea rocked her. A crazy, impulsive idea. What if she got into the water? Would everything reverse itself? Hope surged. If the ocean was how she got here, it could very well be her way back. Then she'd see a rescue helicopter. Or the carrier.

She jogged out of the cabin and across the deck. Leaning over the railing, she found the long, narrow shelf below. The chains. There was one on each side of the ship. They anchored the ropes that supported the masts, because the towering poles could not withstand the strain of the wind on their own. No one dared sit on the chains when the ship was running full speed. They were only six feet wide. But getting home was worth the risk, wasn't it?

She glanced behind her. The captain and crew had returned to their duties. No one was watching her. If she was going to try out her plan, now was her chance.

Hurry. She gripped a rope attached to the side of the

ship, tested it, then rappelled down, landing hard. Her ears popped with the pressure of the thundering sea. The spray-laden wind slapped her wet hair against her neck, her cheeks. It was like standing two feet from Niagara Falls. She kept one hand on the rope, fighting the urge to chant, "There's no place like home. There's no place like home."

Suddenly the wind died. The silence that followed was oppressive. The wind had shifted.

The ship pitched sideways, almost jerking the rope away from her. In her haste to clutch the lifeline with both hands, she lost her balance and plunged backward. Frothing gray-green seawater rushed into her nose and mouth. The rope scored her hands like razors.

"Help!" she shouted.

"Man overboard! Man overboard, I say!"

Carly shot a wild glance up to the railing. Andrew was there, shrugging off his coat, his boots. "Amanda! Good God, hold fast!" he roared, fastening a rope ladder to the railing. "I'm coming down!"

Aw, hell. Her foolishness had gotten her here. Now she was dragging Andrew into the mess she'd created, putting him at risk. She shouldn't have called for help.

Gulping air, she fought to climb higher on the rope. The cords seared her palms. The waves battered her against the hull. Suddenly she didn't care what century she'd dropped into or whose identity she'd taken. All she wanted was to survive.

On the chains, Andrew fell to his stomach and grabbed hold of the rope. "Pull yourself to me!"

Her left hand cramped, shooting knifelike agony up her arm. "I can't!"

Then the greedy swells seized her thighs and hips and dragged her down into the sea.

Chapter Four

For one excruciating instant, Andrew thought he had
lost her. Her panic, her desperation, rushed into him as
though it were his own. But she stopped her slide with
the knotted end of the rope.

The ship was slowing, but not fast enough. If he
didn't act fast, she'd be left behind. The ship would
return for her, but there were no guarantees that she'd
be found.

Gritting his teeth, he pulled the rope toward him,
hand over hand. "Now!" he commanded, reaching
for her.

She swiped for his fingers and missed.

"Again!" he implored.

Grimacing, she extended her arm, her fingers
splayed wide. He lunged for her. The muscles in his
back and arms quivered with the strain. When her

cold, slippery hand wrapped around his, relief beyond his experience squeezed his insides. He muttered a prayer of thanks and hauled her onto the chains, supporting her by hooking one arm under her bottom. "I've got you," he murmured against the pulse beating wildly at her throat.

Amanda's thin arms coiled around his neck. "Thank God."

He tightened his embrace as an overwhelming need to protect her, to care for her, surged through him. He fought the urge to cover her mouth with his and kiss her with as much passion as he had in his soul.

A resounding cheer erupted.

His men were gathered at the railing above. "Fine show, sir," Cuddy called down. "Carry her on up. We'll help at the top."

Andrew moved her back. He gestured with his chin to the roughly knotted rope. "Are you able to climb?"

"No problem," she said steadily, though her hands shook when she grabbed the ladder.

He followed close behind, supporting her wriggling, round little rump with one shoulder, while Cuddy helped her over the railing.

"Mr. Egan," Andrew said to Cuddy, keeping his voice on an even keel to camouflage his roiling emotions. "Let us get underway. South by southeast."

"Aye, Cap'n."

Andrew turned his attention to Amanda. Her golden brown eyes were downcast. Droplets of seawater clung to her pale cheeks like tears. She looked positively forlorn. A sense of helplessness quenched his fierce relief. She had meant to kill herself, he thought numbly. Short of locking her in his quarters, how would he prevent her from trying again? Weary and feeling far older than thirty years, he asked, "Is it so horrible here that you must take your own life?"

She squared her shoulders. "I wasn't trying to commit suicide."

"Then what the bloody hell were you doing on the chains?"

"I thought if I stood near the water, I could get home. But the wind changed directions, and I fell in." She beseeched him with her eyes. "Accidentally."

Surely he had not heard her correctly. "You intended to go . . . home?"

She nodded.

"To India?" he exclaimed.

"Well, no. The United States."

A choked laugh escaped him.

"I was in the ocean when you found me," she said in a rush of words. "So I thought that maybe . . ."

Seeing him tighten his jaw, Carly quickly summed up her position. "I hoped I'd go back to where I started. But it didn't work, so I'll have to try something else."

He grabbed her upper arms, hauling her toward him. "I thought your odd behavior was because you were reacting badly to your captivity. After all, you've known so little hardship in your short, privileged life."

"My life's been a lot of things," she snapped, "short and privileged not among them."

He leaned closer, his voice dropping. "But now you tell me that you intended to swim home. I hereby reconsider. Would you like to know why?"

"Not particularly."

"Not only are you daft," he informed her glibly, "but you are dimwitted, as well."

Something close to a growl escaped her, and he laughed, actually laughed, pure delight dancing in his eyes.

Whatever gratitude she'd felt toward him dissolved. "What I did was impulsive and stupid. I put you in danger, and I'm sorry. But you've rubbed my nose in it long enough." She squirmed to put more distance between them, but he gripped her firmly. "Let me go."

"Hell, no." He brought his lips to within inches of hers. "I rather like this."

She froze. Her gaze flew from his lips to his eyes, which he'd focused securely on her mouth.

"Have you ever been kissed, I wonder? Properly kissed."

She reared back as he leaned toward her.

"Ah, but I suppose I mustn't toy with the merchandise," he drawled, releasing her. "Else the duke may balk at the high price I've set on your head. We'd be reduced to bargaining."

"Good luck," she said sullenly. "The minute he finds out I'm not Amanda, you won't get a nickel."

"Haven't let go of *that* bone, eh? A regular spitfire, you are, and as mad as a snowstorm in July." He rolled one shoulder, then the other, as though to relieve stiffness pooling there. "But I do enjoy your feisty banter. It invigorates me."

Heat rushed to her cheeks. The man was playing with her, had been all along. But it was more than that. He was regarding her with blatant interest, making it clear that her totally inappropriate, utterly misplaced attraction was mutual. Oddly, exhilaration shot through her. But she used her discovery to her advantage, instinctively, the way she would in a dogfight upon uncovering an opponent's weakness.

If anyone needed to be put in his place, it was him.

She smiled sweetly, and sighed for added effect. "You are so selfless, so brave. You've saved my life twice now. I want to thank you."

He preened. "No need."

"No, I must. And *properly,* too."

Wary of the glimmer in her eyes, Andrew folded his arms across his chest. She seized his shoulders. Standing on her toes, she brought her face to his. Her zeal ignited a sharp rush of desire that buried its heat deep in his groin. He tried to push her away, but she pressed her soft belly to his. "Milady, shouldn't you go inside and change into dry clothes?" he asked weakly.

Her lips curved into a mischievous smile. "Hell no. I rather like this."

With that, she planted a firm, closemouthed kiss on his lips and marched off. He gazed after her, stupefied.

Blast. He'd been thoroughly trounced.

"Well done," he muttered, adjusting his collar. Then he picked up his boots, slung his coat over one shoulder, and followed the little spitfire to the main deck.

It took a week for Carly's palms to heal. The day her bandages came off, she gathered most of her possessions, save her handgun, gloves, watch, and pocketknife, and stuffed them into a sack. Then she waited until late afternoon before making her way to the bow of the ship.

She'd decided to give herself a funeral.

A symbolic, spiritual cleansing. A farewell.

The *Phoenix* was on its way to an island off the African coast, leaving her no option but to postpone her escape until landfall. Curiously, instead of panic, a sense of belonging had suffused her, blending with the sense of déjà vu that had dogged her since coming aboard. Though probably temporary, her life here left her feeling free and alive.

So unlike her past.

She'd been the consummate good girl, striving her whole life to please. Always the dutiful daughter, the understanding girlfriend, the perfect little soldier.

No more.

She would no longer drag the garbage of her life behind her like Marley's ghost in Dickens's *A Christmas Carol*. It was time to cut the chains.

Theo coughed softly.

The sound pulled her from her thoughts, back to the old-fashioned sailing ship and the innocent cabin boy who gazed at her with wonder. She smiled at him. "I treasure our friendship, Theo."

"Aye, me too. I'm glad for all your tales of the flying machines. I could hear 'em again and again."

She rummaged through her sack of odds and ends. "If you'd been born in my time, I bet you would have been a pilot." She plucked out her flight jacket. "Here you go, kiddo. It's yours."

Stunned, Theo lifted the garment from her hands, holding the jacket at arms' length.

"Put it on," she urged.

His eyes widened as he flushed and hugged it to his chest.

"Go on!"

"Are you certain?"

65

"Yes," she said. "Now go eat your supper."

"Aye, Carly." Grinning, he stepped backward and stumbled over a knotted rope. Righting himself, he let out a whoop of joy and sprinted toward the stairs that led belowdecks.

Carly returned her gaze to the water. She propped her elbows on the railing, cradling her chin in her hands. About the only thing that hadn't changed in the amazing events of the last two weeks was how much she loved the sea and sky. Tonight, the water was alight with brushstrokes of mauve, highlighting the sun, a shimmering white-hot ball poised above the horizon. The sky was an enormous blue dome unbroken by clouds or contrails, the white streaks left by jets in a typical twenty-first-century sky.

No craft would traverse the heavens for another eighty years.

She shivered with a poignant sense of loss. She'd loved flying, the freedom and thrill of it. It had been something she was good at. Her career had brought her pride, a sense of direction. It had taken her out of poverty and given her a life, and the financial means to care for her mother.

Though she missed her mother desperately, Carly comforted herself with the knowledge that Rose Callahan had finally escaped her pain. She had been ill for as long as Carly could remember. Their roles had been reversed throughout her childhood. Carly had been the one to take care of the house, cook their meager meals, administer medicines to ease her mother's pain, using what free time was left to accomplish chores. Which was why, she supposed, she didn't give a second thought to many of the menial tasks associated with nineteenth-century living.

The relentless wind snapped her pant legs against her thighs, reminding her that as soon as the sun set, the biting dampness would return. She'd better get on with it.

She emptied her pockets. Into the waves went her water-warped notepad, a ruined lipstick, and two leaking pens. She hurled them into the waves and watched them disappear behind the ship. Slowly, reverently, she peeled the fabric patches off the Velcro that held them to her flight suit. It was what she'd been trained to do if she were shot down in war. Since no one here believed her identity anyway, stripping away the bits of cloth gave her a strange sense of freedom. Labels; that's all they were.

Name tag, squadron patch, flag—she studied them, tracing the shape of her hard-won aviator wings with her fingertip. Then she smirked at the grinning skull and crossed bones on her squadron patch. VFA-60 Jolly Rogers. What if they'd been known as the Neanderthals, instead? Would she have ended up in a cave with club-wielding barbarians instead of on a ship full of pirates? She shuddered at the possibilities.

One by one, she released the patches. They fluttered in the breeze like lost butterflies before spiraling down to the sea.

She lifted her dogtags over her head. "An interesting bauble," Andrew had called them when she'd tried using them to prove her identity. "Were these all the rage in Delhi?" he'd inquired blandly. Carly snorted with the memory.

The dogtags hit the waves without a splash.

She unfastened the gold chain she'd worn for years. The tear-shaped half-carat diamond was the first gift Rick had given her. She'd come close to throwing it away a million times after he left but never could.

Now she dangled it carelessly from her index finger.

Since childhood, she'd craved a stable family, and the love of a loyal man. That dream had escaped her mother, and Carly had sworn her life would be different.

With Rick, she'd thought it was. He was from a privileged background and had a bright future to look forward to after his stint in the navy. After graduating flight school, they'd shared a luxurious townhouse. He'd paid the expenses, bought her gifts, and taken her on vacation when their schedules allowed.

She'd been seduced by it all. Unlike Rick, she had not grown up surrounded by the trappings of wealth, so she'd mistaken what he gave her for love. That made it difficult to understand why he avoided talking about their future. She must not have tried hard enough to please him, she'd thought. So she'd redoubled her efforts—after all, hard work had earned her everything *else* in her life. She'd given him everything a woman could give—trust, loyalty, love . . . her body. But he'd turned out to be a boy who valued bloodlines above all else.

Wincing, she remembered meeting his parents for the first and only time. In his mother's disdainful, aristocratic gaze, Carly wasn't a twenty-seven-year-old fighter pilot respected and admired by her peers. She was that little girl again; the kid who lived in the broken-down, one-room shack and wore donated clothes, whose mother had to clean houses and use food stamps at the local market.

"I'm through with men like you!" Carly balled the necklace in her fist and hurled it over the railing. It swirled on the churning water, an innocent trinket atop impending doom. Then, without warning, it was sucked under. "Good riddance."

She'd learned her lesson well, from Rick, from her father. Rich men were spoiled and couldn't be trusted. They ran when times got tough. It had taken her awhile, but she'd finally figured it out.

Cinderella was a fairy tale.

As the sun settled below the horizon, so did her old life. This was her second chance. Tomorrow would be the first day of her new life. This time, she wasn't going to screw it up.

Chapter Five

A vibration built above the thunder until the very air drummed with the beat. So hard to open her eyes.

"Come on, stay with me. Don't sleep!"

A flash. Then the deep voice was no longer with her.

"Where are you?" she cried, groping blindly. The world fell out beneath her, a horrible scraping of metal, a chop, chop, chop of blades striking a rock-hard sea. Thrown free, she saw the mangled metal husk sink beneath the swells. Rain pelted her like a thousand merciless needles.

So cold . . .

The deep voice called to her, shouted something. But she couldn't hear him above the roar of wind and thunder.

Lightning ignited the very air, transforming it into a tunnel with walls that glittered like ice and pulsed to the erratic beat of her heart. She floated inside, toward the far end, where a beautiful glow beckoned. Then doubt flooded her. What if she went in and couldn't come out? She tried to stop, tried to resist the pull, but the walls darkened and closed in on her.

"No, no!" Carly heard herself yell.

"Hush. I've got you. 'Tis all right," said a familiar voice.

The voice from her dream.

Strong arms came around her. Suffused with a sense of utter trust, she snuggled into the comforting warmth.

"Amanda. Wake up."

Carly's eyes flew open. The terrifying beauty of the nightmare lingered for an instant longer, then evaporated.

Her arms were twined around Andrew's warm neck, her cheek nestled in the hollow between his shoulder and throat. She breathed in his scent and the faint, sweet aroma of tobacco that clung to his brocade robe. "I'm dreaming," she whispered fervently.

"You were," he said in a low, husky murmur.

His intimate tone reverberated through her. She wanted to hear more and to hold him tighter, as she'd done all her life with moments of pure pleasure, enjoying them as long as possible, squeezing out every last ounce. Deprived as a child, she'd learned anything delicious was rare and fleeting.

In the barest whisper of a caress, his fingers brushed across her back, moving in a way that was both soothing and sensual. "Are you all right, then?"

His question dragged her back to reality. "I'm fine," she stated, extricating herself from his embrace. His arms were slow in releasing her.

He leaned over her as she settled onto the pillow. A flickering candle softened the hard lines of his jaw and high cheekbones, and glinted on the prickles of his beard. For once, he was without his mask of aloofness. The tenderness and concern in his startling blue eyes snatched her breath away.

"A nightmare?" he asked carefully.

She pushed her bangs off her damp forehead. "Yes. I've never had a dream that vivid. There was a storm. I could hear it. And *feel* it." She exhaled slowly. "Whatever I was riding in crashed into the sea."

His eyes flashed with her last statement. He shifted position, causing the bed to swing and creak. His robe fell away from his chest, far enough for her to see the play of his stomach muscles beneath smooth, tanned skin.

Her body responded instantly. Unexpected and unwanted, a surge of desire kicked her pulse into high gear and made the cabin seem twenty degrees warmer.

Hastily she glanced up. Candlelight and unmistakable interest warmed Andrew's sapphire eyes. It was more than a hot stare. His gaze drove deep into her soul, smashing every barrier, dismantling her defenses, leaving her open.

And vulnerable.

She broke eye contact first.

"I have had several odd dreams, myself," he said after a long pause. "They began as yours did. With a tempest. Then I lost something . . . or perhaps someone was taken from me." His lips thinned. "Whatever the case, the sensation was not pleasant."

He stood, adjusting his robe. "I will speak to Willoughby. Perhaps the man's been a wee bit generous with the curry." Andrew smiled slowly, a genuine grin that reached his eyes.

She smiled back, twisting the blanket in her hands. The sound of distant thunder interrupted the almost companionable silence between them. She took advantage of the moment. "Tell me about Lady Amanda."

Andrew walked to the curtains. He pushed aside one corner and peered outside. A burst of lightning turned the raindrops into shooting stars. "I was told she . . . or rather, *you* . . . were dark-haired. And fifteen. Which we both know is not the case."

"See? I'm not her."

He gave her a slanting glance and let the curtains fall.

"You don't believe me yet," she said. "But you will. Then you'll help me get home."

The ends of his mouth twitched. "To the future."

Hope flared. "Yes."

He combed the fingers of both hands through his wavy chestnut-colored hair. "Your stories are entertaining, to say the least. However, I suggest you save them for the duke."

Sighing tiredly, he settled onto the chair by the bed. "You were raised in America, a proper upbringing befitting a young lady of your station, save the obvious failings of your governess. If the sound of your speech is any indication,'twould appear you were raised by savages," he declared with obvious amusement. "Your American ways baffle me. You mangle the King's English with every word."

"That's because—"

His broad hand shot up. "You are the older of Lord

Paxton's two daughters. Your mother died years ago, before your family moved to Delhi. You have a sister, Lady Augusta. She is the one who is fifteen, I now believe. Since you are fair, *she* must have the dark hair." His brows drew together as he massaged his temples.

"There are a lot of variables here," Carly pointed out.

"I did not undertake this on a whim, milady. You were aboard the *Merryweather,* were you not?" He steepled his hands, contemplating his fingers as he spoke. "Yet, there is the question of your odd attire, your mannerisms and speech."

"Exactly—"

"Easily explainable as the affectations of a bored, petulant, and most likely deranged heiress."

A quick laugh escaped her, despite her irritation.

A smile tugged at his mouth. "I do have proof of your identity—however vehemently you deny it. The sapphire known as the Blue Star of Delhi was in the hold. It was part of your dowry, something Richard wants badly. I cannot fathom why your father would have sent the dowry with anyone other than the duke's betrothed."

Doubt crept over his features once again. "The only thing that surprises me is that Paxton would toss you into London society," he said, as though thinking aloud. "However, in your lucid moments you are quite charming."

She hurled the pillow at him.

Grinning, he rose to his feet and poured himself a brandy. "Since your mother's death, your father has devoted himself to his business. His company is known for opening new trade routes into the Orient. He imports teas, spices, silks . . ."

Carly visualized majestic merchant ships laden with riches.

"Lord Paxton—your father—is but a baron's younger son. Yet, he has amassed a fortune that rivals the throne's. Which is why, I suppose, he was given his peerage."

"Peerage?" Carly asked.

"Paxton was made an earl by the king for his service to the realm. But the title is such that it cannot be passed on to his progeny."

"I understand why Lord Paxton would want his daughters to marry well," she said thoughtfully. "But why would the duke of Westridge bother to import a merchant's daughter from India when he has his pick of *genuine* aristocrats floating around London?"

Andrew crossed his legs at the ankle. The slippery material of his long robe parted to his knees, revealing solid calves and a pair of very nice feet. Carly did her best not to wonder whether the robe would part further.

"Richard's assets are tied up in land, homes, and estates. He likes to spend freely and is quite desperate for cash. You are a cash-rich heiress. Thus the perfect mate."

Carly scowled. "This marriage-as-a-business-arrangement turns my stomach. I wonder if Amanda had a say in the matter."

He shifted his gaze to the sputtering candle. His shoulders were bowed, and he looked older, tired. "What good would that have done? You do not understand what Richard is."

"You hate him, don't you?" she asked gently.

The raw anguish in his eyes sliced through her heart.

"I'm sorry," she whispered hastily, knowing she'd

overstepped her bounds. "That was none of my business."

His mouth twisted. "Richard destroyed everything I had. As if that was not enough, he saw to my complete ruin. He will pay. I will see that he does." He rose. "And that, milady, is why I have captured *you.*"

The breeze from the closing door snuffed out the candle.

Carly rolled onto her side, staring unseeing into the darkness. The unmistakable grief shadowing Andrew's face lingered within her, as though it were hers, too.

Now it made sense—why Andrew refused to believe her, why he ignored evidence most would consider overwhelming: the last name on her flight suit and dogtags, her speech and appearance.

Hatred blinded him.

Whatever the duke had done had wounded Andrew profoundly.

In one month, she would have to face the duke herself. If he was a violent man, which she now suspected, he might react in a dangerous, unpredictable way when she informed him that she was bowing out of the marriage.

Dread unfurled inside her, making sleep impossible.

Rain hissed against the windows. Wind clattered through the masts and riggings with eerie sounds ranging from low, miserable moans to ear-splitting shrieks. The timbers groaned and creaked as Andrew's silverware and decanters quivered, adding their delicate accompaniment to the chaotic symphony.

At dawn the storm intensified. Except for the helmsmen, and the men needed to work the sails, no one went outside. The swells that washed over the deck could easily sweep a man overboard.

Trapped indoors over the next five days, Carly learned how excruciatingly confining a small ship could be. She read, and mended her uniform and socks. She exercised by doing crunches, stretches, and by dancing barefoot with an imaginary partner to the music in her head.

When the gale finally subsided, the men set to work cleaning and repairing the ship while Andrew and Cuddy checked their charts and took readings on the sextant to determine their position. The sun burned off the remaining moisture in the air, and the *Phoenix* coasted over waves soaked in joyous summerlike weather.

Gulping fresh sea air, Carly reveled in the beauty around her, something she could not recall taking the time to do before. Drugged by spring fever, she used her pocketknife to cut off her sleeves. On the main deck she luxuriated in the simple pleasure of afternoon sunshine on her bare arms, wishing she'd cut her pants into shorts. But when she noticed the sailors gaping at her exposed arms, she nixed the idea.

The men watched her walk past, their eyes bugging half out of their heads. Even Jonesy, the grizzled helmsman, whistled. Nothing like this had ever happened to her. Her petite bone structure and A-cup bra size had never earned her any second glances, let alone downright wolfish stares.

Now she felt like Mae West. And liked it, too.

"What have you *done?*"

Carly whirled toward the fury-filled voice. Andrew

was storming across the deck. Apparently, the rumors of her state of undress had reached him.

"Return to my quarters," he bellowed. "I will not allow you to run around half-dressed!"

She lifted her chin. "No."

He reared back in obvious and thoroughly entertaining shock.

"You're too late," she said breezily, folding her bare arms over her chest. "I threw the sleeves overboard. I'm cutting off my pants, next."

"You would not dare."

"Try me."

They exchanged frowns.

"I'll make a deal with you, Captain," she said. "If you let me stay like this, I'll leave my pants intact."

He struggled with his outrage, pointedly keeping his gaze from her arms. "Do I have your word?" he growled finally.

She raised one hand. "Scout's honor."

He stared blankly at her crossed fingers. Then he gave her a curt nod and marched back to the helm.

Smiling, she watched him go. The man was a downright sore loser.

Carly stole away to the quiet stern. Lying on her back, she inhaled the tangy scent of the sea and savored the mellow sunshine warming her skin in contrast to the rough planks beneath her head. It felt good to be alive. Particularly after all that had happened during the past few weeks.

Look.

She lifted her arm to study the tiny silver hairs dusted with salt. Beneath, faint blue veins carried her blood.

Listen.

She heard her own soft, steady breathing, the wind

whistling through the rigging, the swells hammering the sides of the ship.

Taste.

She drew her tongue across the hint of sweetness left on her lips from the sugared coffee she'd sipped earlier.

She closed her eyes in bliss, drifting between wakefulness and sleep until something solid bumped into her thigh, jolting her back to consciousness. She prayed it wasn't one of the resident rats.

Whatever it was poked her leg again, more insistent this time. Shielding her eyes from the sun, she found a tall figure looming over her.

"Why, Captain, are you the rude individual kicking me?" she asked in a sleep-thickened voice.

Andrew's eyes sparked with humor. "I am not kicking you. I merely nudged you with my boot to assure myself that you are alive."

"Ah," she said. "Looking after the cargo."

"Aye. It disturbs me to see it lying upon the deck."

She gave a soft laugh.

"And what, may I ask, are you doing?"

"I was napping until you kick—er, nudged me. Before that I was taking each of my five senses and concentrating on them one at a time. It was lovely. Want to try?"

"No."

She patted the planks next to her. "Come on. You'll like it."

Andrew clasped his hands behind his back and intentionally ignored her invitation. He allowed himself a slow perusal of her long, slender thighs, outlined rather nicely by her ridiculous trousers. Lying in the sunshine, her silvered hair tumbling over her neck and shoulders, Amanda was all mischief and sweetness.

79

Her full lips curved in a smile, and the sun had left behind a hint of pink on her cheeks.

In the deepest reaches of his soul, he knew the way she would feel in his arms.

He remembered.

Yearning swept through him. Not merely arousal, but something else, something more. A basic need that had always eluded him. Had he been another man, perhaps he could have traded his heavy heart for the lightness she seemed to possess. To laugh and talk of whimsical things such as senses, sunshine, and silly tales, to lie next to her and breathe in her scent. To touch her, taste her—

Blast! She was like a spark in the powder room, and twice as dangerous.

"Well?" she asked, propping herself on one elbow.

"I think not, milady. I have no time for frivolous pursuits."

She lay back down. "I bet you're fun when you loosen up."

He gave a quick, surprised laugh. She was nothing like the women he had known. His chilliest retort did not intimidate her, nor did anything else he threw her way. He rather enjoyed not having to tread carefully for fear of frightening her.

"Come inside before twilight, milady," he said in the sternest tone possible. Then he strode off with one purpose: to put as much distance possible between himself and temptation.

"See the red . . . duh-ah-guh. Dog."

"Good job, kiddo."

Theo grinned as Amanda ruffled his hair.

"Now let's try this." She scratched more words onto the slate and propped it on her lap. "Go ahead. Make me proud."

Theo drew his finger over the slate. "*That* one I don't have to sound out."

"So what is it, smarty pants?"

"Pilot."

"Very good!"

Amanda ducked as Theo swerved both hands past her head in what the lad called a mock air battle.

Andrew chuckled. Observing the lessons was a pleasant addition to his daily routine, and he'd been loath to miss a single one.

"I'll be reading the captain's books next, won't I?" he heard Theo boast.

The boy probably would, at that. Any sailor who could read and write was a valuable addition to the crew—there were logs to be kept, ledgers to be gone over. Had anyone told him last summer that the scraggly orphan he'd found on the docks would soon be reading and working with figures, he would not have believed it. It was a pleasure to be proved wrong. Until Theo joined the crew as his cabin boy, there had been nothing but misery in the lad's short life. And now that Amanda had been taken aboard, the boy had blossomed, thriving on the maternal attention she so generously gave him.

Lord knows, a boy needs a mother.

Something deep inside Andrew stirred. Time alone with his mother had been rare. Her life had not been her own, for the demands on a duke's mistress were enormous. Subsequently, as a child, he'd endured long periods of loneliness.

Cuddy settled beside him, a rolled navigation chart in his fist. "The lad's turning into a regular little gentleman, ain't he?"

"Aye. After only a month, she's taught him to read and write."

"Patient, she is. And sweet. Not at all what I'd expected."

"Nor I," Andrew confessed. God's truth, the last thing he'd expected was that he'd develop tender feelings for the chit. "Perhaps not all aristocrats are cut from the same cloth."

" 'Tis what I've been trying to tell you," Cuddy said, a hint of a grin tugging at his mouth.

"Worthless waste of human flesh, the vast majority," Andrew said sourly. "But the lady had a sheltered upbringing. She hasn't had a chance to be ruined yet." He took the chart from Cuddy, unrolled it. "Give her time."

Amanda cried out more words of praise and stood, hugging a blushing Theo to her chest.

"Lessons are over," both men chorused.

Cuddy said on a sigh, "Perhaps I could beg a reading lesson or two myself."

"I do not believe Theo would be inclined to share."

"Then you must step in. As the captain, you have the crew's morale to consider. I ask you, sir, is it fair that only the lad has her full attention every morning?"

Propping the chart on the railing, Andrew yanked out the wrinkles to better see the figures Cuddy had written. "Your duties as first mate keep you too occupied for lessons you do not need. However, if you desire more tasks heaped upon you, I shall be happy to oblige."

Cuddy pointedly ignored him. "How 'bout yourself? Whether you need lessons or not, rank has its privileges. The way she looks at you—"He fluttered his lashes and pursed his lips. " 'Tis an invitation."

Andrew lowered the chart. "God's teeth, man, you've been in the sun too long."

But there was more truth in Cuddy's words than Andrew cared to admit. By keeping his mind focused on the business of revenge, he hoped to bury his highly improper physical and emotional attraction to her. "She's good with the lad," he said casually. "Her children will be lucky indeed."

"Aye. As lucky as Richard will be, having her as a wife."

Andrew blinked away the unwelcome image Cuddy's remark conjured. He pretended to study the marks denoting latitude and longitude, but all he saw was Amanda with Richard, in his arms . . . his bed. Was Richard capable of fidelity, of tenderness? Certainly, he was a stranger to compassion. Andrew scowled, feigning concentration, while reminding himself not to allow Amanda's future welfare to concern him. After all, he wasn't changing her fate, simply profiting by it.

"I say spend some time alone with the lass," Cuddy said. "She's not Richard's yet."

"You're as mad as she is!"

"Aye, she has a colorful imagination. Her stories alone will keep you entertained for hours. Has she told you of the buildings in her fanciful cities of the future? Hundreds of feet tall, thousands of people housed inside."

"My point precisely, Mr. Egan." Andrew returned his attention to the chart. Though he dared not admit it, he found Amanda's imagination fascinating. Particularly her comments on the theories and possibility of human flight, the study of which had inexplicably fascinated him all his life. A woman willing to discuss scientific imponderables and natural philosophy? In all his life, he hadn't thought such a creature existed.

A repetitive rasping sound tore into his musings. "What is that infernal noise?" He directed his irritation with Cuddy's meddlesome banter at Theo, who had settled beside a coil of rope. The boy wore an intense look of concentration on his face and had laid Amanda's odd leather coat in his lap. "Theo! Cease that . . . sound!"

Theo's eyes blazed with wonder. "You ought to see this, sir." He thrust the coat toward him.

Andrew recoiled, held up his hand.

" 'Tis called Velcro," Theo explained cheerily. "It holds the patches in place. 'Tis sticky, but 'tis not."

Cuddy chimed in. "An ingenious invention. Even more so than the zippers. Wee hooks and eyes fasten together—"

"I'm not interested in fanciful inventions from any of the colonies, thank you." Andrew handed his first mate the wrinkled chart. "I'll see you at the helm shortly."

Cuddy clicked his heels together and strode off toward the main mast.

Andrew gripped the sun-warmed railing and looked out over the water, not to admire the gentle swells, but to scan what lay ahead with seaman's eyes. The slowly undulating water shimmered silver in the heat, and for days now the horizon to the south had been crowned with distant purple-gray peaks. The thunderstorms were the border of the approaching doldrums, the equatorial zone where the trade winds died. A ship could languish for weeks, or months, in the doldrums.

Thankfully, their crossing north had been swift, and

he prayed the return journey to Emerald Isle would be as well.

Gradually, his tenseness dissolved, as it always did when he sought the horizon. The endless, open expanse of the sea—he craved it, went half-mad without it. Yet, even with the horizon before him and a fine wind filling the sails, his thoughts circled back to Amanda, and to her father.

Lord Paxton was said to be a devoted father, not the sort who would knowingly give such a free-spirited daughter to a vicious, callow man who played with people like toys, a man for whom murder was a casual act.

Worse yet, Andrew was a partner to this madness. Amanda deserved to be cared for, protected. Instead, with his help, she was being sold to the highest bidder.

Unexpectedly, her laughter rang out, sending sparks of light into the gloom of his soul. Cuddy was chatting with her—flirting, more likely.

Amanda laughed again, smoothing pale wisps of hair off her forehead. Glancing away, Andrew tried in vain to shrug off the familiar gnawing ache.

She was not his, he reminded himself. She would never be his, and by summer, she would be out of his life forever.

* * *

"In Calleo there lives a gal whose name is Serafina.
She sleeps all day and works all night in the old Cally Marina.
Serafina! Serafina!
She guzzles pisco, beer, and gin. On rum her mum did wean her."

Carly rocked back on her heels and laughed at the

song. It was wash day. The men had brought up their damp and dirty clothes, from stockings to trousers, to wash them in a tub on the deck. After the clothing had been scrubbed, and the garments been towed overboard for an hour, Andrew sent her to the cabin while the men bathed. When she returned, she barely recognized the lot of them.

Now the men were hanging their clothing from the rigging to dry, entertaining themselves, and her, with one chanty after another.

> *"Serafina's got no shoes—I been ashore an'
> seen 'er.
> She's got no time to put them on, that hard-
> worked Serafina."*

Carly laughed and glanced across the deck to Andrew. He was slouched on a wooden chair in the sunshine some distance from the men, his feet propped on a barrel, a book in his lap. In a ludicrous contrast to his handsome features, his glasses sat on the bridge of his nose, bestowing the hardened warrior with a sexy vulnerability.

"How about something spicier!" she called out when the song ended.

Delighted, the men laughed. Andrew removed his glasses and captured her with a long, indecipherable stare. She certainly enjoyed teasing him with her carefree and very un-nineteenth-century ways.

Jonesy asked, "Will Barnacle Bill do ya, miss?"

"Clean it up some, first," Cuddy warned.

"Aye," Jonesy said. "The ladies' version."

"Not the watered-down version," Carly protested. "Give it to me straight."

Cuddy and Andrew exchanged glances.

"Blush once and 'tis over," Andrew said, then resumed his reading.

It was nice, for once, to have someone watch out for her, even if it was over something as simple as a song. Only she wasn't going to let herself get used to it.

It wouldn't last.

Jonesy belted out a lively ballad. Carly climbed atop a barrel to listen. The shadow of the main mast hovered over her neck and shoulders. The breeze held steady, teasing tendrils of hair from her braid, tickling her sun-warmed cheeks as she rested her chin on her knees.

" 'Who's that knocking at my door? said the fair young maiden,' " Jonesy sang in a hilarious falsetto, deepening his voice for the next stanza, then alternating as he switched between the man's role and the woman's.

" 'It's only me from over the sea, said Barnacle Bill the Sailor. Hurry 'fore I bust the door. I've newly come upon the shore, and this is what I'm looking for.

" 'Oh, your whiskers scrape my cheeks, said the fair young maiden,' " Jonesy warbled, to the men's laughter. " 'My flowing whiskers give me class, says Barnacle Bill the sailor. The sea horses eat them instead of grass. If they hurt your cheeks they'll tickle your—' "

"Jonesy!" Andrew yelled, ending the risqué ditty.

Carly pressed her palms to her cheeks and swung her gaze to Andrew. "Okay, so I blushed."

"Mr. Gibbons," Andrew said, "sing for us, if you would be so kind."

While the men brought up buckets, mops, and brooms to clean the deck, Gibbons crooned a melody about a woman left alone, waiting for her man to return.

Alternately singing and telling tales, the men scrubbed and scraped the decks, railing, and furniture until the ship gleamed and the sunset transformed the sea into an endless, undulating sheet of gold.

In the deepening twilight, the men gathered on the deck to mend clothes, smoke their pipes, read, and chat. The hum of conversation and the masculine scents of perspiration and beer surrounded Carly as she gazed at the sea.

Alarmed, she shoved aside a quiver of contentment. She must not allow herself to forget the threat of her uncertain future. Because unless she convinced Andrew that she wasn't an English heiress in the short time left, she'd be handed over to a stranger—for money.

Chapter Six

"Bravo, Mr. Willoughby. That was delicious." Carly scraped the bottom of her plate with a biscuit so she wouldn't miss a drop of thick, spicy stew. Along with hunks of salty smoked pork, the broth had contained onions and greens from the small garden she tended near the pen where the livestock was kept. The average nineteenth-century sailor's understanding of scurvy came as much from folklore as it did science, but Willoughby had bowed to her urging and was adding vegetables to their meals more often.

They were nearly upon the equator. The Neptune ceremony, a traditional mariner's rite upon crossing the line of zero latitude, was only days away. For the past hour, Willoughby had been regaling her with stories of how the custom was practiced onboard the *Phoenix*. In between, she'd shared her recollections of the hedonistic celebrations onboard her carrier. By combining the two, she and the cook had hatched the makings of a fine party.

In the past, the sailors on the *Phoenix* had solved the dilemma of dancing without female companions by drawing sticks. Those left holding the shortest ones had to don dresses.

"But this party will be different," Willoughby declared, opening a small cask of beer. "No man will want to dance with another man if he can dance with a lady. You'll be on your feet the entire night."

"I don't mind a bit. I love dancing." Carly looked forward to being the only belle of the ball. The experience was not a new one. She'd spent the last decade almost exclusively among men, two years of that time onboard the *USS Eisenhower,* a veritable bastion of masculinity. Although there were nurses and other female officers stationed aboard the carrier, Carly had often ended up as the sole woman in a group of men.

Two cups of tepid beer in his hands, Willoughby joined her at the table. It seemed all she drank was tea and beer. No wonder people in the 1800s died young—their kidneys wore out.

Carly unfolded a piece of vellum and dipped a pen into a jar of sour-smelling black ink. "Now, let's finish up the plans for our little celebration. When we're through, I'll present them to Captain Spencer."

By the time Carly returned to the deck, the afternoon had melted into the amber-infused indigo of a tropical evening. The deck was unusually quiet, the air still. Most of the sailors were playing in—or watching—a card tournament on the gun deck.

Carly paused to gaze at the two vast oceans—one of miles-deep water, the other a home for infinite stars.

Her thoughts drifted to the dress she was making. Andrew had found her a bolt of pale coral linen in the hold. All week she'd been painstakingly tracing a pattern on some yards of sail, cutting the muslin with the sailmaker's shears and using fishing hooks for straight pins. Her mother had sewn all her clothes until she'd learned to sew her own, and although Carly hadn't made anything in years, she hadn't lost her skill.

A boot heel scuffed the planks behind her.

"Tsk, tsk, Lady Amanda. What would yer rich mama think of ya out strollin' all by yerself?"

Carly whirled around. Overpowered by the pungent odor of skin too long without a bath, she slammed into a man's hard chest.

Black Beard!

"Thanks for your concern," she said, barely hiding her distaste. "Now, if you'll excuse me, Mr. Booth, I'll be on my way." She made no eye contact as she stepped around him.

His fingers closed around her upper arm. Her heart lurched, and adrenaline surged through her. "Do you mind?" she snapped as she tried to wrench free.

Booth pressed the ball of his thumb into her flesh. "What's yer hurry?"

"Let me go," she said evenly, "or I'll scream."

"No ye won't." He slapped one callused hand over her mouth, clamped the other around both wrists, and shoved her into the dark alcove behind them.

He pushed her backward until she slammed into a wall. The full impact of his hulking body crushed the air from her lungs. Bursts of light flickered behind her eyes. Wheezing air through his thick fingers, she tried not to panic.

"Nice an' private." He ground his pelvis against

91

hers. "Now we can play a wee bit." He eyed her as though he meant to kiss her on the mouth. Instead, he fastened his mouth to the side of her throat, suckling hard. His breath was sharp with the scent of grog. Revulsion quivered through her. She bit his palm, crushing the salty flesh in her teeth.

"Damn you, bitch!" He yanked his hand away, raised it.

She braced herself.

But he reconsidered and pressed his big paw over her mouth and nose. She made a muffled moan.

"What's that, missy? Ya beggin'?" He unbuckled his belt. "Me an' the cap'n, we share an' share alike. If he's helpin' himself to a piece of yer sweet ass, I'm takin' me a piece, too."

She bucked wildly, raking her nails over his coarsely bearded cheek.

Jerking back, he blurted, "Do that again, missy, and I'll kill ya. Then I'll take ya anyway."

He squeezed her neck with one sweaty hand. Her vision grayed; her pulse hammered wildly in her ears. "Do ya understand?"

She nodded, gasping.

Panting moist, hot breath against her throat, Booth unbuttoned his pants, freeing himself. She could feel his erection against her belly. Instinctively, she squeezed her thighs together and whimpered, hating herself for showing her fear.

"Ya want it bad, don't ya, missy?"

With all she was worth, she jerked her knee into his groin. He slammed her head back against the wall. He was too big, too strong. She choked her cry of outrage, fought to keep from passing out as he rubbed himself against her belly, grunting with his sick pleasure. The wall behind her creaked with each thrust.

"You're scum," she mumbled into his palm.

"Aye. I like it, too. I'd be shovin' myself between yer legs every night if I were in charge," he gasped, skimming his dirty fingers over her face and neck. "I'd teach ya tricks, and you'd treat me good. Aye, missy, you'd be my whore. My rich little whore." He expelled a groan.

Now was her chance. She grabbed him by his meaty shoulders and stepped to the left. The move threw him off balance. Jamming her foot into the back of his knee, she pulled him forward. He stumbled, hitting his forehead on the wall. She bolted for the deck. Growling, he snatched her arm, yanking her back.

Somewhere, a door slammed.

They froze, arms extended, as though locked in a nightmarish tango. The sound of several pairs of boots approached. Their gazes locked. The glint in Booth's dark brown, almost black eyes was cold and terrifying.

Utterly evil.

It raised the hairs on the back of her neck. This man would take great pleasure in hurting a woman.

He released her and buttoned his pants. "I was only lookin' fer a wee bit of fun. No harm done. And I wouldn't say nothin' to the cap'n. Or I'll see Theo's next swim's his last."

"Don't blackmail me, you bastard," she hissed.

The footsteps came closer. She craned her neck to see who was approaching.

"Look at me, bitch," he whispered harshly. "Mind my words. The lad will die if ya don't keep yer trap shut. Do ya understand?"

She crushed her hands into fists. "Yes," she ground out.

Buckling his belt, he left her in the shadows. She exhaled in a moan, flattening her palms over her tender abdomen.

Men on the deck strolled by, laughing. She heard Booth joke with them as though he hadn't a care in the world.

Light-headed and nauseated, she crouched, lowering her head between her knees as frustration swelled inside her. Andrew had warned her about being alone on the deck after dark. Why had she let her guard down? Life here was as dangerous and real as it had been in her last.

And just as unforgiving.

When the faintness passed, she stood unsteadily and made her way out of the alcove, using the wall as support. Her breath hissed through her gritted teeth. She seethed with thoughts of revenge. But until she figured out how to keep Theo safe, she could do nothing.

Andrew could help her—he was a man of honor.

But he also thought she was crazy.

If she made an accusation—and Booth denied it—it would cause turmoil among the crew. Worse, Booth likely had allies. Even if Andrew believed her and punished Booth, as he'd once promised, someone else could hurt Theo.

She'd leave Andrew out of this, for now. She understood all too well the consequences of relying on someone else. Trust was dangerous. She'd take care of this herself.

Drawing her shredded confidence around her, gathering it into the cloak of toughness that had been her lifelong shield, she walked slowly to the cabin. Pausing outside, she stared dumbly at the candlelight fanning out from under Andrew's door. He stayed up late every night, and she should have anticipated that he'd be at his desk.

This wasn't her night, was it?

She raised her collar to hide any possible bruises, smoothed her hair behind her ears, and rapped on the door.

"Enter."

She peeked inside. "It's only me." Looking up briefly, she hastened across the cabin to her door.

Shock registered on his handsome features. He put his pen down. "I presumed you were asleep. Why were you out unescorted? 'Tis after dark."

Think fast. "I was talking to Willoughby about the party. The whole thing took longer than I thought. Good night."

"One moment, milady."

She gave a soft but very expressive growl.

He cinched the tie on his robe and stood, his mouth tight as he peered at her from top to bottom. "Tell me, what is the matter?"

"Nothing's the matter," she blurted. Still, because of his few words, she was ready to spill everything. He cared.

"Amanda?"

She met his gaze, his eyes midnight blue, reminding her of the night she'd woken in his arms. She'd give anything to be held like that again. Her face flamed.

"You are flushed." He gestured to her cheeks and peered at her, frowning. "Are you not well?"

She inched her collar higher. "I'm tired, that's all."

"I trust you are telling me the truth?"

"Oh, yes," she quickly assured him.

He raised a brow. He was on to her, like the lead hound on a foxhunt. Glancing behind him to the paperwork on his desk, she sought to throw him off the trail. "May I see what you're working on?"

"If you are so inclined."

Long after she blew out her candle at night, Andrew remained at his desk, and she'd always wondered what he was doing. Shyly, she followed his gaze to a piece of parchment. The sketch was intricately drawn with numbers, notes, and arrows scattered on all four sides. It was a boxy vehicle of some kind, with narrow wings or rotors on top, the figure of a man inside. Impossible. "You're sketching . . . *helicopters?*"

"Rotorcraft. Why, yes," he said, equally incredulous. "Few souls are aware of them. Purely theoretical."

"Not in my time. They are real."

He plunged his fingers through his hair. "Ah, of course." After a pause, he slid a stack of papers toward her. "These are the rest of my drawings." A wry smile formed on his mouth as he gestured to an open text. "This one I cannot claim, I'm sorry to say."

She recognized the famous illustration immediately. "Who wouldn't want to draw like Leonardo da Vinci?"

"Aye, a genius, he was. I fear my study of his scientific sketches has become somewhat of an obsession."

"He was so ahead of his time," she said. "Hard to believe he couldn't convince a single soul in the sixteenth century to look at these."

"Aye. A loss for us all."

"Imagine where we'd be now if someone with

money and foresight would have only listened to him. *Think* of it."

The topic distracted her from her bruised body and spirit. Embarrassed by her rising enthusiasm, she glanced up. To her relief, Andrew wore an expression of boyish excitement.

"I have pondered the same thoughts." He pointed to his drawing. "This one I saw in my dreams of the storm. 'Tis not at all like the hot air balloons that have crossed the English Channel. 'Tis self-propelled through the heavens. And so swiftly that it defies the wind. Indeed, in a craft such as this, vast distances would seem small."

He searched her face, his eyes intense, mirroring her own passion. *He's a kindred spirit*, she realized with a jolt.

"Never in my life have I dreamt so vividly, milady," he said, using his expressive hands as he spoke. "Until the storm wakes me, I am sailing on the air, faster than any ship I have sailed. The clouds are but an arm's reach away. Aye, the stars, too. Yet, the sea is far, far below."

The flickering flame of the candle imbued his skin and hair with an amber glow, and his robe clung to the hard lines of his powerful body. She watched him in awe, drawn to his confidence and masculinity in a way that left her breathless.

For the first time in her life, she understood what it meant to experience desire, true desire. The feelings she'd had for Rick, even from the beginning, now seemed childlike and insignificant in comparison.

Her throat ached, tightening her voice to a whisper. "When you describe it, I feel like I'm there with you."

His eyes darkened to a deeper hue. Overcome by myriad emotions she couldn't explain, she turned away.

Andrew exhaled sharply with the loss. He'd felt the very air between them crackle. He was not the only one affected, judging by the color in her cheeks as she looked down to study the sheets of parchment on the desk. His soul lay open on those pages, yet he revealed it to her without hesitation, without fear. His pulse beat slow and strong as she drew her fingertip intimately over the angles and curves: his figures, his writing. She was touching him in a way no one ever had. The shimmering light of the one lamp highlighted her soft, sensitive mouth, her high cheekbones, the haunting sadness in her eyes that seemed sharper tonight than usual. He fought the urge to pull her close and hold her, kiss her, will her to forget her pain, if only for a little while.

The intensity of his desire reminded him quite clearly that he must not be alone with her. She was not, and would never be, his. She belonged to another. Swallowing hard, he clasped his hands behind his back. " 'Tis late. You ought to be in bed."

"Before I go, I need to discuss something with you."

"Proceed."

"Mr. Willoughby and I have finished our party plans. With your permission, we'd like to hold a bigger celebration than usual."

Andrew rolled up his drawings, one by one.

"We have some great ideas for a party. . . ."

He slipped the rolled parchment into a leather sheath.

"By the way, Captain, Mr. Gibbons mentioned that he'd like the first slow dance with you."

His busy hands stopped.

"Oh, good," she said. "You *are* listening."

"Mr. Gibbons wishes to dance?"

She pursed her lips. "You're a very predictable man, which makes it easier when I want your attention."

"Does it, now?" he asked dryly.

"Yes. Do you want to hear about the party or not?"

"I suppose I have little choice in the matter. However, I must remind you that you are my cargo, not my social secretary."

Her eyes twinkled with mischief. "May I assume then, dear Captain, that you've given *me,* a mere bit of cargo, permission to hold the event?"

"Why, of course," he said crisply. "My men's ability to fight depends on camaraderie as much as it does on discipline and trust. In this respect, music and dancing are as important as gunnery drills."

She rolled her eyes and walked to her door. "I suppose that's the closest I'll get to hearing you say 'fun is good.' "

"I take my amusements, milady, when the time is appropriate."

"Do you? Good," she said. "So do I."

He shared her slow smile. "In that, little spitfire, I do not doubt your word."

Chapter Seven

"No, I won't watch." Theo's blush deepened until he was nearly purple. He rocked back on his heels and swallowed, his Adam's apple bobbing above his collar.

"For God's sake, Theo, she's made of wood. What difference does it make what she's wearing?" How a teenage boy could get so worked up over a piece of underwear, Carly had no idea.

" 'Tis because, well, *you* were wearin' . . ." Unable to finish, Theo shrugged and shoved both hands in his pockets.

Groaning in mock exasperation, Carly wadded the apricot wisp of lace in her fist. She hopped over the railing behind the ship's masthead and carefully shimmied up Savannah's back. Without a trace of wind to mar its surface, the sea below displayed a reflection that was as crisp as a photograph.

Straddling Savannah's hips, Carly positioned her bra over the carving's two perfectly shaped polished breasts. "I'm jealous, Savannah. They must have cut down an entire tree for your chest alone." Her attempt to make Theo laugh elicited little more than a muffled cough.

Fuzzy and faded from too much washing and more than a month of wear, the lace stretched and crackled as she tried to fasten the hook-and-eye closure in back. Gritting her teeth, she winced at the twang of bursting elastic. With one last hiss of rending fabric, the bra snapped into place, thanks to the statue's totally unrealistic, male-fantasy, itty-bitty, twelve-inch waist. Naturally, the bra was ruined, but now that she'd sewn three camisoles and pairs of underpants with extra yardage from the dress, she'd planned to retire it, anyway. "You'll look beautiful at the party, Savannah, girl."

Carly slid down to the deck. "It's over," she said, flinging her arm over Theo's shoulder. "Come on, kiddo, open your eyes."

Warily, he asked, "What's next?"

"More decorating, I'm afraid. Captain Spencer said we'll cross the equator before dawn, which means we have a lot of fixin' to do to this ol' sloop before tomorrow. I say we start with the railing and the masts. What do you think?" Carly lifted her arm from Theo's shoulder to ruffle his thick, sun-bleached red hair. His grin returned. Unlike the teenage boys she'd known— the sons of friends, mostly—Theo seemed to enjoy her public physical displays of affection. "Look, here comes Mr. Gibbons with the ribbons now."

Gibbons strode toward her, a bulky basket in his arms. Squinting from the glare of the sun on his white hair, she tugged her collar away from her neck. It was going to be another scorcher. The men had hung tarps to keep as much of the midday sun off the open deck as possible. Away from the protective shade, the hot, humid air was almost unbearable. "Are the ribbons dry yet, Mr. Gibbons?"

"Aye, dry and hot, like everything and everyone on this ship, milady." Gibbons lowered the basket so she could peer inside.

She'd spent hours dying the strips of sailcloth. Sweating over a cauldron of boiling water and saffron, she'd made one batch after another until her stained hands were blistered, sore, and as orange as a pair of Halloween pumpkins. The color on her fingertips was only now beginning to fade.

Carly plucked out a length of yellow sailcloth and yanked it taut. It had dried stiff, but she could soften the material by rubbing it between her fingers.

"I trust the festoons meet your approval?"

She mimicked his imitation of an aristocrat's pompous airs. "I daresay, Mr. Gibbons, we've done a fine job." Lifting a finger imperiously toward the stern, she suggested, "Shall we start at the rear, gentlemen?"

"What in God's name have you done to my fine vessel?"

On her knees, yards of sailcloth ribbons draped across her shoulders, Carly shaded her eyes from the brutal midday sun. " 'Done'?"

"Aye." Wet from a swim, Andrew stood above her, his arms folded over his chest. His damp hair curled around his shirt collar, and he'd rolled up his sleeves. The sodden material of his white linen shirt was almost transparent in several places, revealing a shadow of dark hair across his broad chest. The darkness descended in a narrow line that dipped tantalizingly into the waistband of his pants.

"Captain," she said as she stood. "The rest of the crew thinks it looks pretty nice." She propped her hands on her hips. "I get the impression you don't."

He resumed his slow and deliberate study of his festively outfitted ship. "My *Phoenix* looks like a warrior dressed in petticoats."

Gibbons and Theo let out delighted laughs.

Carly pursed her lips to hide her smile. "Thanks a lot."

"My pleasure," Andrew said, his eyes glinting.

He was flirting with her, she realized with a jolt. Every nerve ending in her body tingled, making her feel suddenly and vividly alive. She tucked a stray lock of hair behind her ear and said, "Those who haven't helped don't get to criticize."

"I see." Holding her gaze, he slid a strip of cloth from her shoulders. "I shall begin where you left off." Crouching, he secured the ribbon around the base of the railing with a perfect square knot. Pausing every few seconds to inspect his work, he wound the strip of cloth around the railing in that peculiar, extremely cautious way she'd seen men use when performing a task they considered "women's work."

Carly felt a rush of tenderness toward the battle-hardened warrior on his knees, several yards of bright yellow ribbon in his hands.

"Oh, Lord have mercy," Gibbons wheezed at the sight of his captain decorating the wooden post, while Theo rolled along the railing, hiccuping and holding his sides.

Carly pressed one finger to her lips. "Hush."

Gibbons waved feebly and coughed, and Theo tried to muffle his hiccups with both hands.

Andrew stood, hooking his thumbs behind his belt. Those adorable dimples of his never failed to send her resistance into a nosedive. "Finished, I believe. Do you agree, milady?"

"I honestly do. It looks great."

He inclined his head slightly, cleared his throat, and drew himself up to his full height, something several inches over six feet. "My ship will be the laughing-stock of the seven seas."

"Laughingstock!" Carly aimed a playful punch at his stomach.

He caught her fist easily. With his other hand, he curled one finger under her chin. "I earned that remark, milady. 'Those who help get to criticize.' As I recall, those were your words, more or less." He gave her hand a gentle squeeze before walking off, whistling one of the more popular chanties.

She touched the place where his warm finger had rested under her chin. "Something will have to be done about him," she murmured.

"Milady, you've done a great deal of good already," Gibbons said. "He may not know it yet, but his men do."

"He says a king's ransom couldn't make up for the trouble I've caused him." She shrugged. "The sour-puss does laugh more, though."

"Aye, he does at that." Gibbons flashed her a broad, white-toothed grin.

Carly settled to her knees. As she slid a length of ribbon from her shoulders, she hummed the tune Andrew had begun, some ditty about a wayward mer-maid. Theo and Gibbons joined her. Within minutes, they were singing the bawdy song aloud.

* * *

The *Phoenix* spun in languid circles atop a glassy sea. Ribbons dangled from the railings and rigging, and near the bow, the men had strung lanterns.

Glad to leave the stifling cabin, Carly strolled outside toward the bow of the ship. The party was well underway. She leaned over the railing, propped her chin on her hands, and paused to absorb the tranquil peace of a tropical evening. The air was thick, primeval. Here, atop the earth's equator, far from any rocky shore, the ship was nothing more than a speck on a vast sea. Gooseflesh raised on her arms. She savored the beauty of the ocean a while longer before leaving the stern.

Her skirt fluttered over her bare legs, brushing her ankles as she walked. She'd dried her hair in braids, creating a myriad of waves that hung to her waist. When she reached up to fluff her hair, one of her cap sleeves slipped down her shoulder. She tugged the sleeve higher, cursing the fact that no one had thought to invent elastic yet. What made it such a difficult concept? Her other sleeve sagged. She gave up, letting it fall. There wasn't much to reveal anyway. She'd spent her teenage years wishing for cleavage, or at least enough on top to hold up a dress. Nevertheless, her body matured late. Not until her twenties had she developed a more womanly figure. Too bad her hips had outpaced her chest!

Food was a sore subject with Andrew these days. They'd gone past the six weeks he'd originally calculated it would take to reach the island. The winds had eluded them, he'd said, making the crossing unusually slow. It might take as long as another month to drift south to the trades. If supplies ran low, they'd be forced to sail to a port on the African mainland to buy more beer, flour, and beef—further delaying their arrival home. Still, it gave her more time to figure out her options before she was forced to leave the *Phoenix* and the only people she knew in this century. Once the duke saw she was little more than a pauper, she figured he'd let her go. Yet, being flat broke in a strange century presented a problem all its own. Short of urging someone to invent an airplane she could fly, she'd be forced to earn her living from the most basic of skills—reading, writing, and sewing.

This evening, though, she promised herself she'd keep those worries shelved. It was time to taste the freedom she'd long denied herself. Tonight was more than a party. It was her personal celebration of life.

A gibbous moon rose opposite the setting sun, casting an otherworldly glow over the festive ship. With the bobbing lanterns and stars above adding their sparkle, it had the makings of a magical night. Her step quickened as she headed toward the sounds of laughter and music, and the smell of sweating bodies, tobacco, and grog.

The men clapped and cheered at her arrival. Only Black Beard and his cronies glowered at her.

She ignored them.

Since Booth had assaulted her, she had carefully avoided being alone on a deserted deck. She dodged him during the day, as well, to keep the extent of their mutual animosity from Andrew's keen eyes.

"My queen," Gibbons said. Dressed as Neptune for the night, he offered her his arm. Size alone was enough to make him appear regal, but with his cape of painted sailcloth, a cowhide belt with a buckle shaped like a sun, and the dented tin crown that sat atop his cottony hair, he looked like the genuine article.

"I do believe I am in the presence of King Neptune himself," she said.

He eyed her in open appreciation. "You're a sight for these old man's eyes, if I may say so."

Her cheeks warmed with his compliment. She searched the crowd for Andrew, half hoping that he'd look at her the way Gibbons had. Disappointment flickered when she saw he wasn't there.

"After you, my queen." Gibbons waved his hand above one of two roughly hewn thrones. "Let the celebration begin!" he bellowed when she sat.

Jonesy was playing the fiddle, singing as his friend blew into a short wooden tube that resembled a flute.

> *"Now let every man drink off his full bumper,*
> *And let every man drink up his glass.*
> *We'll drink and be jolly, and drown melancholy,*
> *And here's to the heart of each true-hearted*
> *lass."*

Carly tapped her foot to the jaunty tune. She was dying to dance with Andrew. Where was the man hiding?

"Sire, I should like the pleasure of a dance with your queen," Cuddy asked Gibbons, dipping in a courtly bow.

"Aye. Permission granted."

Cuddy offered her his arm. He wore a cropped royal blue jacket over a white shirt, spiced up by a jaunty crimson scarf tied around his neck. He led her to the center of a crowd of sailors, all of whom were drinking from tin cups filled with grog.

As Cuddy whirled her around in moves reminiscent of square dancing, Carly had little difficulty learning the steps. "Have you seen the captain tonight?" she asked.

"Aye, on his way to his quarters to fetch a brandy. He doesn't care much for grog." Cuddy must have detected her disappointment, for he assured her, "He'll be back."

"Think he'll mind if I ask him to dance?"

Cuddy laughed and spun her out to arms' length before reeling her close. "I'd give a month's wages to see you two dance. I told him so myself."

"Way to go, Cuddy. Now I'll have to drag him out here."

"And I'll give my next month's wages to see ya do that."

The song ended, and he returned her to the throne. Breathless, she accepted a goblet of diluted grog from Gibbons. She managed one swallow before Jonesy, the helmsman, approached her.

"May I have this dance?" the grizzled sailor asked.

"Why, certainly." She hooked her arm under his. She was ready for some fun.

Freshly shaven, Andrew settled himself against a coil of rope, his bottle of brandy within easy reach. He had a clear view of the dance area but would not be easily seen from it.

Amanda had returned to dance with his helmsman. The dress she had donned completely altered her appearance, changing her from pretty sprite to alluring woman. He did not know which Amanda he preferred, and decided he liked them both. In his days as a young naval officer, and during that one season in London, he'd bedded his share of women—aristocrats, courte-

sans, exotic foreign beauties. But none had so capti-
vated him as this little spitfire.

Absently, he stroked the cool glass of the liquor bottle, watching Amanda as she laughed and danced with
complete abandon. He felt a flash of envy. Her past
was as unblemished as the future of comfort and riches
that awaited her in England. True, she had not all her
wits about her, but in a way, that protected her, making
life nothing more than a game.

He pondered how his own life might have been different had he gone mad from grief rather than bearing
its crushing weight after Richard had destroyed his
family. Perhaps madness would have blunted the
knifelike guilt that pierced Andrew still.

Suddenly cold, despite the tropical heat, he shuddered. No, madness would have done little. His
mother and Jeremy were gone, innocents caught in a
maelstrom of revenge. 'Twas a fact he would never be
able to change. Only avenge.

The thought brought his attention back to the very
instrument of his retaliation: Amanda.

An innocent, as well.

For as long as he could remember, anger and pride
had guided him, the desire for retribution his greatest
passion. Yet, Amanda made him question that self-
imposed isolation.

Rolling a sip of brandy over his tongue, he watched
her chest rise and fall with her exertions. He remembered well the feel of her small but strong body, her
soft curves. Her skirts lifted as she twirled, revealing
the shapely form of two long, deliciously bare legs. He
pictured her round bottom, and how that warm flesh
would feel cupped in his palms.

The ache in his groin echoed a need too powerful to be deadened by liquor, and he weighed the consequences of giving in to his desire for one night. Later, as every other night, he and Amanda would be alone in his quarters. If he chose to seduce her, no one would be the wiser. Lying awake at night, he'd often imagined how she would look wearing nothing but her silky skin, her nakedness for him alone to see. He'd longed to press every tempting inch of her to him, her sweet mouth welcoming his kiss . . . as he hungered for her body to welcome him.

Damnation. He grabbed the bottle and drew on it long and hard. Speaking of madness, his inappropriate lust would surely have him at Bedlam's doorstep before the voyage was over. Amanda scuttled his ability to function as a logical, reasonable man. Indeed, to regain his wits, he had no choice but to use her to satisfy his physical cravings, his erotic curiosity. 'Twas a matter of survival. Aye, he'd have her; then he could sleep at night without her visiting his dreams.

A sudden sickening shame roared through him. Had his father's blood corrupted his very soul? If he were to sell Amanda after they made love, he would be branding her a whore. He would not, could not treat Amanda, or any woman, the way his father had treated his mother. At all costs, he must keep away from Amanda until he was free of her.

Carly's heart skipped a beat when she finally spied Andrew. He was leaning against a coil of rope, his face drawn into a scowl. Oh, for Pete's sake. Of all nights for him to be in a bad mood. She'd cheer him up—as soon as her duties in the Neptune ceremony were over.

"Time for the hooch!" she cried.

She accompanied Willoughby to a bucket of the foulest brew she'd ever helped create. The cook had poured in two bottles of cheap gin before adding a few rotten eggs—"cackle fruit," he called them—and some watery, fermented cabbage similar to sauerkraut, a dish so putrid that the only reason sailors ate it was because it was rumored to prevent scurvy.

She stirred the mess with a ladle, wrinkling her nose when the pungent odor reached her. Grinning wickedly, she sought out Theo, cowering in the front of the crowd, and winked. He managed a wobbly smile. He and two other young sailors had never yet crossed the equator and would be initiated into the society of Neptune tonight.

"Will the first hopeful come forward, please?" Gibbons called. A shaky-looking young man inched toward him. "Move your arse, lad!"

The sailor bolted, but two burly others dragged him back to Gibbons.

"Men!" Gibbons roared. "Would you like to see what happens to sailors who lose their nerve?"

"Aye!" they answered.

Carly grimaced and turned away. This was one revolting tradition she hadn't been able to convince Willoughby to drop.

"Surgeon!" Gibbons beckoned to Willoughby.

For reasons Carly would rather not contemplate, the cook was referred to as the ship's "surgeon."

With uncharacteristic ferocity, Willoughby waved a bloodied knife through the air. "Where is the coward?"

Gibbons commanded, "Answer him!"

111

"Here, sir," the young man whimpered. "Oh, I beg you—have mercy. Have mercy!"

"Gut him, Doctor." Gibbons sounded cold, indifferent.

Willoughby grabbed the struggling youth from behind. Carly cringed at the sailor's pitiful sobs. She covered her eyes but peeked through her fingers.

A piercing shriek tore through the night air. The crowd howled in delight as blood and entrails slithered to the deck.

Carly squeezed her eyes shut, fighting the nausea that rose in her stomach. That chicken had been killed this morning, and the sack of guts Willoughby had hidden beneath the boy's shirt to simulate cutting him had sat in the hot galley the entire day. It would be putrefied by now.

With theatrical realism, no doubt enhanced by the foul odor, the youth sagged to his knees, moaning hideously and clutching his bloodied middle.

"Stand aside!" Theo yelled.

Grumbling vibrated through the crowd.

Carly lowered her hands.

Theo explained, "There is a man down." He crouched next to a third young man, who had fainted. The candidates hadn't been told that the execution was staged.

"Move back, I say!" Theo fanned his hat vigorously over the unconscious fellow's white face.

Booth shouted, "Gut the swoonin' jellyfish!"

The crowd echoed his jeer.

Theo rose to his feet. "No. Take me, instead." Though his wan face revealed his terror, his steady voice resounded clearly across the deck.

Carly glanced behind Theo and locked her gaze

with Andrew's. His frown had vanished. Propping his arms on his bent legs, he shared her smile of pride.

"Come forward, lad." Gibbons's tone had softened, revealing the respect he had for the boy. "Are you prepared to become a son of Neptune?"

"Aye, I am," answered Theo solemnly.

At Gibbons's nod, Carly scooped up some hooch with a ladle and dribbled it into a cup. "I'm so proud of you, Theo," she whispered. "The captain is, too."

Theo nodded, wide-eyed, and took the cup from her. To her delight, he raised it high with unexpected showmanship. "To King Neptune!"

Gulping the cup dry in one swallow, he handed it back to Carly. "Whew," he gasped, his blue eyes watering.

She framed his face in her hands and kissed him on the forehead. As the crowd roared their approval, Theo blushed brighter than the moon.

Gibbons and Cuddy poured a bucket of seawater over the fainted sailor. As soon as his eyes fluttered open, they gave the sputtering youth a mouthful of hooch. "To King Neptune," he gasped and promptly got sick over the side of the deck.

Someone fired a pistol shot into the air, then another, and the rowdy celebration resumed. Jonesy picked up his fiddle, stomping his boot as he played.

As the men gathered in groups to talk, sing, and laugh, Carly crossed the dance floor. Bombarded by sailors eager to dance, she shook her head, discouraging the men as politely as she could, and moved just beyond the crowd, into the shadows at the edge of the lantern light.

Half-reclining against a coil of rope, his shirt unbuttoned partway down his chest, Andrew should have looked like the other drunken sailors but did not. He was magnificent, as regal and elegant as a lion at rest.

And just as potentially dangerous.

Tossing her hair over her shoulders, she gave Andrew the sultriest come-hither look she knew how. Though his eyes blazed, he did not rise to his feet.

"Playing hard to get, is he?" she said under her breath. "Fine. I'll do this by myself."

Facing Andrew, she swayed slowly. Using all her other senses, she savored the magic of the tropical night. Moving her hips in a primitive, undulating invitation, she raised her arms.

Andrew watched her intently.

The beat drummed faster. Letting go, she arched her back, shaking her hair until it was wild and tangled, tumbling over her heated face and bare shoulders. She was vaguely aware of the raucous sounds of the party far behind her, but she ignored them, becoming lost in a world that was nothing but stars and sea and freedom such as she'd never known before. Drunk on life, she let out a whoop of joy, whipped her hair, and twirled on the balls of her feet, dancing faster and faster, her bare feet slapping against the deck planks in time to the feverish, hedonistic beat deep inside her.

In the end, satisfaction eluded her. Her steps faltered. She slowed, panting. She needed more than the sensuous caress of linen clinging to her moist skin, more than the excitement the music brought her. Her heart was tired of dancing alone, always alone. She wanted Andrew. She wanted his strong hands to pull her hard against him, holding her until the sweaty heat of their bodies melted away all the reasons they shouldn't be together. A hundred rational, haven't-you-learned-your-lesson-yet reasons.

She dropped her arms to her sides and peered past the ropes and rigging until she found him. *Target at twelve o'clock.*

Smiling, she armed her weapons and rolled in for the kill.

Chapter Eight

Sitting up with some effort, Andrew lowered his bottle of brandy. Amanda was walking toward him, her cheeks flushed, her hips swaying, her skin slick from exertion.

The way she would look when he made love to her.

He choked on his brandy. His head was already swimming with the effects of too much liquor, yet he tilted the bottle a second time, drinking deeply and then swiping the back of his hand across his mouth.

She stopped directly in front of him and leaned forward. Her bodice gapped slightly, revealing the rounded tops of her small breasts. He tightened his grip on the bottle, crushed his other hand into a throbbing fist, and somehow resisted the urge to slip his hand inside the muslin to caress one of the exquisite mounds.

She is your cargo, Spencer. She differs from the other booty aboard only in her potential *value.*

In a breathless, husky voice that shuddered through to the very core of him, she asked, "Would you like to dance?"

He stifled a groan. The way she'd danced for him had aroused him completely, set on fire the deepest, most primal male part of him. He'd never felt anything like it.

"Andrew?"

The sound of his name on her lips nearly undid him. Dizzy from the alcohol, he peered at her, steeling himself against her invitation.

He did not consider himself a religious man, nor a believer in miracles. His skills and instincts had kept him afloat these past few years. Not faith. Yet, there were times, after his dreams, when he'd entertain the notion that he and Amanda had been brought together for a reason.

"Come on. . . ." She raised her hand, palm up, beckoning. It was so simple. He merely had to touch his fingers to hers—

No. He had to see through his revenge.

It was all he had left.

"I don't dance."

"Oh, that's okay." Her lips curved in a sweet smile. "I'll teach you."

"I do . . . not . . . dance."

Disbelief, then hurt flickered in her eyes, but she recovered swiftly. "You know, Mr. Holier-Than-Thou, you could try being a little more polite."

"Polite?" He snorted. He was ready to detonate, and she was questioning his social graces? Good God, if he was any more polite, he'd explode.

117

"You think you're better than me, don't you?" She gave a quick laugh that hinted at bitterness. "Guys like you haven't changed one bit in the past hundred and eighty years. All you care about is money, and you'll roll right over anything and anyone in your way to get more, won't you? You're not better than me. You're nothing but a rich man's bored and spoiled son."

He raised one brow.

"Well, you're not spoiled, exactly." She paused to catch her breath. "All right, 'bored' is pushing it, too. But that leaves duke's son, and believe me, that's plenty."

He stared at her. "A duke's legitimate son? Wherever did you get such a notion?"

His astonishment escaped her notice. "Listen," she said, "I don't know what happened to you to make you such a jerk, but it has nothing to do with me."

"It has everything to do with you, milady."

Her eyes flashed. "It has everything to do with *her.* Amanda. My name is Carly. Why don't you try saying it? Maybe it will help you figure out that the night you thought you saved Amanda, you saved me instead. Carly. Go on, say it."

Watching her, he brought the bottle to his lips.

"Say it!"

"The dress—it suits you," he offered, making certain she saw his appreciative perusal. It was an attempt to dilute her growing fury, but it did quite the opposite.

She rolled her hands into fists. "I've had it. You've ignored everything I've said since the day I got here. All you care about is *your* revenge, *your* plan, what benefit I will bring *you.* I'm sick of it." Her voice trembled, and she swallowed. "You aren't the only one with a grudge

118

to bear. You aren't the only person in the world who has been wronged by someone else. Or has felt pain."

"You know nothing of pain, milady."

He heard her sharp intake of breath, as though she'd been struck. Her eyes glinted with sudden tears. She bit her lower lip and raised her face to the stars. "You know nothing about me," she whispered. "Nothing."

Her anguish smashed his heart into a million pieces.

"Milady, I—'twas wrong of me to say that," he heard himself say in a hoarse, alcohol-slurred voice.

She would not look at him.

Andrew rubbed the palms of both hands over his eyes. He was fighting on two fronts now—one against the woman he was dangerously close to falling in love with, and another with the man she would marry.

"If you think that I'm going to go to this duke-guy willingly, then you're more nuts than you think *I* am." Pausing, she silently mouthed the words she'd uttered. Apparently satisfied that she'd gotten the statement right, she bent forward and tapped her finger on the top of his head. "I ain't going. Got it? Work *that* into your brilliantly calculated strategy, Captain."

With that, she left him.

"Cuddy," she called out, smoothing her skirt, "how about another dance?"

Every part of Andrew cried out to run after her but, drawing on years of discipline, he did not. The beginnings of a headache throbbed behind his eyes. He set aside the bottle. He'd had more to drink than he'd intended, and he did not need more.

For hours, he listened to the music, the laughter, the lusty celebrating of his men. He was their purpose, their livelihood. He'd worked hard to earn their respect, and judging by the eagerness with which they followed him into battle, they trusted him with their very lives. With the exception of Booth, who he tolerated because the man had helped him escape from prison, the men had served with him in the navy, where Andrew had been known for his rather unconventional thinking.

Unlike most of his contemporaries, Andrew had welcomed new ways of solving old problems, opened his mind to all possibilities, and then made his decisions heedless of tradition.

When had that all changed? When had he become so set in his ways?

He pressed his face to his open palms, massaging his temples with his thumbs. He thought of Amanda—her sweetness, the vulnerability that she tried so hard to conceal. And at odds with it all, her iron will. He'd called her daft, but his heart told him otherwise. For months now, she had been trying to tell him something. Perhaps it was time he listened.

"Sail ho!"

The cry startled Carly awake. She was still on her hands and knees, blinking, groping around in the bright morning sunshine as the crew sprang into action.

After the party had died down, the sour stench of sweat, grog, and rotting food was nearly overwhelming in the cloying, humid air, but the heat in the cabin had been worse. She'd slept on the deck protected by Gibbons and Theo.

Hastily weaving her snarled hair into a braid, Carly sought out Andrew. Deep in conversation with Cuddy, he was holding his telescope to one eye. She followed the direction of the telescope to the horizon. Her heart lurched. She could barely make out the speck of white, but there was no doubt about it. It was another ship.

"Who is it?" she asked, joining the two men.

Andrew calmly handed the telescope to Cuddy. "'Tis a man-of-war."

Absorbing his statement, she started to chew on a fingernail, then forced her hand away and into a fist.

"Aye. Too far yet to see her flag." Cuddy lowered the telescope. "What do you make of it?"

"They may simply be running along the same route." Thoughtful, Andrew squinted through the telescope. "Or they may be after me. Or perhaps the lady. Only time will tell. We shall be ready for them in either case."

"Aye, sir. That we will." Cuddy left to shout some orders to the weary, hungover crew.

Though Andrew hadn't given Cuddy specific instructions on what to say, she knew the orders were Andrew's. Cuddy spoke often of his years with Andrew. In situations like this, she surmised that they anticipated each other's thoughts.

"May I see?" she asked with strained politeness.

Andrew gave her the telescope. She squeezed one eye shut, focusing on the ship as he moved behind her. His warm breath stroked the side of her neck. "Three masts, square-rigged—'tis a monster, armed to the teeth," he said.

Her insides felt watery with his description of the threat. What if it was the duke's ship? What if they took her aboard against her will? How would she ever find her way home then? Worse yet, what if they harmed Andrew and his crew? Willing herself not to show any emotion, she placed the telescope in his open hand. She gripped the railing until her fingers throbbed. "Thank you," she murmured, her back to him.

Andrew hesitated before leaving her side. "It frightens you."

"Yes." It seemed she could not hide anything from him. She exhaled slowly. "But not in the way you think."

"In what way, then?"

She stubbornly kept her gaze on the water below, avoiding his eyes, avoiding the warship. "I don't want to be taken against my will. I . . . feel safe here."

I feel safe with you, Andrew, was what she wanted to say. *I could love you.*

Heat spread over her cheeks with the revelation.

She lifted her gaze. "I'm not Amanda," she said quietly. "Help me get home."

He winced, and that familiar look of pain clouded his tender gaze. This time, he was the one who glanced away.

Could it be that he didn't want her to leave? Had he changed his mind? Hope buoyed her. "Andrew, don't make me go aboard that ship. If Amanda's who they're after, and I'm not her, I don't exactly relish the idea of being onboard that ship when they find out."

"There is no wind, milady. We cannot move. Nor can they."

"So, what you're saying is, don't pack my bags yet."

A moment of uneasy silence ticked by; then he faced her, his face contorted with what had to be honest-to-God guilt. "Later, I should like to speak with you, milady. About last night."

The memory of his rudeness pulled her thoughts

122

from the warship, the possibility of her capture. She waved her hand and said almost airily, "Let me guess. You want dance lessons."

His expression darkened. "Stay out of my men's way this morn," he said in an equally frosty tone. "The hammock in the rigging, too. That is an order."

"Aye-aye, *Capítan.*"

He scowled, then strode off, his cutlass slapping against his tight blue pants, while his knee-high boots thudded on the deck.

It was childish bickering, and she hated it. Sighing, she sagged against the railing. Why was she pushing him away when she needed him most?

As the morning wore on, the whisper of a breeze that had arisen at dawn died off. Andrew had ensconced himself at a small table with Cuddy and several other men in a tarp-shaded nook near the helm. He smoked a cheroot, occasionally rubbing his eyes tiredly as he leaned back in his chair. Though he looked haggard and hungover, there was no doubt he was in command of his men and his ship. She felt safer for it, admired him for it, too. After a while, her anger began to fade. Maybe the snob really didn't know how to dance. In light of the present crisis, the whole thing seemed like a silly argument anyway.

By noon, the other ship's position on the horizon had not changed. The men not immediately involved in hauling gunpowder and cannonballs from belowdecks were edgy and went about their chores quietly. Carly untied the festive ribbons and carefully folded them into the basket. She reclaimed her bra from Savannah, only to give it a well-deserved slingshot burial at sea. She watered the ship's vegetable garden and played with the new litter of rabbits. The ship grew some of its own food, of course. As the temperature climbed, she and Theo spent the remainder of the afternoon in the shade reading *Rob Roy*.

Finally, when the supper whistle blew, Andrew stood and stretched. He crossed the deck to where she sat with her plate. "Would you care to join me for dinner?" He gestured to the same table he'd been sitting at all day.

"Sure." She walked alongside him, stealing glances at the stubble on his jaw, the shadows under his eyes. "You're looking a little rough around the edges."

He pulled out her chair as she sat, then took his place opposite her. He propped one long leg across his knee and regarded her with thoughtful blue eyes. "Rough around the edges, is it?"

"It was a long night for all of us, I suppose," she said, grateful that she'd danced instead of drinking grog.

Gibbons brought a tray with two plates of roast pork, biscuits, a side of pudding—which wasn't much more than boiled flour and molasses—and two cups of warm beer. They thanked him, and he rejoined the other men.

Andrew cut into the pork and gestured with his chin to the horizon. " 'Tis too far away to see who she belongs to, but she has the lines of a new warship. If her captain is intent on catching us, he will."

Carly's heart thudded in her chest. "How long?" she asked, lowering her fork.

"In the absence of wind—days, perhaps weeks."

"That's the best news I've heard all day."

His expression softened. "Do not worry. No one will force my hand. I will not give you up before the appointed time and place."

"Was that what you wanted to tell me?"

"No." He spread his hands flat on the table. "I was rude last night, milady. 'Twas a consequence of reacting before thinking. I do not wish to lose the pleasure of your willing companionship, so I pray you will find it in your heart to forgive me." He reached across the table and grazed his fingertips over her bare arm.

She shivered, and her eyes prickled with unshed tears. What was it about the man that made her carefully dammed emotions gush to the surface? "I didn't want to argue, either," she said softly. "Apology accepted."

Andrew felt his tension dissolve. "I am certain the duke received the news of the kidnapping weeks ago. Since our progress has been slow, this could very well be a ship dispatched to apprehend us."

She sipped her beer. "They outgun us, don't they?"

"Vastly." He noted that she did not flinch. Would not a gently bred lady fall to pieces? Perhaps she was indeed his muslin-wrapped warrior. "This is the reason why I drill the men twice a week. Our twelve-pounders—our cannons—are no match shot for shot against the bigger guns on a man-of-war, but we can fire, reload, and fire again in under four minutes."

"Can't they?"

He cut off a piece of pork and chewed thoughtfully. "Most captains rarely drill their crews. Gunpowder is expensive. Prowling the seas in the most powerful ships in the world has made them complacent."

"And thus speed is their weakness," she said.

"Precisely."

Her luminous eyes glittered with interest.

Encouraged, he continued, "I've accumulated a vast store of gunpowder. My men and I have often gone without other necessities in order to purchase it . . . or take it."

"From other ships?" She leaned forward, her lips slightly parted.

He forced himself to ignore the temptation of her sweet mouth. "Aye. The only way to fight sheer muscle is to be quick and clever—"

"And unconventional."

"Well put. I learned that lesson during this last unsuccessful war with the Americans. The closest I came to defeat as a naval officer was to those former colonist upstarts. I daresay they earned my hearty respect."

Smug, she sat up straighter.

"You haven't yet touched your food," he said. "Eat, milady, or I shan't tell you another thing."

She gave a soft laugh. She picked up her fork and regarded him from beneath her thick, dark lashes. "I suppose you think I'm too skinny, too."

"You are not skinny. Slender, yes, but with curves in all the proper places."

Her cheeks reddened as she shyly averted her eyes. The amber light of the setting sun illuminated the skin on her neck and bare shoulders. He felt a jolt of arousal as he imagined exploring her smooth, sun-warmed flesh with his lips. "You are no longer among polite society, milady. Unlike the men you are accustomed to, I speak my mind."

"Please do. And don't stop." She flashed him a

saucy, flirtatious smile that made him want to kiss every freckle on her little nose. "I wasn't fishing for compliments, but thank you."

"Whyever would you need to 'fish' for compliments?" He was astounded to see her blush brighter than before. "You are enchanting. A beautiful woman. Surely men have told you that before."

"No," she said softly, tucking a strand of hair behind her ear. "Not like that."

Clearly distracted, she pushed her dinner about her plate. He could see her pulse ticking in her throat.

He folded his arms over his chest, drumming his fingers on his upper arms. He must cease this dalliance immediately. It would only make matters more difficult for both of them when the time came for her to leave. "In the morning I will be meeting with Cuddy in my quarters to discuss our, ah, unexpected guest. You may join us if you like."

She appeared relieved by the change in subject. Then her eyes sparkled as an eager grin lit up her face. "I don't know much about sea battles, but I studied them in my history classes at Annapolis."

"Ah, the military academy you spoke of. Where you were a midshipman."

She looked at him askance. "You're not going to add something snide? I don't believe it."

"Let's just say I have decided to keep an open mind." He pointed to her plate. "Eat."

With a victorious smile, she dipped her fork into the pudding.

Agony exploded down his back, pulsing in white-red flashes behind his eyes. Panic squeezed his insides. He had to stay conscious so he could keep her warm. He mustn't lose her. Blinded by saltwater streaming into his eyes, hands numbed by the cold, he reached for her. She slipped from his grasp.

"Stay with me!"

"Blast!" Andrew struggled upright in his hammock, his hands clutching air, his heart thudding in his chest. Drugged by the intensity of the dream, he glanced wildly around the darkened room as he slowly slipped from the dream back to reality. His heart lurched. "Amanda," he murmured and headed for her door.

Moonlight drifted into the cabin. The faint light eased his journey to her bed. Relief flooded him at the sight of her. Dressed in Theo's shirt, she was sleeping on her back, one arm thrown casually over her head.

Tonight's dream had been the most vivid of all. He'd tried to protect her, ignoring the pain that threatened to render him helpless. But in the end, as always, he lost her.

Yet, here she was, unharmed—his spitfire with the face of an angel.

He moved closer, smiling in spite of his thundering pulse and the fear reverberating inside him. Carefully, so he would not wake her, he caressed her soft, warm cheek with his palm. She stirred and flung her arms to either side. The linen shirt drew taut over her breasts, revealing the hazy silhouette of her nipples.

His heartbeat quickened anew. He wanted to climb into the bed and feel her arms come around him.

Again he touched her, his fingertip to her lower lip. He smiled at the way she pursed her lips in her sleep. Lifting a lock of her hair, he rubbed it between his fingers and savored the weighty, silken texture.

He looked down at her face once more. Her eyes

were wide open, watching him. His throat went suddenly dry.

"Milady," he blurted hoarsely, yanking his hand away as though he'd been burned. "I had another dream. I was merely assuring myself of your well-being."

"You don't need to explain," she murmured sleepily, pulling the blanket higher. "I know what your dreams are like. Sometimes I come in to check on you."

"Do you now?" He reached down to smooth her hair away from her forehead. Then he slipped his fingers into the hair bunched at the nape of her neck and massaged her gently. She made a sigh of contentment. Pushing aside his inner warnings, his better judgment, he leaned down to brush his lips over hers.

Her lips parted beneath his gentle pressure. Groaning, he slipped his tongue into her warm, wet mouth. He heard her utter a muffled cry as her hands locked behind his head, pressing him to her as her tongue stroked his in an unexpected intimate, erotic welcome. He shuddered. Good God—the woman could kiss!

Urged by her eagerness, he kissed her deeper, wanting more, much more. His arousal strained against the flimsy covering of his robe. He supported the weight of his upper body by propping his arms on the bed. Although he ached to touch her, to hold her close, he grasped fistfuls of the bedsheet instead, lest he lose himself and allow the kiss to go too far.

In the end, he lost track of time, loving her with his mouth until he feared her lips would surely be sore.

He pulled away to gaze at her in wonder. "I don't believe I've ever shared . . . a finer kiss."

She smiled with her gold-brown eyes. "I was thinking the same thing."

Overcome by emotions he could not begin to decipher, he framed her face with his hands, stroking his thumbs over her cheeks. The way she combed her fingers through his hair sent tingles careening down his spine.

"Just one more," she whispered. "One more kiss."

"Aye . . . one more." The bed creaked as he shifted his weight. He took his time answering her request, suckling her kiss-swollen lower lip, teasing her with tiny nipping kisses on her nose, chin, and neck, before covering her mouth with his, taking her deeply, desperately, the way he yearned to make love to her.

His groans, her whimpers, their panting breaths filled the quiet cabin. Never in his life had he fought so hard to maintain control. Never before had it mattered.

She arched her back. He moved his hips farther away from her belly, and his arms trembled with the awkward position. Then, when she slipped one hot, smooth hand inside his robe, he forced himself to pull away. "We mustn't."

She frowned, but her eyes sparked with amusement. "Oh, 'we mustn't,' " she teased, mimicking him. "So proper. You British and your stiff upper lip." She trailed one finger over his mouth. "Well, not so stiff, maybe, in your case."

He nipped her fingertip, then kissed the inside of her wrist. "I will not compromise you, milady." He pushed himself off the bed. It swung with the release of his weight. He cinched the knot on his robe, then smiled down at her, thoroughly enchanted.

The moonlight mingled with the silver highlights in her hair, magic that spilled over the pillow and onto her shoulders. He regretted that he'd never see her, *all* of her, in the light of the moon. Alas, she was not his. She would never be his. Perhaps that was what his dreams were telling him. Rueful, he brought his hand to her cheek.

She kissed his palm, a sweet gesture that sent a tidal wave of pleasure crashing through him. "I have the feeling that you won't want to talk about this in the morning," she said.

"This . . . 'tis not proper."

"If you say so."

He opened his mouth, then closed it. There was nothing more he could say. "Sleep well, milady."

Closing the door behind him, he eyed his hammock with reluctance. He was too sharply aroused to sleep. He stripped out of his robe, donned his trousers, and walked onto the deck of the sleeping ship, welcoming the blessedly cool air on his heated skin.

He climbed into the ship's longboat, lay on his back, and watched the stars until the last one faded with the rising sun.

Chapter Nine

When Carly woke, the memory of Andrew's kisses wrapped her in blissful warmth. She rolled onto her back, then touched a fingertip to her tender lips as she listened to the familiar sounds of early morning aboard the *Phoenix*. Boot heels thumped, men whistled and shouted, water sloshed as several heavy wet mops were pushed over the deck, but the tell-tale hiss of wind in the sails was thankfully absent. If the *Phoenix* couldn't move, neither could the other ship. Heartened, she climbed out of bed and jumped to the floor.

He was one hell of a kisser.

With a shiver of pleasure, she relived Andrew's kiss—how impulsive it was.

And wonderful and sexy and . . . perfect.

132

But judging by how quickly he'd left, she doubted he cared to repeat the deed any time soon.

Thank goodness, one of them had the common sense to stop before things got too hot. Flirting and kissing were one thing—but if she and Andrew became lovers, she might fall for him. She couldn't risk that. Not now. Not when it was so important that she keep her wits about her. At any moment, the warship could attack and take her aboard. That would thrust her into a situation that very likely might prevent her from ever making it home.

Someone knocked on the outer door as she dressed in her flight suit. She heard Cuddy, the scraping of chairs, and the sound of Andrew's deep, resonant voice in her head. *"I don't believe I've ever shared . . . a finer kiss."*

Groaning, she slapped two handfuls of cool water onto her face, then two more, dousing a new brushfire of desire. Only after a good deal of effort did she manage to compose herself.

Pausing at the door to Andrew's cabin, she recalled her former skipper's words: *"No matter what kind of night you had, or what may have happened to you on your way to work, you come to my briefings with a clear head and ready to work."*

With Commander Martinez's voice fresh in her mind, she took a deep breath and pushed open the door. "Good morning, gentlemen."

Immediately, both men stood. Andrew's bloodshot, blue-eyed gaze hesitated for the briefest instant on her lips as he pulled out a chair for her to sit down.

Her traitorous heart leaped at the sight of him. He wasn't smiling exactly, but his glacial facade had thawed considerably.

"I trust you slept well, milady."

"Best night in weeks," she replied. "And you?"

"I feel particularly well-rested this morn."

"The weather was quite warm last night, wasn't it?" She thought she saw a flicker of amusement in his eyes.

"Indeed," he said. "Unusually so."

"I like the sudden change. Think it'll continue?"

He contemplated her for a good long moment. "The weather at the equator is often unpredictable."

Stamping out more brushfires, she exhaled slowly. Then she turned her attention to Cuddy. "And good morning to you, Mr. Egan."

Looking mildly confused, Cuddy smiled and scratched his fingers through his silver-gray hair. "Good mornin'."

She sat, followed by the two men. The small table was cluttered with charts and a battered, salt-stained Royal Navy textbook.

There was another knock on the door.

"Enter," Andrew called over his shoulder.

Theo walked in, his back straight and his chin up. "You summoned me, Cap'n?"

"Aye. Hoist the English flag, if you would, lad."

"Aye-aye, sir," Theo said gravely.

"Please have Mr. Gibbons fetch breakfast for Lady Amanda, Mr. Egan, and myself."

"Aye, Cap'n. Will that be all?"

"That will be all." Andrew unrolled a chart and took what looked like a pair of dividers, used for measuring, from a leather pouch.

"Expecting our friends a little sooner than planned?" Carly asked after Theo had closed the door.

"The winds may change this morn. And again, they may not." Andrew twirled the divider between his

134

thumb and forefinger. "From this day forward, we are the *Sea Slug,* a simple English merchant sloop minding her own business."

"The *Sea Slug*?" Carly laughed. "Now, don't you think that's overdoing it a little? There have to be more . . . noble names. Sea Hawk, for instance, or—" She drummed her fingers on the table.

Cuddy said, "We have christened ourselves far worse. 'Tis the best we could manage, with a lady onboard." He gave her a shy smile.

"But *Sea Slug*? Spare me."

" 'Tis done," Andrew said. "Mr. Gibbons will paint her with the new name." He waved vaguely in the direction of the bow before unrolling a piece of parchment. The change in his demeanor implied that the time for chitchat was over.

Carly crossed her arms over her chest and settled back to listen. This was serious business. She guessed that she had been invited here to learn, perhaps to help, if possible.

Andrew lit a cheroot and propped his elbows on the table. A silvery thread of smoke coiled upward, briefly obscuring his features. The man revealed as the smoke dissipated was composed and resolute, a leader. His lips were set into an unyielding line. Yet, they were the same lips that had that kissed her with such aching tenderness last night. The change only made her want him more.

"If my instincts are right about the man-of-war," Andrew continued, "we shall be meeting in battle in highly irregular circumstances. In the near absence of wind,'tis often said a lucky shot determines the victor." Thoughtful, he gazed at the burning tip of his cheroot. "I say luck has nothing to do with it."

"Meaning?" she asked.

"Luck is naught but skill and preparation." He balanced his glasses on the bridge of his nose. Then he smoothed the parchment until it lay flat on the table.

Carly's breath lodged in her throat at the sight. Andrew had sketched, in detail, the ship that might very well try to take her aboard. It had more sails and more deck levels than the *Phoenix*. And—if the drawing was accurate—twice as many guns. As she flattened her hand over the drawing, her fighter-pilot instincts surfaced. *When up against overwhelming odds, use your strengths to exploit your enemy's weakness.* Her fingers traced the length of the tallest mast. She tapped it thoughtfully.

As though reading her thoughts, Andrew said, "There must be wind to topple a mast—unless we score a direct hit."

She glanced up to find his penetrating gaze fixed on her. Her hunch was right. He had already determined his strategy—yesterday, during his day-long meeting with his officers. By asking for her help this morning, he was merely giving her the chance to prove she was who she said she was—a navy officer.

She returned her attention to the sketch. Frowning, she studied the picture, chewing the inside of her lip. There were many similarities between ships and planes. *Find some.* Her fingertip hesitated over the cannons. *No.* The powder room? *No.* If it was like the one on the *Phoenix,* it was lined with lead and deep in the bowels of the ship. *Where is this monster's weakness?* Her finger drifted aft toward the stern. From the corner of her eye, she saw Cuddy straighten. Ah, she must be getting warmer.

The stern. The rudder was in the stern. It was connected to the tiller, the wheel used to turn the ship. She felt a surge of excitement. If there was no rudder, a ship couldn't be steered. And the *Phoenix* was a smaller, more maneuverable ship. She might not be able to out-gun the man-of-war, but she could out-think it.

"Here," she said, unable to keep the enthusiasm out of her voice. "They are most vulnerable *here*. If you aim for the rudder and break it off, even with the biggest cannons and all the wind in the world, they wouldn't be able to catch us. They'd spin in circles."

"Precisely, milady. Well done." Andrew tamped out his cheroot in the ashtray and removed his glasses. His smile was one of admiration, warming her from head to toe. "Now we will discuss how this presumably impossible feat will be accomplished."

That evening, as the sun drifted down to the glassy sea, Carly stared at the innocuous speck of white on the horizon. "We'll be like David and Goliath," she remarked to Cuddy, who stood by her side.

He nodded. Pushing his tarpaulin hat higher on his forehead, he eyed her with a good deal of affection. "In battle, no ship is better than her captain. When it comes to captains, there are none better than Sir Andrew Spencer." He returned his keenly intelligent gaze to the horizon. "None better."

The warship had not budged from its place on the horizon. The crew's adrenaline had peaked weeks before. Without a battle for release, the men had become grouchy and argumentative.

Fresh water was rationed. Bathing had to be done with seawater. Carly felt as dirty and miserable as the crew looked.

Their supplies dwindled. They'd used the last of the turnips, potatoes, and onions while Carly's precious garden shriveled in the unrelenting heat. The chickens were gone, as were the rabbits. She'd become attached to the innocent fluffs of energy, and steadfastly refused to eat the meals Willoughby prepared from their meager flesh.

The only thing that wasn't in danger of running out was her desire for Andrew. She wanted him more than ever. He swam daily. The sight of his suntanned, muscled upper body as he emerged dripping wet from the sea simply took her breath away. Having tasted the passion of his kiss, she was grateful that he'd moved his hammock outside to the deck, taking away the temptation of knowing he was next door.

But her feelings ran deeper than mere physical attraction. The recent harrowing days had proven that Andrew was a born leader: courageous, inventive, and honorable. Not the aimless aristocrat she'd assumed him to be. She could almost believe that he was the reason she'd been taken from her home and brought here.

To a life that became more dangerous each day.

One afternoon, a man fell from the rigging. He died two days later because of an infection from rope burns. After the funeral, the crew's spirits plummeted.

It was a turning point for them all.

Andrew was a man possessed. To Carly it seemed his sole reason for living was to keep morale high, to keep the men focused on their task. He seemed to be everywhere on the ship—all the time. He used humor; he was approachable. He organized impromptu gatherings to sing seamen's chanties and frequently mentioned the island hideaway off the African mainland. "A gem, a piece of paradise," he'd remind them, quoting Gibbons. Many of the men had wives and families waiting. They were anxious to return. It had been nine months since they were last home and Andrew made sure they knew his goal was their safe return.

Through it all, he slept little. If not for Carly's constant badgering, she was sure that he would have forgotten to eat. Her impression was that this encounter was more than a sea battle. Andrew wasn't fighting a ship; he had declared war on his tortured soul.

To Carly's dismay, the ship started gaining on them. At first, she'd thought she was seeing things. But by the second morning, she was positive. The sail had grown larger.

"How are they doing it?" she asked Cuddy.

"In a dead calm, some captains will order the men to tow the ship."

She peered through the telescope. "How in the world do you tow a ship?" The man-of-war was sitting still at the moment. Certainly, nothing was in front, towing it.

"They use the longboats at night." Cuddy said grimly. "They send the men down in shifts to row. 'Tis exhausting work. In weather such as this 'twill wear a crew down quicker than the scurvy."

"Their captain must be absolutely mad. Or heartless."

"If I was to judge by the rate they're closing on us, I would say both, lass."

With Cuddy's words, icy fear crystallized inside

139

her. Whatever the silent behemoth on the horizon wanted, it was ready to kill its crew to get it.

After the midday meal, while the crew rested in the shade of the tarps, Andrew informed them that the war ship was now also being towed during the hot daylight hours. His mouth curled in disgust. Clearly, he did not approve of how the ship's captain was driving his crew.

How would that captain fight the actual battle? Carly wondered with a great deal of trepidation. Would he be as brutal, as merciless?

She prayed she'd be of use to Andrew when that time came. She was a warrior, but one with clipped wings, a trained soldier who knew little of cannons or cutlasses or gunpowder. But she'd offer her expertise all the same.

As the afternoon wore on, the *Phoenix* lolled on the gentle swells, her sails unfurled and limp. Soon Carly grew drowsy in the muggy heat. A strand of limp hair tickled her cheek. She brushed it away impatiently.

"Rain!" the cry rang out.

Carly scrambled to her feet. Light-headed, she nearly passed out. As she hugged the mast for support, she heard the deep, resounding boom of thunder. A cheer went up. Storms meant wind, and the thunderstorm bearing down on the *Phoenix* promised to deliver more than its share. If the winds were harnessed properly, and luck was on their side, the *Phoenix* could leave the war ship behind.

But the storm teased them.

It moved away . . . stalled . . .

Then came closer, only to repeat its tantalizing dance.

A gaggle of drumming fingers and tapping toes, the crew lined the decks, awaiting the rain in a silent vigil throughout the long afternoon.

Except for Andrew.

He was in constant motion, pacing up and down the length of his ship, consulting his charts, barking orders. It exhausted Carly to watch him. He was wound up so tightly that she feared he would snap in two if the storm passed them by.

The sails billowed hesitantly. The crew waited.

And waited.

The air was thick with the scent of thunder, and crackled with electricity. When the roiling clouds finally engulfed the sun, the temperature plunged.

Carly's heart fluttered with anticipation. In the chill of the monstrous shadow, the thunder rumbled on and on, raising the hairs on the back of her neck. It was hard not to think of her dreams.

When the great sails exploded with the thunderstorm's first gust, the *Phoenix* lifted like the legendary bird she was named after. It was the finest moment of exhilaration and escape Carly had ever experienced. She cried out her joy. The sailors bellowed theirs. She raised her hands above her head and lifted her sunburned face to the cooling drops. Then the deluge was upon them.

She loosened her hair from her braid and shook the heavy tresses free. Soon she was soaked to the skin. She inhaled the scent of rain, the salty sea, the resinous vapor rising from the parched, overheated deck planks.

"You'll never catch us!" she shouted in the direction of the war ship. "Nature is on our side, not yours!"

Unfortunately, the victory was short-lived.

When the storm passed, none replaced it. To no one's surprise, the war ship reappeared two days later.

Chapter Ten

"Hi."

From where he sat on the chains, Andrew glanced up at Amanda's greeting.

"Nice evening, huh?" she said. "Mind if I keep you company?"

"Please do." Wearily, he patted the planks next to him.

Dressed in a shirt and trousers, she climbed down. Her hair was still damp from her bath in seawater, and she busied herself combing out the snarls.

Andrew leaned against the ship's hull. A dull headache throbbed behind his eyes. The exhausting weeks of tension had taken their toll. When he'd last used a razor, days ago, he'd seen the strain in the lines bracketing his mouth and in his dark-circled eyes.

Distant lightning pulsed on the horizon.

"Maybe it'll rain again," Amanda said fervently.

He gave an indifferent grunt, understanding all too well why she had joined him tonight. He kept up the crew's morale by day, but in the evenings, Amanda boosted *his* spirits. He allowed her to do so only because he had come to trust her. Cheering him tonight, however, would be an impossible task.

"Come on, Andrew. Chin up."

He snorted. "I have resigned myself to it; they will catch us. But we shall be ready. My only regret is the possibility of you and my men being injured in battle."

She said quietly, "Just promise me you won't try to be a hero. I'd die if anything happened to you."

His heart leapt. Did she care for him? Something deep inside him stirred with the possibility. "Milady, I shall do whatever must be done."

"I know. That's what I'm afraid of," she said somberly, then tended to her hair.

In the silvery moonlight 'twas easy to believe she was a mermaid intent on enchanting him. Moonlight and magic—were not sailors warned of this? Nearly a month had passed since the last full moon, and he remembered well the mischief it had wreaked on its previous visit. A man wouldn't soon forget a kiss such as the one they'd shared.

He stared at the comb as she rhythmically sifted it through her glowing locks. If she were his, he would comb her hair each night. "Aye, I would comb it," he said under his breath.

Andrew clamped his jaw shut, praying she hadn't heard him.

Her arm hesitated. "Sorry, what was that?"

He felt a flush creep up his neck. Bloody hell. Had

he actually said he'd comb her hair? He must have lingered in the sun too long today.

The silence between them stretched out into long moments. Then, to his utter amazement, she nonchalantly placed the comb on the wood between them. "If you want to, I don't mind."

Andrew's heart thundered in his ears as he curled his fingers around the ivory comb. He swallowed, gathering her thick, damp hair in his hand. It was like wet silk. Reverently, he stroked the comb through it.

A shiver ran through her, and she arched her neck as he patiently worked through the tangles.

"This is unearthly wonderful," she whispered.

Andrew barely heard her voice above his ragged breathing. He lifted her hair from her neck to gaze at the curve of her pale shoulder, revealed by her too-large shirt. 'Twas all too easy to imagine kissing the side of her throat, touching his lips to the pulse he saw there.

She was meant to be made love to in the moonlight.

Aye, he would take her here, loving her as their bodies moved in rhythm to the gentle swells.

His swelling manhood throbbed painfully. "Blast."

"What is it?"

"A splinter," he growled.

She laughed softly. He immediately tugged on her hair. She yelped.

"No laughing, milady. Or I shall comb your mane out by the roots."

Amanda held up her hands in surrender, then hitched up her fallen sleeve, fastening a button at the collar.

Andrew exhaled.

"Do you have any sisters?" she asked.

He frowned. "No. Why do you ask?"

"Just curious. I thought maybe that's why you wanted to comb my hair—that you'd done this for your sisters."

"Humph." What he was feeling for her was anything but fraternal.

"Do you have any brothers?"

"One."

"Older?"

"Younger."

After a pause, she asked, "What is his name?"

"Was."

"Was?"

"*Was* his name," Andrew said. "He died."

"I'm sorry." She cleared her throat. "He must have had a name, though."

"Jeremy."

More silence.

Sighing loudly, she scooted around to face him. "Do you have any idea how hard it is to have a conversation with you? Oh, sure, you can talk the fur off a cat when it comes to sailing or thunderstorms or your precious helicopters, but when it comes to your family or any other normal topic that two people can talk about, I get *this!*"

His gaze dropped to her mouth.

Carly hadn't forgotten *that* look. "And furthermore," she said, "if you keep looking at me like that, I'll kiss you like there's no tomorrow."

His shoulders rocked with laughter. "Good God," he said, wiping his eyes. "I never know what will come out of your mouth."

She turned away from him to hide her smile. "Is that why you were gaping at my mouth?"

"Hardly," he said. Curling a finger under her chin, he angled her face toward him. His own was shadowed, his eyes dark. "Have you any idea how much I want you?" he asked and lowered his mouth to hers.

She sighed as honeyed warmth spread through her. His kiss was deep, hungry. She'd never dreamed kissing could be like this. And it felt right, somehow familiar, his tongue velvet against hers, fingertips deftly skimming across her throat and jaw, to her ear, circling, over and over, fanning her desire into languid heat.

Threading her fingers through his silky hair, she cuddled closer until he simply lifted her onto his lap. He moved her shirt aside to nibble her shoulder, and she half-laughed, half-moaned at the sensation of his raspy whiskers mingling with the softness of his lips.

"You are sweet," he said, his voice huskier. "So delicious." He buried his face between her breasts, his strong hands kneading her back, lifting her to him. With the flimsy barrier of her shirt in place, he coaxed her nipple into his mouth with gentle suction. She panted with the intimate attention, thinking she would never again catch her breath.

He took his lips from the tight peak, blew a stream of cool air on the linen moistened by his hot, wet mouth, and she gasped with the sudden, sharp pleasure. She knew then that if he were to touch her where she so desperately ached for him, her last shreds of resistance would blow apart. She would give him everything. . . .

Her heart, her soul.

But if Andrew believed she was Amanda, the love shared would be a lie.

"Andrew—" She could barely form a single coherent thought, let alone utter a sentence.

Yet, he knew; somehow he knew. He hauled her to him with enough force to knock the breath from her. She lay with her cheek crushed against his chest, listening to his thudding heart. He was just as affected by the embrace.

"I can't," she whispered.

"Aye, I know."

Curling her arms around his broad shoulders, she hugged him with all her might. Above, a sentry strolled by. When the sound of the man's boots faded, Andrew cradled her face in his roughened hands and moved her head back. "I apologize for my impudence."

Is that what he thought, that she objected to his impudence? "I *wanted* you to kiss me," she said, expecting him to make a remark about her loyalty to her betrothed. "I stopped only because you think I'm someone else."

"Give me reason to believe otherwise."

"I've given you plenty!"

He regarded her. "Tell me about you, then. The woman you claim I do not know."

With his words, Amanda's mouth curved ruefully. Andrew was amused by her sudden reticence. He kissed the tip of her freckled nose, then ruffled her damp hair. He used the comb to fix the chaos he had wrought. "Did you have a special acquaintance at home? A suitor, perhaps?" *Or a lover?* he asked silently, his gut twisting with the very thought.

She stiffened. "No."

"No suitors before the duke?"

"One."

"Was he saddened by your departure?"

Her lips thinned.

"Milady?"

"No, I said!" She spun away from him.

He brought his thumb to her chin and turned her head. "Have you any idea how hard it is to have a conversation with *you*, milady? Indeed, you can talk the ears off a dog when it comes to your imaginary world of the future. Or your bloody flying machines. But when it comes to family or any other normal topic that two people may discuss . . . I get *this!*"

She laughed in delight. "Touché."

Andrew picked up the comb and resumed where he'd left off, although any tangles were long since gone. "Tell me," he said.

"I didn't leave Rick. He left me. We were engaged, but he changed his mind. We'd lived together for—"

Andrew yanked the comb, pulling several strands of hair out by the roots.

She peered at him with accusing eyes. "Will you please stop doing that?"

"You lived as husband and wife without vows?"

She winced. "I'd rather you didn't announce my personal life to the entire ship."

"I apologize. Now, answer me."

"Yes, I lived with him for two years."

"A bloody scoundrel."

"Actually, he was. But that's not *why* he was. It is common for couples to live together before getting married. So you can get to know each other."

"That is the purpose of courting," Andrew stated. "An honorable man does not bring a woman into his home and soil her, all without a legal commitment."

Her mouth crept into grin. "Dr. Laura would love you."

"Who is this doctor?"

"She's a therapist . . . a radio talk show host." She shook her head. "Never mind. I met Rick when we were

149

cadets at Annapolis. I was born and raised in a tiny town in Virginia, and it was my first time away from home. Boy, was I ever innocent." She signed. "I fell head over heels. Rick came from a good family. Old money, he called it. To me, money meant security. When he bought me things, I thought it meant he loved me. He did, I guess, but other things were more important."

"Like what?"

She gazed out to sea. "He left me . . . because his family told him to. His mother didn't think I was good enough—rich enough—for her boy. To be perfectly honest," she said, "all I've ever wanted was my own family—a husband who loved me. And children."

" 'Tis not much to ask," he said gently.

"My childhood wasn't easy. I worked when I should have played. I had to be an adult before I was ready—" Her voice caught. "Dreaming about a real family made it better, somehow."

Andrew admitted, "As a child, I, too, was often lonely."

"Tell me more, please. I know so little about you."

"My father never acknowledged me," he said to his astonishment. This he had never told another soul.

Had you been worthy, he would have loved you.

Andrew grimaced as the mantra of his childhood sliced into him. He thought he had buried it where he could no longer hear it.

"My father never acknowledged me, either," Amanda said bitterly. "He got my mother pregnant and left. The usual story. He was rich. My mother was dirt poor. He accused her of wanting to trap him." Her mouth twisted.

Andrew gathered her close, fitting the curve of her spine against his stomach. He rested his chin on her shoulder.

"He left to attend a university a month before I was born," Amanda said. "He was the president of his own company. But my mother said it was dangerous relying on anyone else. She was too proud to ask him for money. Or to force him to accept me as his daughter."

" 'Twas his loss."

"I'd say your father lost out, too."

Her confession smashed through every barrier he'd erected to cover the old pain.

He closed his eyes as a shudder coursed through him. Never had he felt so close to another.

"My mother was everything to me," Amanda whispered. "She told me I could grow up to be anything I wanted. Everything I went on to achieve was because of her. She gave me the wings to fly."

He exhaled slowly. "My mother was an extraordinary women, as well. She was Italian, came to London as a girl."

"Yes," she coaxed when he paused. "Tell me."

He drew her closer.

Carly felt the prickle of his whiskers against her cheek, the heat of his broad chest through her thin linen shirt. Despite the warm night, goose bumps raised on her arms. To be held like this was something she'd waited for her entire life. To feel safe, secure, cherished. She wished the moment would last forever. Warily, tentatively, she opened the door to her heart. Just a crack.

Andrew found her hands and laced his fingers with hers. "Richard's uncle, the elder duke of Westridge, was my father. My mother was the duke's mistress. I am a bastard."

"That's why Richard inherited, not you."

"Aye." He tightened his grip on her hands. Odd, but

151

she appeared pleased with his announcement. It was the first time a woman had met that news with anything other than distaste. "I grew up in a town house near Hyde Park. Close to where Westridge lived with his family. I rarely saw him, though. He did not meet with my mother at our town house—not after I was born, at any rate. He maintained yet another residence for that purpose.

"There were many demands on her. Yet I never doubted she loved me. She may not have been able to give me time, but she showed me love with her deeds. For instance—and this was highly irregular, mind you—she wrote Westridge's name on my record of birth. Then she insisted that I receive an education. When I expressed a desire to go to sea, she had the duke buy me a commission." As a younger man, Andrew had been mortified to learn that the man who had not thought him worthy of a second glance had been goaded into buying his bastard a livelihood—by his mistress, no less! He'd felt indebted to his father, although he resented the man's absence. It had taken years, but Andrew finally understood that all Westridge did was gain him entry. He now realized that his success had been up to him. He'd achieved it. Despite his father. Only to have Richard wrest it away.

"My mother may not have had the best judgment," Andrew said tightly. "But she was fiercely loyal. She would have fought to the death to protect her own."

Which was precisely what she did, Spencer, he said to himself.

Amanda covered his hands with hers and squeezed. "Now I know where you get it from."

"Sorry?"

"You're the same way. You'll fight to the death to protect what's yours, won't you?"

He inhaled the scent of her hair. "Aye," he whispered, tucking the locks spilling over her shoulder behind her ear. He kissed her there, eliciting a shiver. In a surge of affection, he wrapped his arms around her and pulled her flush against him. "I never could understand why someone so beautiful appeared so melancholy," he said.

"Your mother."

"Aye. I don't know precisely how it came to me, but I knew Westridge was to blame. From the time I was six or seven, I hated him."

"Which is why you've sworn revenge on his nephew."

Among other reasons. He gave a curt nod. If not for the vengeance he so desperately sought, he would have no reason for living at all.

The moon rose higher. Reflected in shimmering bands of light on the water, its timeless tranquility cooled Andrew's anger. He hugged Amanda close, breathed in her scent. She was all that was sweet, all that was good.

The very opposite of him.

Slowly, he rocked her back and forth, holding her until he'd lulled her to sleep. Then he held her for hours afterward, until the stars in the eastern sky began to fade.

At dawn, he reluctantly carried her to his bedchamber. After tucking a light blanket over her legs, he brushed his finger over her soft cheek. "What am I to do about you? You will marry another, Amanda. Losing you will torture me all the days of my life."

153

Chapter Eleven

"H. M. S. *Longreach*," Andrew read aloud.

Cuddy took the telescope. "Never heard of her."

"Nor I." Thoughtful, Andrew stroked his chin. "I can only assume she's recently commissioned."

Carly stood quietly as the men discussed the warship. A light breeze had come up during the night, bringing the vessel close enough to see in detail. If the wind continued, the ships could engage each other within hours.

Her stomach clenched. She wished she had something constructive to do to calm her nerves. She walked to the bow, where Jonesy and Theo were wrapping Savannah with ropes and hammocks.

"It looks like a cocoon," Carly remarked.

"If you'd been the least bit willing," Jonesy said, "Cap'n would have the same done to you."

They exchanged knowing grins. So much for her participating in the battle, Carly thought.

"She's overseen every battle, with nary a scratch," Jonesy explained, finishing the job with several strong knots. "Patience, sweet Savannah. We'll be unwrappin' you before you know it."

Carly continued her inspection of the ship, sensing the tense anticipation of the men as they readied the guns. The cannons weighed thousands of pounds each, and it took several men to operate them. It was sweaty, strenuous, exhausting work. The great guns had to be pulled backward, loaded with a ball and gunpowder, pushed forward, aimed, and fired, before starting all over again. There was no room for error. If the fire wasn't out before fresh gunpowder was added, the mistake could trigger an explosion. With only fifty sailors aboard, the *Phoenix* could fire no more than half her guns at any particular time. This further added to her vulnerability.

A distant sound—like the backfire of a truck— erupted from the direction of the warship. Carly's heart echoed with her own thunder. "Are they firing already?"

She hadn't realized she'd actually voiced the question until a sailor nearby answered, "She's wantin' to test our mettle."

Carly hastened back to Andrew and Cuddy. "Explain 'test our mettle.' "

"She's firing her long nines," Andrew replied. "Testing her range, and hoping we'll fire an answering volley." He exhaled. "They'll not risk your life, though. I suspect the captain will try to ascertain whether you are aboard before he commences firing in earnest."

155

Her throat went dry. "How's he going to do that?"

"Dispatch a party, a longboat or two."

She started at another sharp bang, and forced her mind away from Andrew's grim reply. "The 'long nines' are the smaller guns, aren't they?"

"Aye."

"They sure don't sound small." She ought to be used to the noise of cannon fire—she'd been through dozens of gunnery drills since coming aboard. But when the cannonballs were aimed their way, it was a different sound entirely.

Again the crack of distant guns echoed.

"Milady,'tis time."

She glanced up at Andrew's words. "The cabin already? I'd rather stay and fight."

Andrew wiped the back of his hand across his sweaty brow. He swallowed, then exhaled slowly. "Mr. Egan, I need a moment with the lady, if you don't mind."

"Understand, sir." Cuddy tucked the telescope under his arm and left them.

Andrew lifted one arm as though to touch her. Catching himself he clenched his hand into a fist and let it fall to his side. Like her, he tried not to display their growing closeness in front of the crew. "We have been over this time and again. There will be no more discussion on the matter. You have disobeyed me in the past. Do not do so today." Though the words were harsh, his tone was gentle, almost pleading. "I do not want to see you killed."

For a brief moment, they stared at each other as though nothing existed but the two of them. His gaze was unguarded, exquisitely tender, revealing the depth of his feelings for her.

Her chest squeezed tight. What if this was the last

time they saw each other? A wave of light-headedness hit her as she tried to catch her breath. She wanted to throw her arms around him, beg him to be careful, tell him she couldn't bear the thought of losing him. There were no antibiotics; he could catch a fever and die from a cut or a broken bone.

"Go on," he coaxed. " 'Twill be over soon."

She took a deep, shuddering breath. "I'll hold you to your word, Captain."

Andrew's eyes glinted strangely. Turning away, he called to a group of men nearby. "Booth!"

She stiffened, heat flooding her face.

"Escort the lady to my quarters. Ensure that she bolts the door."

Black Beard looked as though he'd just won the lottery.

"No!" Carly blurted, drawing Andrew's astonished stare. "That's not necessary. I'm sure Mr. Booth is quite busy with his other duties."

"Yer a more important duty," Booth drawled, offering her his arm. She drilled him with a touch-me-mister-and-you're-history stare.

His eyes turned dead cold.

Apparently, none of it was lost on Andrew. "On second thought, return to your duties, Booth," he said, eyeing Carly curiously.

Booth hesitated. "Cap'n?"

"Go. I want you manning your gun."

"Aye, Cap'n."

"Before you do . . . I have a bit of strategy to discuss."

Booth trailed Andrew just out of earshot. Uneasy, Carly watched the two men converse. Booth's face turned crimson. But Andrew appeared calm. The only words loud enough for her to hear were: "—not a request, Booth. An order."

Glowering, Booth returned to his cannon.

Carly wondered what had transpired between them, and immediately thought of Theo's safety. Maybe it was time to tell Andrew what had happened between her and Booth. For Theo's sake, anyway. But now was clearly not the moment.

Andrew cupped his hands around his mouth and called for Cuddy to take her to the cabin. She and the first mate walked side by side in silence. Before stepping inside, she looked over her shoulder for Andrew. Immersed in his own thoughts, his hands clasped behind his back, he faced the sea. She said a silent prayer for him and the others, then squeezed Cuddy's arm. "Good luck."

"Superior skill and preparation, not luck," Cuddy reminded her with a grin.

"I'll pray for all three, then."

Cuddy walked away only after she'd slid the bolt in place. Sighing, she leaned tiredly against the door and faced the empty cabin, which no longer resembled a cabin. To her right, where there used to be a wall, was the shadowy interior of the ship. Before today, she'd never known that the wall was hinged, allowing it to be raised and hooked to the ceiling in times of battle. To further reduce the chance of injury, the furniture and the glass panes from the windows were stowed in compartments below the waterline. Unlike the missiles she had fired from her jet, cannonballs did not cause fire when they hit. They plowed through wood and masts and fragile sails like wrecking balls. She'd learned from Andrew that most injuries and deaths in a sea battle weren't from the rounds themselves, but from splinters hurled like spears.

A hammock and mattress-padded corner had been prepared for her protection.

Just like Savannah.

Sitting cross-legged in her odd nest, Carly removed the handgun she'd hidden in the thigh pocket of her flight suit. She ran her thumb over the cold steel. Sleek, almost futuristic in appearance after so many months, the gun was out of place in this world. She turned it over and over in her hand until she'd reacquainted herself with its weight and feel.

Six shots.

If she was to fire, she'd need to choose her targets wisely. And quickly. She leaned back against the padded wall and took deep breaths.

By the time evening fell, she was stiff, and her legs were cramped from heat and dehydration. The darkness was almost suffocating without candles or lamps to illuminate the now cavernous room. Sea battles, she'd been told, were fought in daylight, and, clinging to that thought, she allowed herself to relax somewhat.

Around midnight, she guessed, Gibbons brought her dried beef and a flask of beer before leaving to rejoin the men. With the food and beer filling her stomach, she could no longer fight her drowsiness, and she surrendered to exhaustion soon after.

She slept poorly. Twisted visions and bits of restless dreams mingled, whipped together, and spun around like dead leaves on an autumn wind. Fitful and perspiring, she hovered between wakefulness and sleep.

She thought she was still dreaming when the first war cries tore through the predawn silence.

She bolted to her knees. There were more shouts, followed by the popping of pistols and the firecracker smell of black powder. *This is no dream.*

Ignoring Andrew's earlier warnings, she crept to the side window. Two unfamiliar longboats were docked alongside the *Phoenix,* and one more was coasting up. *Crap.*

They were under attack.

Apprehension uncoiled inside her as dozens of soldiers clambered aboard; it was a raid to weaken the *Phoenix* and her crew before the sun rose and a full-fledged battle began.

The crew met the onslaught with chilling howls. Carly steeled herself. Her years of training for war came back with startling clarity. She narrowed her eyes and set her jaw. Then she closed her hand around the gun.

More men scrambled over the side of the ship. Some were cut down instantly by cutlasses, axes, and clubs. Pistol-fire flickered like an army of flash cameras at the scene of a horrific accident.

The screams of the wounded were the hardest to take. Her prayers flowed faster than her lips could form them.

Haze and smoke drifted across the deck where pistols exploded and blades glinted. She saw Theo run past, wild-eyed with fear and excitement, his red hair poking up in all directions. "Oh, God," she said softly, and bit the inside of her lower lip.

Amid the confusion, Andrew's purposeful stride caught her eye. He'd shoved his pistol into his belt, and now gripped his cutlass with his right hand. His hoarse voice rang with authority and purpose as he pointed feverishly in one direction, then the other, shouting orders to his men.

Carly's heart sank. There was blood smeared across his forehead, and more trickled from his matted hair.

Something, or someone, slammed into the cabin door behind her. She whirled to face the sound, aiming her gun as she did. Her heart pounded frantically.

She waited for what seemed like an eternity.

The door handle turned.

Another thud . . .

The bolt held firm. She heard a curse and whoever it was moved away.

The sound of feet running drew her attention outside, just as sunlight burst over the horizon and fanned out over the calm sea. Two of the enemy longboats were on their way back to the man-of-war, no doubt to deliver the news that she wasn't aboard. The few soldiers left onboard the *Phoenix* were desperate, slicing and shooting their way to the one remaining longboat. Now that it was full daylight, and Amanda hadn't been found, the real sea battle would begin. Knowing that their presence would hardly keep the larger craft from firing as soon as it got into range, the trapped soldiers fought viciously to escape.

Andrew jogged past the window. Carly ducked. He didn't see her. Gulping smoky air, she peered over the window ledge once again.

Andrew had run to a man writhing in agony. Cutlass in hand, shoulders heaving, he hunkered down next to him. Jonesy! The helmsman's shirt was soaked with bright red blood. Andrew was talking to him, patting him on the cheek to keep him conscious.

Yellow-gray smoke floated at knee level across the

deck, imparting to the scene an eerie, nightmarish quality. Something caught her gaze: a movement, to the left.

A shadowy, pistol-toting figure slowly closed in on the pair.

Horrified, she swerved her attention to the men. Didn't anyone see him? Jonesy's head had sagged to one side, and Andrew was so immersed in loosening the man's collar that he did not notice the would-be assassin.

She raised her handgun. "Andrew, turn around," she urged under her breath, but he he simply stood and wiped sweat and blood from his eyes with the back of his hand.

The soldier's hand raised, but Carly fired first.

Blood sprayed from the soldier's head. Andrew wheeled around, yanking his pistol from his belt. The mortally wounded man advanced still, but with a strange, wobbly-legged gait. Before Andrew had time to shoot at the odd sight before him, Carly fired a second shot, hitting the soldier in the neck. His pistol discharged harmlessly in the air as he fell face-first with a dull thud.

Andrew gaped at the fallen man, then looked incredulously across the deck to where she stood at the window.

Overcome by the enormity of what she'd done, Carly staggered backward. The gunshots and her heartbeat rang in her ears. Strange emotions swirled through her. She had killed a man—and saved Andrew's life. She didn't know whether she wanted to cheer, cry, or be sick.

"Amanda!" Andrew pounded on the door like a madman. "God's teeth, woman. Open the bloody door!"

Her hands shook as she released the bolt. He

crashed inside, almost knocking her down. His breath hissed in and out as he bolted it closed.

"Andrew. You're hurt." She reached up to push his bloody hair off his forehead.

He reared back. " 'Tis a scratch." He was taut, gruff, and had the wild eyes of a warrior in battle. "Where is the weapon?"

"Jonesy. Is he dead?"

"No, he is not! The pistol. Hand it to me."

She placed the still warm gun in his palm. He gingerly turned the weapon over, looked inside the barrel, sniffed at it. "I have never seen workmanship such as this. Who built this? Where did you purchase it?"

She answered the easiest question first. "It's a Glock 26 handgun."

His head jerked up. "I have never heard of 'Glock.' 'Tis not at all a conventional pistol."

"It sure as hell was conventional in my time."

He lowered the gun. "Your time . . ."

"Yes. Almost two hundred years from now."

His inner struggle was evident in his distracted gaze. He paced several steps and stopped. Exhaling a rough breath, he turned to face her. "You are not Lady Amanda."

"You believe me!"

He nodded.

Joy and relief surged through her. She clutched her hands, fought to keep her breathing even. "Had I known the gun would convince you, I'd have shown it to you long ago."

With bloodshot eyes, he contemplated the weapon in his hands.

"Would you like to see how it works?" Tapping the gun with one finger, she raised her brows in silent entreaty. The ammo was precious, but it was worth a bullet to ensure her victory.

"Aye."

Cautiously, she covered his hands with hers. Standing beside and somewhat behind him, she gently guided his fingers around the gun. "See? Not so different than your pistol."

His dark brows drew together. He lifted the weapon, pointing it out the window that faced the stern. " 'Tis prepared?"

"No powder," she told him. "Now all you do is fire."

A muscle ticked above his stubbled, sweaty jaw. He aimed steady and true, then fired a single shot out to sea.

"Holy Mother of God," he muttered. Holding his arm rigid, the gun firmly in his grip, he closed his eyes. "It has the gentle kick of a babe," he said finally.

"Compared to your pistols, yes."

"No powder is required?"

She shook her head. "It's inside the individual bullets. The rounds."

"Hide it."

She stepped back. "No. Keep it. Please. You'll need it out there."

"No!" he snapped. "No one must see this. No one must know. Swear to me you will not show any man this weapon."

"I swear. I—" He was regarding her in an odd, intense way. "Andrew?"

Something inside him seemed to snap. He hauled her up against him so fast that her feet came off the ground. His mouth came down hard over hers, and he kissed her with a possessiveness that had not been there before. He smelled of gunpowder, tasted of battle—of salty sweat, the metallic tang of blood. He was impatient, almost rough, and there was both fury and frustration in his muffled, drawn-out groan.

She locked her arms behind his neck, pressing every inch of herself to him. Growling deep in his throat, he dragged his open mouth from her lips to her cheek, her ear. His hot breath sent streaks of pleasure up her spine, raised goose bumps on her arms and legs.

He gasped, "Carly . . . oh, Carly."

Carly.

Uttering a soft cry of joy, she clasped her fingers behind his head, forcing his mouth down to hers to taste the sweet sound of her name on his lips.

Mumbling something about wanting more than kisses, he pushed her backward to where the hammocks padded the wall. In one swift motion, he caught her thighs and hoisted her up. Molding his hands over her buttocks, he lifted her atop the hard, thick bulge between his thighs.

He buried his face between her shoulder and neck and rocked his hips as though he was already inside her. His whiskers scoured her neck, his hands covered her breasts, and his breathing grew harsh and uneven. Reaching between their bodies, he fumbled with the buttons on his pants.

Driven by the lingering adrenaline from the battle, he intended to take her hard and fast against the wall, so unlike her fantasies, where he'd made slow and exquisitely tender love to her. Yet her need for him was so intense, she'd do anything he wanted.

"Yes, my sweet girl, my fire."

Anything.

"Amanda—"

"Carly," she corrected breathlessly.

He gaped at her blankly, as though he'd woken up to find a stranger wrapped around him.

"What is it, Andrew?"

Anguish flashed in his eyes. He made a choked groan and went rigid. Carly's thighs slid down his legs, and her booted feet hit the planked floor with twin thuds.

"It's okay," she said softly. "I'm sorry I made a big deal out of it. I expect it'll take a little while to get used to calling me Carly."

" 'Used to'?" He slammed his open hand against the wall.

She flinched.

"Where is Amanda?"

"How am I supposed to know where she is? I don't even know how *I* got here."

"You don't know," he repeated in a monotone. Abruptly, he turned his back to her and buttoned his pants. Then he crossed the room to the door.

"A good-bye would be nice."

"Do not seek to detain me, milady."

"Afraid if you stay that you'll soil the cargo?" she quipped nervously in hopes of defusing whatever had gotten him so riled.

He said nothing.

A few steps brought her next to him. "Andrew?"

The veil of icy remoteness that had so characterized his behavior in her early days onboard the ship had returned to his eyes. " 'Tis the way of it, aye."

As if deflecting a blow, she brought her hands to her stomach.

"I don't understand," she persisted, hating the quavering of her voice. "I don't belong to the duke. I don't belong to anyone. I thought you'd be happy about that."

He squeezed his eyes shut. She saw him clench his jaw. "I must see to my men."

"Talk to me, Andrew. Don't do this."

"No?" he bellowed. "What would you have me do? You have proven your identity, have you not? And now you want me to act as though I am pleased? God's teeth, woman!" The very air in the stuffy room vibrated with his rage. "What the bloody hell am I supposed to tell my crew? That I've risked their lives for naught? That instead of the duke's betrothed I've snared some apparition from the future? ' 'Twas a slightly muddled kidnapping, Your Grace. Please accept my apologies.' Oh, bloody hell, I can hear Richard laughing now."

"Damn it, Andrew. Let him laugh! Who cares?"

He glowered at her. "I do."

"I see. Well, I'm glad I found this all out now. Before we . . . you know." Tears stung her eyes as she waved her hand at his crotch.

"Milady, I will say this but once more. I cannot dally, tempted though I am by your, ah, sweet invitation."

"How dare you!" She lifted her hand, wanting to slap away his insolence. Instead, she curled her hand into a fist and pressed it to her thigh. His nostrils flared as though she had indeed struck him.

He looked almost apologetic as he reached for the bolt. "Stay back." He opened the door, then peered cautiously outside, his cutlass poised and ready. "The skirmish has ended. The day, however, is far from over. Stay inside. That is an order, be there any doubt on your part."

"Yes, your high and mighty *sir.*" With that, she slammed and bolted the door.

Chapter Twelve

Andrew stood outside the door, inhaling deep lungsful of air. It seemed he was caught in the momentum of his life, rushing toward a fate his despicable deeds had set in motion. He could no more stop the imminent outcome than he could stop his heart.

There's no turning back.

He plowed his fingers through his sweat-dampened hair and marched away from the cabin. But not from the image of Amanda's—*Carly's*—incredulous, anguish-filled gaze. He remembered well the wariness in her eyes during her first days on the ship. Now it was back. *He'd* brought it back.

His chest squeezed tight. *Damn her eyes*. Damn her for making him believe he could be like other men. That he could love.

And for making him love her.

"Mr. Egan," Andrew called out upon sighting his first mate. "I take it you've disposed of the last of the *Longreach*'s milksops?"

"Where were ya?" Relief was etched on Cuddy's exhausted face. "I thought we'd lost you overboard."

"There was a problem at the stern. 'Tis solved." The lie tasted bitter. "As soon as we are in range, Cuddy, have the men aim for the rudder post."

"Aye, sir."

Andrew clasped his hands behind his back and walked toward the helm. After surveying the damage to his ship and discussing the casualties sustained with Willoughby, he spent the last tense moments before battle pondering the identity of the woman in his quarters.

The extraordinary pistol had scuttled his lingering doubts. She was not Lady Amanda; thus she was not betrothed to the duke. The possibilities frightened the hell out of him.

She could be yours.

But this was a woman who could vanish into the future as abruptly and unexpectedly as she'd come into his life.

Don't let her, he thought crazily.

If she stayed, what then? What had he to offer her save a nomad's life and the shame of his sorry past? Furthermore, his loyal, profit-driven crew expected to divide the promised ransom upon her release. Andrew's honor and his word as their leader were at stake if he did not follow through with the plan.

Bloody hell. 'Twas a seemingly unsolvable dilemma.

* * *

A cannonball tore through the ship with a hideous screech of splitting wood. Carly dove into her nest of rolled hammocks and flung her bare arms over her head—flimsy protection should one of the twenty-five-pounders hit the cabin.

The *Phoenix* answered with cannonfire of her own. Carly prayed the men would be successful in their dogged attempt to hit the warship's rudder.

The *Phoenix* shuddered and turned. There was a moment of blessed silence. Then Cuddy bellowed, "Fire!" and it started all over again.

It reminded her of the time she'd served temporary duty in the Middle East and the Iraqis had shelled the barracks in which she'd been sound asleep. It had scared the stuffing out of her. But this—hands down—was a hundred times worse.

More silence followed as the ships maneuvered in the breeze that had strengthened as the morning wore on.

Carly detested the silence. Even the terrifying interruption of the cannons was preferable to the quiet, aching emptiness in her heart.

What a fool she was! How could she have misinterpreted Andrew's friendship as something more?

He hadn't developed feelings for her. He'd intended to trade her for a few gold coins—and still did. End of story. Still, unlike Rick, at least Andrew had been truthful about it all along. Give the man two points for honesty. And another for remaining loyal to his men. Duty above all else—that was Andrew's credo. In a way that made her feel better, but not much.

She touched her fingertips to her puffy lips, the tender places on her chin and cheeks where his whiskers had scraped her, remembering the joyous relief on his face after he'd fired her gun and accepted who she was. But she must have misinterpreted it. Lovemaking was the farthest thing from his mind this morning. He'd only wanted to rut with her like an animal. He'd been on a combat high, fueled by the adrenaline and aggression that filled men whose lives were on the line, the same emotion that caused some soldiers to rape. But he'd come to his senses; his icy aloofness had returned.

Carly got the message loud and clear. Andrew didn't want anyone too close to him. He preferred isolation to revealing who or what had hurt him in the past. *That* at least was something she could understand.

"Fire!" Cuddy shouted from the deck. The cannons thundered in answer.

. . . Because until recently you felt the same . . .

"Fire!"

. . . and would have lived your life that way . . .

"Fire!"

. . . had Andrew not smashed the door to your heart wide open.

A cheer went up, louder than the cannons themselves. She popped upright and looked expectantly out the long window that faced the stern. Within seconds, every man onboard the ship was yelling, whistling, and whooping.

Only victory could make chaos sound sweet.

Carly leaned over the sooty windowsill. Turning southeast, the *Phoenix* leaned into the wind that had eluded her for so many weeks.

The warship didn't follow. Because she *couldn't* follow.

"Way to go, guys!" Carly raised both fists in victory. "You did it! You really did it!"

* * *

At twilight, Carly lit more lanterns, placing them close to the wounded men who had been brought to the makeshift sickbay—a partitioned area with a hatch in the ceiling as its only source of light. Because it was where she figured she'd be the most useful, Carly had offered to help Willoughby tend the wounded.

The cook was as skilled using the primitive tools and medicines of nineteenth-century healing as he was at creating meals from the limited resources onboard the ship. She'd helped him clean an assortment of cuts and burns, and even a few bullet wounds, though Willoughby had dug out the balls first. Luckily he hadn't asked her to stitch the wounds. It was not a task for the fainthearted. She'd felt the blood drain from her face the first time she watched him push a needle through a man's skin. Upon hearing her muffled moan, Willoughby had said, "I left a kettle of broth in the galley. See if it's bubbling, milady." It had given her an excellent opportunity to escape.

Now only two men remained in the hammocks. Jonesy—who'd been stabbed in the shoulder—and a cheerful, burly man with a broken leg: Angus MacVey. They were resting quietly, thanks to liberal swigs of gin and doses of what she guessed was a form of opium.

So far, Angus hadn't developed a fever. His color was good and his eyes were clear. Poor Jonesy, on the other hand, had a fever that defied all attempts to bring it down. Willoughby had confided to her that his chances of recovering weren't good. Again, she'd found herself wishing for the miracle of antibiotics.

Amazingly, there had only been two deaths.

Andrew had conducted a brief funeral before their hammock-wrapped bodies were gently tipped overboard. After a pensive moment of silence, the raucous sounds of hammers, saws, and shouting resumed. Only at twilight had the repairs ceased. Carly was certain the crew was on the deck by now, drinking their grog and solemnly toasting their fallen comrades in the starlight.

Carly settled onto a stool between Jonesy and Angus. She lifted a wet rag from Jonesy's forehead. "Can't wait to hear you play your fiddle again."

He licked his dry, cracked lips and tried to smile. "Can't think of anything sorrier than a one-armed fiddler."

"If you keep talking like that, sailor, I'll pour the rest of your gin overboard."

He chuckled, then gave a raspy cough.

She wrung out the cloth, still hot from his skin, and dipped it in a bowl of cool, precious fresh water. "Well, you'll be back fiddlin' before you know it."

"Aye," he whispered. "That I will."

With a light, tender touch, she stroked his hair with her flattened palm, the way she used to do as a child when her mother was bedridden. When she'd been in pain, this had never failed to put Rose to sleep.

Jonesy closed his eyes. "Feels nice, miss. 'Tis like bein' cared for by an angel."

"Aye," Angus piped in. "And we thank ye."

She shook her head. "I thank *you*. You and Jonesy and the rest of the crew sure beat the pants off that ol' man-of-war."

Both men chuckled.

"Captain Spencer's fortunate to have such a courageous crew," she insisted.

174

" 'Tis the other way around, miss," Angus said. "We've served with Cap'n Spencer since he was our lieutenant in the navy. We'd follow him anywhere. He's the best there is. He was knighted for valor by the king himself. For his deeds in the war."

"I know," she said quietly.

"The Americans outnumbered him that day. Everyone said he'd lose the fight, but win he did."

"Like he did today," she murmured.

"He'd be on his way to bein' an admiral if it weren't for that blasted duke."

Her mouth tightened.

Angus looked positively stricken. "My apologies, miss, but there's bad blood between the two. 'Twas a shame about the court-martial. Lies, all of it. Cap'n's an honorable man. He wouldna done what the duke said he done."

Jonesy patted her hands with his hot, dry palm. "When Cap'n came for the *Phoenix*—he and Booth— he told us we were free to go. We said we were staying. Ain't that the way it was, Angus?"

"Aye. And we stayed."

"Cap'n didn't like it much. Said he didn't want us tossed in prison for his sins." Jonesy, too weak to continue, lay back against his pillow. "Tell her, Angus," he rasped, closing his eyes.

"The cap'n's only sin was sharin' the duke's blood." Angus's ruddy cheeks colored further. "Something he's been payin' for all his life."

Heavyhearted, Carly propped her chin on her hands. Angus and Jonesy were telling her what she already knew: Andrew possessed every quality she'd ever admired and wished she'd find in a man. He was brave, loyal, honorable . . .

Considerate and loving . . .

He'd held her in his arms as though she was the most precious thing in the world.

Passion and power; that was Andrew. A magical combination that had unlocked her heart. They might have had something wonderful had she meant more to him than a profitable piece of cargo. Or an instrument of revenge.

"His loss," she muttered with a conviction she did not feel.

"My apologies, miss." Angus was peering at her. "Me and Jonesy, we shouldna gone on about the duke so. Frightened ye, we have. I pray ye find happiness with the duke."

"You didn't frighten me. I couldn't care less about Westridge. I'll go to him, so you can get your money. But I'm not going to marry him."

Angus shifted in his hammock, wincing. "Where will ye go?"

"Probably America. As far west as they've settled. I'll be a seamstress, or maybe a teacher. Independence is what I'm after," she declared, lifting her chin. "Relying on no one but myself." Then she sighed. Her lifelong I-can-take-care-of-myself credo seemed to have lost its appeal.

"Whoever wins yer heart someday will be a lucky man," Angus said quietly.

Tears blurred her vision, and she glanced away. She must be more tired than she'd thought.

She remained with the men until they'd fallen asleep. Worn out, she rose to her feet, massaging the small of her back.

Willoughby walked into the sickbay holding his

ledger in one hand, a towel-wrapped teapot in his other.

"They're asleep," she told him.

"You look weary yourself. I'll fetch Mr. Gibbons to bring you back to your quarters."

The last person she wanted to see right now was Andrew. "Can I sleep here? Come on, I know you could use the help with your galley duties and all."

The cook smiled at her with gentle eyes. "I can manage, Miss Carly."

"Please. I don't want to go back to the cabin tonight."

"Then I'll tell the cap'n you'll be staying." He lifted the ledger. "After I tally the day's figures."

"Thanks," she said as she trudged toward the extra hammock.

Willoughby extinguished the lights, save one candle on his desk, and sat down to work on his ledger, while Carly crawled into the hammock. Every bone in her body creaked and ached as she settled onto her back. Her stomach rumbled, too, but she'd lost her appetite for dried hunks of beef and couldn't face the stale biscuits that even the bugs had abandoned lately. She yearned for fresh fruit and real bread. A huge crunchy salad. And french fries, a bowl of cookie dough ice cream, and . . .

"Oh, what I wouldn't do for a slice of pizza," she murmured.

Willoughby glanced up. "Was Pete your cook in Delhi?"

"In America."

"America," he repeated dutifully, stroking his wispy beard.

She lifted her head. "Wait a minute. Pete who?"

"You said you wanted a slice of Pete's *zah.*"

"*Pizza,*" she said with a soft laugh. "It's an Italian dish."

"Italian, eh?" He raised his brows in interest. "How is it prepared?"

"Well, you start with dough. The best pizza places toss it—like this." She lifted both palms, then jerked her hands upward.

He glanced warily at the ceiling, then at the planked floor. "I fear I'd drop it."

"Nah, you wouldn't. Then you top it with tomato sauce, cheese, and then anything else you want—sausage, mushrooms, onions, green peppers. Sometimes Canadian bacon and pineapple. Once I even tried pizza topped with broccoli." She grinned at his expression of unadulterated horror.

"Dough . . . sauce . . . mushrooms—I don't know, miss. Sounds a bit odd to me. Give me a plate of kidneys and eggs, toast, aye, and a rasher of bacon. Or perhaps a bowl of that fish stew the ladies make on the island." He patted his belly. "I can taste it now."

Gibbons climbed down the ladder from the deck. " 'Tis getting dark. Cap'n asked me to escort you to the cabin."

"He hasn't spoken to me all day," she retorted, "but it's heartening to know he still wants his cargo close by."

"Christian," Willoughby cut in, calling Gibbons by his given name, "I'd like to keep the lady here. I have two sick men. Two more hands is what I need, tell him. She'll be safe."

Gibbons nodded.

Despite her hurt and anger, Carly worried about Andrew. "How's he doing?"

The big man frowned. "He's in a foul mood."

"What else is new?"

For once, they all laughed at their captain's expense.

"I was hoping you'd be done here," Gibbons told her. "So you can talk to him in that way you do."

"You'd think we lost the battle, the way he's carrying on," Willoughby said.

"Cap'n's still fighting his battle. Here." Gibbons tapped his thick finger against his head. Then he drummed his finger on his chest. "Here, too."

Gibbons bid them good night and headed up the ladder back into the starry night. His words lingered in the stuffy, medicine-scented air long after he had gone.

" 'Rolling home, rolling home, rolling home across the sea; Rolling home to dear Emerald Isle, rolling home, dear land to thee,' " sang Gibbons in his deep, rich voice.

It was another funeral. Carly sat on the deck, Theo by her side. She wiped a tear from her cheek with the back of her hand and put her arm over Theo's shoulders.

Jonesy was weak but was growing stronger every day. The funeral was his first foray up to the deck since his fever had broken a week ago.

Angus had been laid to rest, but the shock of his unexpected death from infection lingered. She was not the only one affected; the entire crew was subdued despite the brilliant blue sky and the southern Atlantic trades swelling the mended sails above.

"Up aloft amid the rigging, swiftly blows the favoring gale,
Strong as springtime in its blossom, filling out each swelling sail.

*The waves we leave behind us seem to murmur
as they rise,
We have tarried here to bear you, to the land
you dearly prize."*

Since the *Phoenix* had no chaplain, Andrew had conducted his third funeral in less than two weeks. Somber, he'd read from the Bible and added a brief eulogy before the crew joined him in singing "Amazing Grace." By the time Angus's flag-draped body had been placed on a grate at the lee side of the ship, quite a few of the rough-looking pirates were wiping their eyes. After the ship's bell had tolled three times, two men hoisted up one end of the grate, allowing the body to slide into the sea.

*"Full ten thousand miles behind us, and a thousand miles before,
Ancient ocean waves to waft us to the well-remembered shore.
Cheer up, Jack, bright smiles await you from the fairest of the fair.
And her loving eyes will greet you with kind welcomes everywhere."*

Carly raised her face to the sun and hummed along with the final chorus to the song.

*"Rolling home, rolling home, rolling home
across the sea;
Rolling home to dear Emerald Isle, rolling
home, dear land to thee."*

* * *

"No!"

"No!" Andrew's own yell yanked him from his

nightmare. Skittering at the edge of panic, he was out of his hammock and on his way across the deck before he'd come fully awake.

Where was she? Had he lost her?

Raw fear propelled him forward. He had to know she was safe. He did after every dream, those inexplicably lifelike, turbulent nightmares in which he flew a rotor-craft—one he couldn't keep from crashing into the sea. Carly was always there—and he could never save her.

He opened the door to his quarters, peering in. In the moonlit darkness, he made out her slender form under the blanket. Relief surged through him. "Why do you slip from my grasp?" he asked in an anguished whisper. "Why can't I hold you? What does it mean?"

She stirred. Hastily he shut the door. Leaning his forehead against the cool wood, he squeezed his eyes shut, until the familiar scents of oiled mahogany, leather, and tobacco erased the last vestiges of the dream.

He trudged back to his hammock and climbed into it. The sky was so dusted with stars that it had taken on a silver cast. It reminded him of the night he and Carly had spent on the chains . . . her back nestled against his chest, his arms around her as they'd gazed at the heavens, laughing and making wishes when they'd spied a shooting star.

Making wishes.

Nonsense! By the time he was six years old, he'd given up on wishes. Why then, with Carly, did everything seem possible? What was it about that woman that made him believe all over again?

He closed his eyes.

And saw the heart-stopping expression of affection and admiration and trust she wore on her face whenever she gazed at him. He knew she was quite capable of looking after herself, but that expression made him want to protect and defend her against all the ills life might conjure.

He rolled onto his side and stared at the rigging. The faint perfume of flowers on the breeze mingled with memories of her warm skin's sweet scent.

He flopped onto his back. The moon had risen higher, casting its magic through the ropes and rigging, bathing him in silver.

Silver.

Strands of silver-blond . . .

Blast!

He was sick of it, sick of it all. He had wasted his life locked in a pointless feud with Richard. He'd dragged others into his battles and put innocents at risk to further his selfish ventures.

No more.

He might not be ready to forgive, but he was bloody well tired of seeking vengeance. Perhaps he could salvage what was left of his life. If it was not too late.

He'd begin by thanking Carly; her faith in him had prompted what he could only describe as an emotional awakening. Then he'd tell her what he had decided. Aye, at first light.

He ground the heels of his palms into his eyes and climbed down from the swinging hammock. The air tasted earthy, alive, hinting at land nearby. Although nothing had been sighted yet, he knew land would come soon—unlike a good night's sleep, which clearly was beyond his grasp.

Andrew walked barefoot toward the stern, nodding to the sentry on duty. The sailor returned a hushed greeting and strolled in the opposite direction, toward the helm, where another man stood watch at the wheel.

The deck was silent but for a few faint snores of sleeping men. Most slept belowdecks, save a few, like Andrew, who preferred to sleep under the stars should the weather permit.

The moist, tropical air clung selfishly to the heat of the day. Even the deck planks felt warm under his feet. If it had not been the middle of the night—and a fool-hardy thing to do—he would have taken a swim.

Silhouetted in the moonlight was the longboat on its mount above the deck. He sauntered over to it, propped his back against the rough wood, and crossed his arms over his chest. Drumming his fingers on his upper arms, he willed sleep to drift over the railing and claim him. He forced a yawn.

The longboat shifted slightly with his weight. The movement set off a sudden scratching and scrambling from inside the vessel. Vermin? Peeking inside, he made a mental note to toss Jonesy's one-eyed tomcat in there on the morrow.

Carly gasped in surprise.

"Ah, 'tis but a woman rattling about," he said, his heart leaping at the sight of her. "I thought it was a family of rats."

Her mouth curved ruefully. "Been called worse."

"Why, may I ask, are you not in your quarters?"

"Couldn't sleep. I heard you check on me. After that I gave up and came out here." She gazed skyward and sighed. "It's incredible tonight, isn't it? I've never seen so many stars."

"Nor have I." Andrew watched her as she watched the stars. Good God, how he dreaded telling her. But he must. 'Twas the fist step. "Ah, Carly," he said, clearing his throat. "I've something to discuss with you."

"I have something to tell you, too."

"Oh?"

She patted the bench opposite her.

He hoisted himself up and over the edge of the long-boat. 'Twas the oddest thing, but he had the feeling that by doing so, he'd committed himself to a battle in which he was outmanned and outgunned. Settling himself on the bench, he propped his arms atop his knees.

She picked at the fabric of her trousers. "We haven't had much time to talk recently."

Guilt swamped him. He cleared his throat and glanced away.

"I can't blame you," she said. "You promised the men their share of the ransom before you found out I'm not Amanda. I don't envy your position."

"Carly, I—"

She held up her hand. "One more minute, okay?"

One minute, hell. He'd give her a lifetime if he could. "Go on."

"Getting to know you has meant so much to me," she said softly.

He expelled a breath. It was the first volley, and she'd hit him broadside.

"The past few months have been, by far, the happiest of my life."

He was taking on water and sinking fast. "Mine, too," he said.

Moonlight glinted in her wide golden eyes.

Framing her upturned face with his palms, he kissed the warm, downy place on her temple where her hair met her skin. "Know this. You are free to go."

She shook her head, seemingly confused.

He forced himself to say the words. "You may go to England with the duke's men. Or," he said with a sigh, "if you wish to return to your home—to your own time——I will do everything in my power to help you."

"No." Her soft, husky voice was emphatic. "I want to stay here . . . with you."

He wanted to cheer. However, it was ill-advised to claim victory before the battle was over. Once he told her the truth about himself, she would turn away. She would never want to touch him again. "Carly, do not make that decision until you hear what I have to say."

"I doubt you'll be able to change my mind." The old vulnerability flickered in her eyes. "Unless, of course, you don't want me—"

Incredulous, he blurted, "Carly, I'm in love with you."

Her eyes widened, and she took several deep breaths.

Before she could reply, he gripped her hands in his. "I've agonized over how to tell you this. And I've determined that there is no best way. So I'll just tell you." He swallowed hard. "My father never recognized that I existed. I despised that, despised *him*. This you already know. When he passed away, I acted on that bitterness. As a result, my family is dead."

Iron bands of self-loathing and grief constricted his chest. Holding her rapt gaze, he said quietly, "Their blood is on *my* hands."

Chapter Thirteen

Carly stiffened. Thankfully, she did not pull away.

Andrew said, "I told you I was summoned to court and knighted."

"Yes."

" 'Twas five years ago. My mother was living in the town house with Jeremy. Westridge bequeathed it to her before he passed away. For his generosity in that regard, I am grateful. Jeremy was lame, you see."

"Your younger brother," she murmured.

He nodded. "When I was eight, my mother discovered she was with child. She tried to comply with the duke's wishes and rid herself of the pregnancy."

Carly's expression was one of utter grief. Even in the moonlight she looked pale. "What happened?"

"Something went wrong. She bled for days. I was so frightened, Carly. I feared she would die. To this day I remember her maids pulling me from her side because I wouldn't stop crying."

"Oh, Andrew." She squeezed his fingers.

"The botched procedure damaged Jeremy's legs, I believe. Afterward, my mother had something done that would prevent further pregnancies. She was never the same again."

"No," Carly said grimly. "She wouldn't be."

Andrew exhaled and began again. "After my presentation at court, I stayed on in London. It was the beginning of the season—when society attends one ball after another and parents try to marry off their daughters," he clarified, so she would understand. "As a bastard, I was considered too scandalous to be an acceptable marriage prospect. But because of whose bastard I was, I amassed enough invitations to paper four walls."

"What was it like at those parties?"

"Interesting, to say the least. My appearance caused quite a stir. I was the image of my father. A man who was legendary for his, ah, abilities as a lover. It seemed every woman in the *ton* thought I'd inherited his charms. Or hoped I had," he added wryly.

Carly tried to tug her hands away. "Do I want to hear this?"

He pressed her palms to his mouth, then kissed the insides of her wrists. Her golden eyes deepened to the sultry shade of melted caramel. "I was living the life I believed was my birthright. 'Twas an exceedingly pleasant experience for a young man who'd spent five years at sea. Until it occurred to me how often I was called 'Edward,' my father's given name. Nonetheless," he said on a sigh, "being a vigorous young rake, I endeavored to look beyond their passion-induced confusion."

Carly's mouth curved in amusement.

"I digress," he said ruefully, peering at the sky. It had changed from a inky black to deep indigo. Dawn was not far away. "Several titled young gentlemen joined me in my carousing. My scandalous mixed blood and my ability to attract the opposite sex won me their acceptance. Hellions we were. Somewhere along the way, they convinced me that I ought to wrest my father's title from Richard."

"Richard, duke of Westridge," Carly said uneasily. "Amanda's fiancé."

Andrew gave a curt nod. "I was Westridge's eldest son. His child. I deserved to be the duke . . . or so my companions told me."

"Were you able to reclaim the title?"

"As a bastard, no." He combed his fingers through his hair. "But I was young and naive and full of myself. I had a desperate, misguided need to be looked upon as an aristocrat." His lips thinned. "A twisted way of gaining the acceptance my father never saw fit to give me, I suppose."

Carly frowned. "You're too hard on yourself."

Oddly, the protective anger in her voice gave him the will to continue. "I craved the title and the lands. And more. I wanted my mother to be treated with respect, Jeremy to be protected and cared for. I was so consumed by my desires that I did not consider the consequences of flaunting my parentage in front of Richard. And worse—I truly believed my companions were assisting me because they cared about my welfare." Shuddering with pent-up anger, Andrew snarled, "But all I was to them was a game. A bit of sport, a dress-up toy duke they paraded in front of Richard to provoke him.

"Naturally, he lashed out," Andrew said tiredly.

"And my so-called friends simply sat back to watch the cockfight. Richard responded to my challenge by giving me a well-deserved lesson on the balance of power. But he waited until I returned to sea—and my first command."

Andrew swallowed hard as remorse swelled inside him. "He had my brother arrested for stealing. Stealing! The lad was a cripple, for God's sake. Sweet and gentle. Jeremy died in custody, Carly. Beaten to death."

"Oh, Andrew—"

"My mother demanded an investigation. Richard silenced her by having her thrown in debtor's prison. By the time I returned to London eight months later, she was dead." Andrew stared out to sea, fighting to breathe past the tightness in his chest.

Carly drew him into her embrace. "Oh, sweetheart, it hurts," she murmured, pressing her lips to his throat. "I know how much it hurts."

He was tense with the old shame, the fury, but her caresses and soothing murmurs guided him home through the haze of pain.

This is what it feels like not to be alone, he thought, allowing himself a moment to savor the embrace—for it would soon be gone.

"That despicable coward destroyed the only two people I loved," Andrew ground out. "But it wasn't enough. He wanted my very soul. And I suppose I wanted his. But he had power and money, which I did not. In a blink of an eye, he blasted apart my career, my reputation—"

"How?" she asked, incredulous. "You were a war hero."

Self-loathing shuddered through Andrew. "An

earl's young daughter was raped and strangled. The evidence against me was overwhelming. They found bits of my clothing in the field where they found the poor girl, strands of hair that matched mine."

"Richard," Carly said flatly.

"I cannot think of another explanation. He was quite vocal about his desire to crush me." He moved her back, studying her sweet, forlorn face as he spoke. "I was placed under house arrest to await my court-martial. 'Twas the talk of the *ton*. I was a threat to society, they said. And far too dangerous to remain at home. That's how I ended up in a remote prison on the Welsh border. I met Booth there. He helped me escape."

She recoiled. "I detest that man."

"He is not a likable sort."

She set her jaw.

Her forced composure didn't fool him in the least. "What did he do?" he demanded. "Tell me. I can see it on your face, Carly. He's bothered you."

"It was a misunderstanding," she said stiffly.

Andrew slammed his palms onto the wooden bench. "He *has*. I suspected as much. 'Twas why I warned him not to speak to you."

"No harm done. I don't think it'll happen again."

"Nay, it will not!" Anger vibrated inside him. When he'd questioned Booth, the man had denied having spoken to Carly. Andrew made a mental note to watch him more closely, and to have Cuddy do the same.

Carly shrugged. "Now I understand why you keep him around. I didn't before." Her voice dropped lower. "He isn't like the rest of the crew."

"Nevertheless, I owe him. Revenge was what I sought, and he was eager to help. We escaped. Then I hired a rig, and we sailed to Liverpool. The *Phoenix* was there, awaiting her new captain. I told my former crew that I was taking her to sea. Any man who wished to join me was welcome. Two thirds said 'aye.' 'Tis why I value their loyalty above all else."

He gathered her close, gazing over her head to the stars fading on the eastern horizon. "All these years I have blamed the duke when I should have blamed myself. 'Twas my own selfishness and stupidity that killed my mother and brother. And the earl of Cheshire's daughter as well. But instead of learning my bloody lesson, I pursued what I considered the ultimate act of vengeance: kidnapping Amanda. Putting you, yet another innocent, and my men at risk, so I might exact my futile revenge." His mouth twisted. "Now the real Amanda and her crew are dead because of it."

Carly regarded him.

Andrew searched her eyes for the disgust he expected to find there. Instead, he saw the unconditional love he'd dreamed of all his life.

"You may have provoked Richard," she said. "But in no way does that justify his actions. What he did was evil. *He's* evil. You're nothing like him," she said with conviction. "You're a good and honorable man."

Andrew bowed his head.

Fighting her rising emotion, Carly curved her hand over his cheek. His sharp whiskers pricked her palm, just as his undeserved self-blame pricked her heart. "The blood is on the duke's hands, sweetheart, not yours."

Andrew's eyes flashed with something precious and wonderful, filling her with love.

"I intend to pay the men from my own funds once we arrive at the island," he said. "No ransom will be collected."

Carly's heart soared. He would stand by her! He wouldn't leave as Rick had, as her father had.

"No one needs to know why," he assured her.

She laughed softly. "They wouldn't believe it anyway."

Andrew's grin formed a dent in each cheek.

She touched them with her fingertips. "You have the most adorable dimples."

He wove his fingers through her hair and drew her to him. "And you, my little spitfire, have the most kissable mouth," he murmured against her parted lips, tasting her with each word. " 'Tis hard to believe that I am kissing a woman one hundred and eighty years my junior."

"Mmm. You're a pretty good kisser . . . for an old man."

"Old man!" Growling, he nibbled her ear. "I demand to know what you mean by *pretty* good," he said, nipping the side of her throat.

"I mean *very* good!" she yelped.

Laughing, they fell hard onto the blankets on the bottom of the longboat. He propped himself over her, fitting himself in the cradle of her thighs and pressing the small of her back into the musty wool. She worked his shirt out of his waistband, slipped her hands under the damp linen. His mouth came down over hers in a deep and sensual kiss that scattered her senses like blossoms in a spring wind.

Desire flared deep in her belly. "Andrew," she whispered, dragging her thighs higher on his back. "I've wanted this for so long, wanted you—"

"Not nearly as much as I've wanted you, love." His powerful muscles flexed beneath her palms as he pressed feverish kisses along her throat. "Not nearly as much . . ." He cupped the sides of her breasts and buried his face in the small valley between them.

"Land ho!" came a shout from the deck.

Carly heard the thudding of running feet. Breathless, she squinted at the lightening sky, then at Andrew burrowing kisses between her breasts.

"Land ho," she repeated, questioningly, wondering why he hadn't leapt to the deck.

He made an expressive growl, grabbed the zipper at her collar, and pulled.

"Andrew!" She slammed her hands onto his thick shoulders. "Didn't you hear it? Land ho."

"Aye. Twin peaks." He cupped her breasts and touched his lips to the sliver of bare skin now between them.

She squirmed, grinning. "For God's sake, I'm not talking about my copious bosom," she said sarcastically.

Suddenly aware of the commotion, he cocked his head. More cries of "land ho" echoed in the early morning quiet.

He turned back to her, his blue eyes as dark and full of promise as the dawn sky. "Damn the island." Grinning wolfishly, he tugged a tarp over their heads.

Chapter Fourteen

Carly laughed. "Dereliction of duty."

Andrew's eager mouth muffled her words before he kissed his way to her ear. "You may file a formal complaint with Mr. Egan," he said, tracing the sensitive lobe with the tip of his tongue. "Later."

He had her under the spell of his hot, exploring hands before she could form another coherent thought. She was lying on her back in a rowboat lashed to a heaving ship, a moldy wool blanket abrading her skin. But none of it mattered. She had never been kissed so tenderly, so thoroughly.

"Captain Spencer! Sir!"

Andrew growled, this time in irritation.

Cuddy's voice echoed from across the deck. "Check his quarters. Come to think of it, has anyone seen the lady?"

Andrew reluctantly rose to his knees. "I fear they're on to us. They'll be bloody well hopping in here in another moment." He reached down as she reached up. Lacing his fingers with hers, he pulled her to a sitting position.

"There, my little spitfire. We're home."

"Home?"

He nodded and moved aside the tarp. "Emerald Isle."

She zipped her flight suit and peeked over the edge of the longboat, shadowing her eyes from the rising sun. Off the starboard side, hazy in the morning mist, was a fog-shrouded, emerald-green island. Her chest constricted strangely.

"Aye," she whispered in the tongue of her new world. "I'm going home."

Andrew vaulted over the side of the longboat. He held up his hands for her, then gently lowered her to the deck. He contemplated her mouth a good long time with what she'd dubbed *that* look.

She eagerly wound her arms around his waist and came up on her toes.

"I'd like to kiss you senseless, woman," he said.

Sighing she raised her chin. She was already putty. Why not be senseless, too?

The dull clicks of boot heels on wood headed their way, yet they stayed like that, poised on the verge of a kiss. The rising sun had turned Andrew's suntanned skin to a deeper bronze. The soft light glinted amber on the prickles of his beard and the curling ends of his brown hair. She savored the heat of his skin through his shirt, the gentle rise and fall of his stomach with each breath. What would his strong body feel like moving over hers—without the barrier of clothing? Skin to skin?

Skin made slippery from lovemaking.

Another sigh escaped her before she could stop it.

"Cap'n!"

As Andrew turned to face Cuddy and Gibbons, his hands were slow in leaving her waist. The other two men exchanged amused glances.

"The island." Cuddy waved in the direction of the craggy hill rising above a thatch of palms. "Seein' as you already know, we'll leave you and the lass alone."

"No need, gentlemen. I'm on my way to the helm." Andrew returned his vivid, blue-eyed gaze to her. "As for being alone," he said under his breath, "there'll be time for that later."

His smile hinted at intimacy to come. To her dismay, she felt her cheeks warm. Although the mesmerizing moment of the almost-kiss had ended, the heat between them still sizzled. Carly had never felt anything like it in her life.

"Milady, the helm is where the view is best." Andrew settled her hand over the crook of his arm. Then they all made their way toward the bow.

There Andrew left her side. He and Cuddy shouted orders to the crew and supervised the maneuvering of the *Phoenix* around a coral reef. Beyond the reef, the water was as clear as a crystal, ruffled only by the light trades, which kept the air blessedly cool. Carly didn't doubt that the sun would soon heat things up, but for now, the temperature was ideal.

Theo joined her. " 'Tis a sight for sore eyes, ain't it?"

"Smells wonderful, too." She savored the fresh, sweet scents floating on the breeze—almost overwhelming after so many months of breathing the salty, moldy odors of the ship.

The *Phoenix* was skating over the smooth waters,

all her sails now wrapped but one. Beneath the surface, a veritable rainbow of fish darted this way and that. Below the glittering creatures lay the beauty of the reef. The coral appeared deceptively close enough to touch, but clearly wasn't, since the ship sailed over it without a scrape.

Carly tingled all over. Every pore felt wide open. She found she had to squint to mute the intensity of the colors. She'd seen beautiful tropical islands before but had never reacted in such a physical way. She inhaled greedily, then again, wishing she could breathe all the colors in. Sand the color of wheat. Turquoise, mauve, and magenta. And, of course, emerald green.

Her chest ached and swelled with the utter exhilaration of being alive. It was akin to stepping into a painting, a brilliantly rendered masterpiece done in a palette using all five senses.

Movement off the bow and distant laughter caught her attention. "Look, Theo!"

" 'Tis the entire village, I'd say."

Wooden canoes overflowed with joyful, waving women, dozens of children, and a few older men. The villagers' colorfully tinted clothing was as vivid as the landscape. Accenting skin that ranged from suntanned cinnamon to a dark, rich mahogany.

Within minutes, sleek vessels flanked the *Phoenix* and stayed by her side, accompanying her into a peaceful inlet, while land-starved, woman-starved pirates lined the railing and the chains. To Carly's delight, the tough-looking group shouted endearments to women she figured were wives and girlfriends. Some women responded by holding up infants being seen for the first time by their fathers.

A familiar longing swept through Carly. Unconsciously, she brought her hand to her stomach. How wonderful it would be to have a husband who cherished her, children they both adored. Would this new life grant her that wish?

Impulsively, she pulled Theo into a hug. He mumbled questioningly into her chest. "I just felt like hugging you, kiddo, that's all." He relaxed against her. Before she let him go, she ruffled his hair.

The *Phoenix* shuddered. The unfamiliar movement was followed by the raucous sound of metal against wood. A loud whistle pierced the rumbling, sending what must be every bird on the island into the sky.

"We've dropped the anchor," Theo explained, sounding like the veteran seaman he was. At thirteen, he'd already experienced more than most men did in a lifetime.

The *Phoenix* bobbed in place like a horse tied to a post after being ridden hard. She heard several loud splashes, then cheers. The men not immediately involved in shipboard duties were diving into the waves and swimming to the beach.

"Come on, Carly," Theo coaxed. "Follow me."

She glanced behind her. As though sensing her question, Andrew strode toward her, all business again. "Find Maria when you get to the village. Tell her I sent you. She'll show you where you may stay."

"Okay," she said.

"Okay-okay-*okay,*" he repeated, teasing her.

She loved the way the words sounded in his clipped English accent.

He seemed pleased when she laughed. "Escort the lady to shore, lad," he told Theo and returned to his duties.

Theo hopped onto the railing. Already stripped to

the waist, his arms extended, he balanced himself on the railing like a tightrope walker. "Ready, Carly?" He dove in with hardly a splash.

Carly paused to twist her hair into a thick knot, then followed. Moments later, she emerged from the turquoise water and trudged dripping wet onto the sand.

Paradise.

A lush forest of palm trees grew to the edge of the wide beach. Birdsong and the chattering of a dozen different animals emanated from the shadows. A boulder-strewn hill rose steeply from the island's center with wisps of clouds floating at its crest.

Theo held her arm at the elbow and led her past a group of sailors and villagers. A path cut into rich dark dirt headed inland away from the beach. When Carly spied pens containing pigs and cows framing a cultivated area and a small orchard, she breathed a sigh of relief. Fresh, crisp vegetables. And fruit, *real* fruit.

Chickens and roosters scurried everywhere, crisscrossing the path, darting underfoot, crowing and cackling.

"I've never seen so many roosters in my life," Theo remarked.

Carly chuckled. "Me neither. I have the feeling no one sleeps late around here."

As they crossed a barrier of palms, the sharp odor of manure and the barnyard sounds faded—except for the crowing of the seemingly crazed roosters. A circular cleared area sat on a gentle rise, with well-made rectangular thatched huts clustered around the perimeter. To the side of a grouping of benches and tables made of halved tree trunks was an enormous shallow pit littered with charred rocks and bones. Near it, Carly smelled the lingering fragrance of old wood smoke. Small fires burned in front of a few huts, bubbling pots hung over the flames.

Carly gazed warily at the surrounding jungle of mysterious shadows. The vines and exotic plants seething at the edge of the cleared area had the look of being freshly hacked away. Everyone must have chores here. She expected she would, too. Only she prayed it wouldn't be weeding.

A squealing pig trotted by, three stick-wielding, long-legged boys in hot pursuit.

"Dinner," Carly muttered to Theo. For the first time in her life, her craving for fresh meat overwhelmed her desire for mercy. It wasn't hard to imagine the pig spitted and roasting slowly over an open fire until rich, savory juices ran from its crisp skin.

Still, she winced when the pig's cries were cut short. With a twinge of guilt she realized that her mouth was watering.

"Welcome!" One of the village women was hurrying toward Carly and Theo. Her wavy black hair swayed with the undulating movement of her hips, while her earrings and the bracelets on her wrists and ankles tinkled with each step. Carly admired the magenta and gold silk wrap she wore. It hugged her ample, curvaceous figure, ending a scant inch or two above her breasts. Just once, Carly wished she could exude that kind of lush femininity.

Reaching them, the woman smiled, revealing a missing eyetooth, which somehow made her exotic beauty all the more genuine. "Lady Amanda, I am glad to meet you," she said in lyrical, accented English. If the woman found her attire strange, her wide-set brown eyes gave no hint.

Awkwardly self-conscious, Carly tucked her damp, limp hair behind her ears and smoothed one hand over her threadbare flight suit before extending her hand. "Call me Carly. I take it you're Maria?"

"Yes." The woman clasped her fingers in a delicate grip. "You will visit with us for a few weeks, yes? While you are here, you will stay with me. I'm so sorry your visit cannot be longer."

Carly shifted uncomfortably. She wondered when Andrew would break the news.

Maria fussed over Theo, making him blush. Then she cried out, "Leila!"

A young girl about Theo's age sidled up to Maria. She was pretty, with long thin arms and legs that had far outpaced the rest of her. "My daughter, Leila."

Introductions were exchanged.

Maria gently pushed the girl toward Theo. "Take this young man with you. Give him something to eat and drink." Maria wrinkled her long, elegant nose. "Then show him where he may bathe."

Theo blushed again as Leila led him away.

Carly followed Maria into one of the rectangular huts. Inside, it was cool and shadowed. The walls were made of dried, woven palm fronds, and the dirt floor was swept clean. Embroidered curtains fluttered over the windows, which were free of screens or glass. On the table, a ceramic vase of flowers spilled petals onto a lace doily.

Something inside Carly softened. After so many months with men, she appreciated the feminine touches. "You have a very pretty house."

"We call it a *choupana,*" Maria said. "It means 'little house' in Portuguese."

Carly contemplated Maria's cinnamon-hued skin. "Are you Portuguese?"

"My father was, yes. A Portuguese sailor. My mother worked on a cocoa plantation on the mainland. Most of us here are Portuguese and African, or English and Spanish . . . a mix of this and that."

Maria handed her a drink. Carly held the cool cup between her palms and sniffed. The fresh scent made her light-headed with anticipation. While Maria busied herself searching through a trunk, Carly savored a tiny sip, rolling the cool, sweet drink over her tongue. "This is heaven. What is it?"

Maria reached for a wooden bowl piled high with fruit. "Mango juice," she said, choosing one. Juice sprayed as she thrust her thumbs through the skin and split it open. "Try."

Carly bit into the pale yellow-orange flesh. "Oh, my," she mumbled, her eyes drifting closed. The uncivilized part of her wanted to cram the rest of the mango into her mouth with both hands, then attack the dozen left in the bowl.

The door flew open. Carly glanced up guiltily, mango juice dribbling down her chin. She dabbed at it with her hand as Maria cried out, "Christian!"

Gibbons crossed the short distance between them and swept the woman into his arms. "I have missed you sorely, wife," he roared, spinning her around the small room.

Carly ducked to avoid being hit in the head by one of Maria's bare feet. Gibbons was married? She'd assumed he was a bachelor like Cuddy and Willoughby.

As the pair kissed, Carly inched toward the open door, taking the remaining mango half with her. "Why don't I come back later? You two ought to be alone."

"I will have months with this man," Maria said, dismissing her comment with a wave of her hand. "I will grow tired of him long before that."

Gibbons's rich laughter filled the room. "Cap'n wants the lady to stay with us," he said, dragging in a trunk and two wooden crates from outside.

"I will prepare a place for her with Leila."

Gibbons nodded. "I'll be back after we unload the cargo."

Maria clasped his hands: "I will make Carly comfortable." Her voice dropped seductively. "Then, my husband, I will make *you* comfortable."

Gibbons looked twenty years younger. He kissed his wife soundly on the lips, winked at Carly, and closed the door.

"I never knew he was married," Carly said. "Or that he had a daughter."

"Leila is the daughter of his heart, not his blood. My first husband was killed when she was two."

Carly's grin faded. "I'm sorry."

Maria shrugged and refilled Carly's cup. "It was a long time ago."

Maria was in her forties. She had a few silver threads woven through her thick curly hair, but her skin was smooth. With a heavy heart, Carly thought of her fragile, sickly mother, old before her time at forty.

Maria crouched in front of a trunk, sifting through its contents until she found a long, brightly colored piece of silk. She folded the silk and placed it in a straw satchel, then tossed in a cake of soap, two towels, and a pair of combs. "Come," she said warmly. "I imagine you would like to bathe."

This time she truly *had* died and gone to heaven.

Carly inhaled the lavender fragrance of creamy French soap. Immersing herself in a fresh-water spring that tumbled over timeworn boulders, Carly took an almost erotic pleasure in the simple act of bathing. She was vividly aware of everything that touched her, and all that she saw, smelled, and heard.

After squeezing the excess water from her hair, Carly gathered the soap and washcloth, then waded out of the spring, wrapping a towel around her as she walked onto the dirt beach.

While she worked a comb through her hair, she reveled in the company of other women. After so many months of deep, masculine voices, the women sounded utterly musical. In accented English, mixed with Portuguese and what she assumed were local tribal languages, they chatted about children, cooking, herbal remedies, and mundane topics such as the early end of the rainy season. They were excited and grateful that the men had come home, not only for the obvious companionship, but for protection as well. Their laughter made Carly smile, and their spicy tales rivaled anything she'd heard onboard the ship.

When she'd finished combing her hair, she spread it over her shoulders to dry. After awhile, the humid air and whirring of millions of insects made her drowsy. She propped her elbows on her knees, her chin in her hand. Her thoughts drifted to Andrew's wide, expressive mouth, the feel of his soft lips on hers. His hands . . .

"Where were you?" the women called to a particularly pretty woman who was just arriving at the spring.

From what Carly could discern, she had lingered overly long with her lover. The other women laughed and teased her.

She gave them a saucy shake of her head and dove into the water. Carly watched, fascinated. The young woman exuded the kind of sexual confidence and comfortable ease with her body that Carly longed for.

Was she Andrew's *lover?*

The thought came to her unexpectedly, and she eyed the woman with new awareness. Was she dipping her nude body in the pool to rinse off the last hints of his spent passion?

Carly's insides clenched with the unaccustomed grip of jealousy. She'd assumed she'd have private time with Andrew, but what if he was busy with a lover, or a wife?

Or kids.

No. He said he loved her and she believed him. He wasn't the sort of man who would be unfaithful.

Or would take another man's woman.

Over the past few months, there had been plenty of opportunities for Andrew to seduce her. Yet, he hadn't—because he thought she was engaged to the duke. And because she would be worth less if no longer a virgin. But now that he'd accepted her identity, that was no longer a concern. Nothing should keep them apart. Unless he was angry over setting her free—and losing an opportunity to punish Richard. As much as Andrew wanted to change, it wouldn't be easy putting years of hatred behind him.

Sunlight filtered through a twisted canopy of vines

and branches. Carly glowered at the shadows cavorting over her bare toes until a hand gently shook her shoulder.

"You are sad," Maria said.

Carly shrugged. "I'm tired. It's been a long day."

"We will return to my *choupana* to sleep." The woman urged her to her feet with motherly bossiness. "Up, up, now. I will help you dress."

The towel fell away as Carly lifted her arms. Maria swathed her in the silk she'd brought along, wrapping it around her torso twice, fastening it with a knot, and tucking the loose ends between her breasts. Carly smoothed her hands over the scarlet and lavender dress as Maria stepped back to admire her handiwork.

"Much nicer than trousers, yes?"

"It's gorgeous. I wish I had more to hold it up, though," Carly said wryly, tugging on the knot at her chest.

Maria made a clicking sound with her tongue. "Why do you concern yourself with this? Leila gives me the same trouble."

"She's thirteen," Carly retorted. "She's supposed to look that way."

Maria rolled her eyes. "I did not mean to compare you to Leila. Yours are the curves of a woman, not a young girl."

"No offense taken. I was joking. That's how I look past things that bother me—I laugh about them."

Maria curled a finger under Carly's chin. "My early years were not easy. I, too, used laughter the way you do. It was not until Leila was born that I learned to see only what I have, not what I do not."

She lifted Carly's hair and let it fall slowly over her shoulders. "So beautiful. You know this? Like angel hair."

"Thank you," Carly squeezed past a lump in her throat. Maria reminded her vividly of her mother. For once, Carly did not flee from the memory and its sharp pang of grief. Instead, she held it close, savoring the image of her mother before tucking it away.

She and Maria resumed their walk along the path to the village. "After we rest," the woman said, "I will help prepare the feast."

Carly perked up. "A feast?"

"To celebrate the return of our men. We will eat and dance until the rising sun sends us to our beds. Unless, of course, our lovers do first."

Carly immediately thought of Andrew, and her cheeks heated.

Maria noticed. "Ah! You have a special man."

"I do . . . I think."

"By sunrise you will *know*," she said pointedly, linking her arm with Carly's. "I will weave flowers in your hair, like I do for Leila. You will change into a different dress, too. I know the very one. It is the color of cinnamon, with threads of real gold woven through. You may use my scents, my jewelry, anything you want."

Carly yawned. "Sorry."

"You did not sleep well last night, did you?"

"Only an hour or two."

"The man in question kept you awake?"

Carly felt herself blush. "Yeah, you could say that." There would be no keeping secrets from this woman.

"All the more reason to rest. Tonight will bring you

207

anything but sleep. Night on this island is magic, and from magic comes love, yes?"

"That's what I'm hoping."

Laughing throatily, Maria squeezed her arm. "Kiss him once under the stars, and your man will not be able to resist you."

Carly grinned. She couldn't wait to test Maria's theory.

Chapter Fifteen

Carly gazed at the swath of night sky visible through the palm trees. No wonder Maria called the nights here magic. The sky was glazed with countless stars strewn across a backdrop of fathomless black.

More than enough to make wishes on.

As smoke from the torches blurred the sky, Carly returned her attention to the party. Jonesy's energetic fiddling was a treat. It was the first time he'd played since being injured. Those not dancing couldn't help but tap toes, clap, or sing along to the music.

She swayed in place to the tune, feeling utterly feminine. Her skin was perfumed with scented soap and she'd woven flowers into her hair. She'd seen no need to borrow more than a pair of hoop earrings; Maria's elegant gold-trimmed, cinnamon-hued wrap was adornment enough.

A dress worn with . . . *nothing* underneath.

Carly had never been a go-out-dancing-with-no-panties kind of person; it had never even entered her mind. What a shame. This was so incredibly sexy and liberating. Her entire body tingled, and she was aware of every blessed nerve, every pore.

It wasn't as though she'd intentionally set out to attend the dance half-naked, but her homemade muslin underwear kept bunching up under the dress, forcing her to remove them. Now all there was between her bare skin and the outside world was an utterly inconsequential wisp of silk.

"Where is the cap'n?" Gibbons asked.

One end of Carly's mouth edged up. She couldn't think of a better reason to be half-naked. "Haven't seen him since we got here. He *is* on the island, isn't he?"

"Aye, milady. He's here." Gibbons exchanged a meaningful glance with his wife.

Maria, in turn, winked at her.

Carly frowned. She'd bet Gibbons, the snitch, had told his wife that he caught her and Andrew in an embrace. "Think he'll grace us with his company, Mr. Gibbons?"

"Aye. I saw him bathing by the falls earlier."

Carly conjured a vivid image of water rushing over Andrew's suntanned, muscular body. "Sorry I missed that," she said under her breath.

Maria gave a conspiratorial grin but did not reveal what she'd overheard.

Carly said gratefully, "You have a wonderful wife, Mr. Gibbons."

"She is that." Gibbons put his arm around Maria's waist. "She keeps me young."

"Young enough to dance?" Maria prompted.

Grinning broadly, Gibbons led his wife toward the music.

Carly's stomach rumbled. Maneuvering around a group of giggling children, two squawking roosters, and a shaggy, flea-bitten dog, she made her way to a table literally sagging under the weight of food. The roasted pig was still steaming, its skin blackened and crisp, its lips curled around a mango.

"Sorry about what happened," Carly said, helping herself to a piece of pork. She laid it on a plate, which was an oval wooden slab. She added a small fish roasted with fins and head still attached, chunks of mango, baked yams, plantains, and a delicious, grainy flat bread fried in the same rich palm oil as the plantains.

She returned to her spot by the dance area. Bathed in wavering torchlight, she tuned out the sounds of the party, luxuriating in the exotic spices, textures, and scents of her dinner. She made the meal a sensual experience, drawing out the pleasure. When she'd consumed every last crumb, save the fins, tail, and fish head she'd tossed to the dog, she mopped up the last of the pork juices with a piece of fried bread.

Setting her plate on the ground, she scanned the crowd. There were no masts or coils of rope for Andrew to hide behind this time. So where was he?

Theo approached her and asked her to dance. Scrubbed clean, his hair neatly combed, he was trying very hard to look grown up.

"I'd never pass up the chance to dance with such a handsome man," she said.

His cheeks reddened—as she knew they would—and he offered her his arm. On the dance floor, Theo's confidence returned, and he led her through a lively waltz.

211

"You ought to ask Leila to dance," she said when the music stopped,

"Leila?" A flush made its way up his neck.

"Yes, you silly goose. Leila. Maria's daughter." Carly lowered her voice. "She's had her eye on you."

Theo's Adam's apple bobbed.

In a surge of affection, Carly squeezed his hand. "Get used to it, kiddo. You're so darling, you're going to have to beat the girls away with sticks."

"Think so?"

"I *know* so."

Theo glanced speculatively in Leila's direction.

As another tune began, Carly steered Theo off the dance floor. Leila sat next to her mother. Her hair was scraped back from her face and hung loose down her back in a wild mass of black curls. She stared straight ahead, her hands clasped primly in her lap, her posture erect. One bare foot tapped to the beat.

"Ask her," Carly whispered, giving Theo a gentle push. She couldn't hear what transpired between the two but was relieved to see Leila bashfully clasp Theo's hand. With the smug satisfaction of a successful matchmaker, Carly watched the young couple move away.

A pair of dark blue eyes watched her intently from across the dance area. *Andrew's eyes.* Her physical reaction to him was immediate. Her skin warmed, and she tingled low in her belly.

He inclined his head slightly. His slate-gray cutaway coat and white shirt, with a starched, stand-up collar and a snowy cravat was more suited to a Regency-era ball in London than a tropical island, but in that uncanny way of his, he managed to look cool and composed.

His long-legged strides quickly erased the distance

between them. At his charming best, he bowed, his boots gleaming in the torchlight. "Milady."

"Hi," she said softly.

Holding her gaze, he lifted her hand to his lips. He was freshly shaven, and she caught a whiff of soap along with his familiar scent. He kissed her palm, then the inside of her wrist. Goose bumps prickled her arms.

"Miss Callahan," he said, "may I have the pleasure of this dance?"

"A . . . *dance?*"

He waved in the direction of the dance floor as though she were the densest individual on Earth. " 'Tis where I get to hold you close as the music plays. Dancing," he enunciated. "Surely you've done it before. In fact, I have seen you engaged in such a manner numerous times."

"You said you couldn't dance."

"Ah, that." He scuffed his boot heels in the dirt. "God's truth, Carly, I wanted to dance with you that night. More than you can imagine. I did not, because one dance would not have been enough. I'd have wanted another and another—" He paused to stare at her mouth. "Then, if I kissed you," he said on an exhalation, "I'd have wanted another and another."

Carly's tingles roared into a full-scale conflagration.

"Since you were promised to another man—or so I'd thought—I decided 'twas wisest I did not dance." One corner of his mouth edged up. "However, Miss Callahan, I don't believe I ever said I *could* not dance."

A laugh bubbled in her throat. She wanted to throw her arms around him, but everyone still thought she was Amanda, so she reluctantly nixed the idea. "I never really believed you anyway."

213

He gave a quick laugh and twined his fingers with hers, leading her to the center of the dancers. He caught her around the waist and pressed her to him, close enough to feel the hard contours of his body through the inconsequential wisp of silk she wore. If she had any lingering doubts as to his abilities on the dance floor, they were erased the moment he expertly took the lead.

"You're a great dancer!" she exclaimed as the couples around them appeared to fly by in a blur. "To think, I was sure you didn't know how."

He slowed his steps. "I didn't know," he said, his expression oddly intense. "Not truly. Not until you came into my life."

She almost melted on the spot. "Me, either," she breathed.

Tenderly, he tucked their entwined hands under his chin. She snuggled against his chest, listening to his heartbeat. Oblivious to the waltz, they swayed slowly in place.

"I apologize for my late arrival," he said.

"I was beginning to wonder if maybe you were with your wife."

He reared back. "My wife?"

"Your lover, then."

His eyes flashed with surprise before the look was replaced by affectionate amusement. "I have no wife."

"A lover?"

"No lover."

"Good. I won't have to cause a scene."

He tilted up her chin. "I was otherwise engaged."

"You . . . were?"

"I swam halfway around the island."

"You did what?" Carly gaped at him.

"Swam around the island. After that, it was a long

trek up to the falls and back. By the time I returned, you had entered my thoughts again, so I was forced to endure another swim."

She saw her plans for the evening dissolve. "And now you're exhausted," she said glumly.

He brushed his lips over her ear. Maria's gold earring clicked against his teeth. "Not in the least."

Her stomach fluttered.

"Care to join me for a stroll along the sea?" he asked. The heat in his eyes alone was enough to make her blush. "Every star in creation is out tonight," he murmured.

Carly peered at the heavens. *Magic.* She tugged on his arm, eager to test Maria's theory. "Let's go."

"When the music stops, I will leave you. Watch me," he said carefully. "When I go, wait for a moment, then follow."

She nodded. Ever the leader, he couldn't risk flaunting a liaison with her before the crew learned of the change in plans.

They danced until the song ended, then bid each other good night and walked to opposite sides of the dance area.

Carly observed Andrew as he accepted a beer from Cuddy and turned down an offer to dance from one of the women. Before long, he settled against the trunk of a palm tree, his arms crossed over his chest, an expression of haughty boredom dulling his features.

Carly grinned. The man of many talents was an actor, too. She sipped her beer and waited. A popular tune began and was met with cheers. The dance area filled with couples. By the time she glanced back at Andrew, he was gone.

Her heart lurched. She craned her neck, searching

until she found him half hidden in the shadows. The moment their eyes met, he turned and walked into the trees.

She steeled herself by emptying her cup of beer. She counted to ten, raced through the numbers, and counted to ten again. Then, like a child up to mischief, she plunged into the trees behind her.

The path wound through waist-high vegetation and a thick grove of palms. Vines above obscured the moon, making the darkness complete and claustrophobic. The sounds of the party grew faint and were soon overtaken by the raucous, exotic sounds of a jungle at night. With each cautious step, the rumble of the surf ahead became louder, and she could smell its saltiness, sense the spray in the muggy air. Gradually, the pebbly dirt smoothed into sand under her bare feet.

The trees ended suddenly. She hesitated at the edge of a pristine beach bathed in golden moonlight.

Andrew saw her the moment she emerged from the trees. He almost laughed aloud from joy as she paused to gaze at the stars while fixing the flowers in her hair. Never before had he felt so full of hope.

He tugged off his boots and silently stole up behind her. She started, then immediately calmed in his embrace. Nuzzling her neck, inhaling her scent, he enfolded her in his arms. "Good evening, Miss Callahan."

"Hi."

He splayed his hands flat over her stomach, stroking upward, stopping at the undersides of her breasts before sliding his palms lower. Moaning softly, the sound that drove him wild with wanting her, she arched her neck. Petals from the flowers in her hair fluttered to the sand.

He was fully aroused, but he kept his hips away

from her tempting round bottom so she would not feel his aching need. More than anything, he wanted to make love to her tonight. But he wanted the decision to be hers.

She twisted to face him. Her fingers glided through his hair and locked behind his head. She pulled him down to her, flicking her tongue over his lips. That was all the invitation he needed. Her arms tightened around him with the kiss. She tasted of beer and the sweetness that was uniquely hers.

To her murmur of protest, he pulled away.

"Kiss me," she cajoled in a whisper.

To appease her, he brushed his mouth over her parted lips, her cheek, her jaw. "No, sweet, not here. 'Tis too close to the village. Walk with me."

She mumbled something about stars. Or perhaps it was magic. But she wouldn't give him a hint either way when he asked her what she'd said.

Under the light of a nearly full moon, they left a trail of footprints along the beach, empty but for the sound of the pounding surf and the calls of night creatures. He led her through a grove of shrubs with enormous scented flowers, then across a stream and up over gritty dunes until they'd reached the far side of the island.

Coconut palms fringed a curving swath of sand swept clean by the tide. "The lagoon," he said simply.

"It's beautiful."

"And private." He moved behind her, stroking her arms. To his delight, he felt gooseflesh rise under his palms. He loved the way she responded to his lightest touch, and, at times, to his words alone. "We're the only souls about. What would you like to do? We can stroll along the water and wake up the crabs. Or perhaps swim, if you prefer."

217

She fingered the knot of silk between her breasts. "A swim sounds nice."

Andrew watched her carefully. She was up to something. He could almost hear the wheels of mischief turning in her head.

As fast as lightning, she yanked the knot open and darted away from him. "Can't catch me!" she cried over her shoulder, flinging her dress into the air as she ran toward the water, treating him to an uninterrupted view of the sweetest bare bottom he'd ever seen.

Already, her feet were a blur as she splashed through the shallows. "Bloody hell," he muttered, and proceeded to undress more swiftly than he ever had in his life.

Chapter Sixteen

Carly surfaced, gasped for breath, then dove under. By the time she burst through the water again, her chest heaved with the effort to catch her breath. The water was waist deep, but only her head poked above the surface. She didn't dare risk standing until her brain caught up with what she'd done.

Boy, talk about impulsive.

Now she'd have to suffer the consequences. Though suffering was not exactly what she had in mind.

Andrew's heavy splashes sounded behind her. She spun to face him. His hair was slicked back from his face, and his incredibly defined stomach muscles flexed as he waded toward her.

Slowly, she rose to her feet.

He faltered almost imperceptibly, his eyes igniting with a primitive, almost feral hunger. In that instant, she wished she had more to offer him—lush curves, womanly breasts.

He closed the distance between them, then stopped, mere inches away. Water beaded and rolled off his strong body, running in rivulets down his stomach as he perused every square inch of her exposed skin.

"Aphrodite," he said quietly. "You are beautiful."

Carly's held-in breath rushed out. *Aphrodite.* So many months ago, he'd used that name to torment her. Now he'd uttered it with such profound sincerity, in a voice so thick with desire, her wish for lush curves seemed ridiculous.

He gathered her into his arms, kissing her with a heavenly tenderness that made her feel cherished, desired.

Loved.

Kneading her back, her buttocks, he chased the water trickling down her body with his tongue. Plumes of pleasure spiraled out from his touch. Light-headed, she closed her eyes and wrapped her fingers in his hair. His warm mouth closed over one nipple, his callused thumb teasing the other. The gentle, insistent suction ignited heat between her legs. "Oh, Andrew," she whispered. Hot, wet suckling, the rasp of his tongue, his knowing hands. Exquisite pleasure. She tilted her head back and uttered a drawn-out, throaty moan.

Kneeling before her, he kissed his way lower to where the water met her skin. Then his hand dipped beneath the surface, between her legs. His fingers slipped in and out, wet from the sea, wet from her, sliding in dizzying circles over the most intimate part of her. She gasped, arching toward him. "Make love to me. . . ."

He made a sound deep in his throat. Sweeping her

off her feet and into his arms, he carried her to just beyond the reach of the waves and lowered her to the sand. The cool, grainy wetness shocked her. She reared away from it and into his powerful warrior's body. Greedy, she met his crushing kiss as he pressed her into the sand, his water-cooled skin heating instantly against hers.

His knees sank into the sand, and she felt him nudging her thighs apart. Then he filled her with his thick heat.

Her fingers bit into his hips.

"Oh, Carly—" His voice was strained, almost unrecognizable.

He anchored his fists in the sand, rocking slowly, his strokes deliberate and deep, lifting her hips off the wet sand. The pleasure was almost too much. Clutching him, she uttered a low, husky cry.

His breaths pelted her chin and water dripped from his hair onto her face. As she slicked his wet hair out of his eyes with her fingers, her gaze locked with his. She saw his love . . . his desire, and it intensified the deeply intimate, aching need only he could satisfy. Desperate for all of him, all at once, she scoured his damp skin with her sandy hands, pressed her open mouth to the throbbing pulse in his throat. Her caresses left smears on his back, his buttocks, his shoulders and arms. She tasted salt, grit, inhaled the sweetness of their passion.

Groaning, he clutched her buttocks with one gritty hand and pressed her to him. " 'Tis heaven inside you," he whispered harshly. "Ah, Carly; you're all I've ever wanted."

Like a ship loosed from its moorings in a storm, she broke free, swirling, surging on a tide of pleasure and emotion too intense to comprehend. She cried out, wrapping her legs around him. Her climax was swift, profound. She bit his shoulder, her release exploding through her with unexpected force, pulsing around his hardness and drawing him deeper inside her. She was vaguely aware of Andrew stiffening, his powerful body jerking. He muffled his hoarse cry against her throat and thrust once more before falling to his elbows.

"I love you," she murmured over and over.

As he kissed the words from her lips, the future became clear for the first time in her life. No matter what country or century she lived in, if she was with this man, she was home.

A wave surged over their twined legs. "Tide's coming in," he mumbled against her mouth.

"Mmm."

He smoothed her hair off her forehead, sprinkling sand onto her face. He kissed her, then laughed and spat out more sand. "I have sand in every imaginable crevice."

"And maybe a few crevices you haven't imagined."

"Aye, and you, too, I suspect."

Gently, he withdrew. She sighed, already missing him.

He rose to his knees. Clumps of sand plopped to the ground with the movement. "Seeing that I've made you a mess, I suppose I ought to wash you off."

"Only if I get to bathe you first."

Grinning, he pulled her to her feet and into the lagoon. They romped like children, diving and splashing.

Carly surfaced. "You're too slow!"

He lunged for her, but she wriggled from his grasp.

"You're as slippery as an eel," he accused.

She flashed him a sultry glance. "This eel likes being caught."

"Does she, now?"

"*If* you can catch her." She dove into the water and shattered the reflected moonlight into a thousand shards of light.

Andrew followed. He was not a man to back down from a challenge, particularly one issued by an impertinent little mermaid who looked to be in need of a kiss—and a thorough kiss at that. Snatching her easily about one ankle, he hauled her to him.

"Drat. You caught me." She didn't sound disappointed in the least.

He wrapped her wet hair around one fist and angled her head back. "I caught you, all right." Her gold-flecked eyes glazed with passion as his mouth came down over hers. He caressed her small, high breasts, kissing her deeply, and with an urgency that swiftly spiraled out of control.

She reached between their bodies, exploring him until nothing mattered but the staggering pleasure given by that one small, strong hand. His buttocks clenched; his thighs quivered. Good God, if he didn't put an end to this exquisite torture—

"Carly, love," he gasped, clamping his fingers around her wrist, " 'tis private here, but not as private as I would like. Come to my *choupana*. There is a lamp, a bed. I want to see you as we make love." With lazy intimacy, he dragged his finger from the hollow at the base of her throat down to the wetness between her thighs. "And I want to love you all night." Then he kissed her. The kiss intensified. Breathless, they both pulled away.

"Are you sure you want to wait?" she asked mischievously, her eyes dark and wanting. She rubbed herself against him, tilting her hips in an almost irresistible invitation.

He gripped the sides of her thighs to hold her still. "Woman, you are playing with fire."

"Hmm. And I might get burned?"

"Burned won't be the half of it."

Her golden-brown eyes glittered with curiosity. "I'll get dressed."

" 'Tis only a recommendation, but 'twould not be wise," he said, taking her earlobe between his teeth, "to tie the knot too tight."

The lamp sputtered and was almost out. Rolling to his side, Andrew locked his arms around Carly, drawing her to him until her sweet, warm bottom rested against his belly. He buried his face in her damp, silky hair, nuzzled the back of her neck, and lazily caressed the length of one sleekly muscled thigh.

Her breathing deepened. He lifted her limp arm, then dropped it. It hit the mattress with a muffled thump. "I've thoroughly exhausted you, haven't I?"

Her languid sigh answered his question in a way words could not. "Sleep well, then, love."

The thought of spending the night with her, protecting her when she was most vulnerable, waking with her in his arms, was right somehow. As if by doing so he was satisfying some primitive, elemental need. With that thought, an almost palpable sense of destiny swept through him, a sensation of having lived this moment before.

Ridiculous. He had never loved a woman before Carly.

He kissed her hair. The damp tresses smelled of salt, the sea, and passion. He slid his hand down her belly to the triangle of flaxen hair, where she was still moist from their lovemaking. The discovery aroused him, and his hardness jutted against her back.

She sighed in her sleep, snuggling against him. He longed to wake her, to love her again, but she was weary and needed to sleep.

Shifting position, he exhaled slowly. He'd taken his time learning what pleased her. He'd used her gasps, the slightest hitch in her breath, the clenching of her intimate muscles when he was deep inside her, to learn what she enjoyed most. Secrets he would not forget. Even now he could see the passion in her eyes, hear it in her voice as she cried out his name.

His name.

With Carly, he'd made love not as his father's son, not as a make-believe duke or would-be aristocrat, but as Andrew Spencer, the bastard, the renegade ex-naval officer, the man who had made many mistakes. Because of Carly, he hoped he'd learn to view his past in terms of lessons learned. He was a good and honorable man, she'd said. He wondered if she knew how much those words meant to him.

"I will not disappoint you," he whispered in her ear. "I will protect you and keep you from harm. I swear it. You will never hunger or want. Or be forced to face fear alone. This I vow, my love. This I vow. . . ."

A rooster squawked long and loud, backed up by a lusty chorus. Carly opened one eye. Wincing at the incessant crowing, she wondered what God had been thinking when he'd created the annoying creatures.

Sunlight flowed past the plain linen curtains drawn

over the windows. Although the trades had cooled the *choupana* during the night, the breeze had died off at sunrise. The muggy air promised another hot and sticky day.

Dogs barked; a baby was crying. Villagers talked and laughed as they walked outside the *choupana*. Not conducive to sleeping late.

The noise hadn't disturbed Andrew. Sound asleep, he had one hand tangled in her hair, his other arm flung possessively over her hip. She brushed her lips over his rough cheek, then rested her head on his shoulder, dreamily sifting her fingers through the dark hair on his chest. With the pad of her finger, she followed the fine trail of hair from Andrew's navel to where it dipped below the sheet. A twinge between her legs reminded her of the passion shared only hours before. She grew aroused with the thought of making love again. She wasn't inexperienced, but until last night she'd never known sex could be so consuming, so *incredible,* leaving her feeling sensual and feminine and fulfilled.

And reckless.

They hadn't used protection. She didn't know what passed for birth control in the 1800s, but she sure as heck hadn't thought about it last night. She was midway through her cycle, so she could become pregnant. How would *that* muddle her already complicated situation?

Her disregard for consequences was yet another reminder of how much she'd changed over the past few months. She'd always lived with the future in mind, not simply day to day. *She'd* been the responsible one, the careful one. Not anymore, apparently.

Something heavy swished by the door, as though it was being pushed over the dirt floor. Carly twisted around in time to see a bracelet-adorned arm withdraw as the door whisked closed. Sometime during the night, Maria must have figured out that her houseguest hadn't made it back to the *choupana.* And why. Carly smiled warmly. Not only was Maria thoughtful enough to bring breakfast, the woman knew how to keep a secret.

Carly inhaled deeply. Mangos! And that delicious fried bread. Enticed by the aroma, she slipped from Andrew's embrace and tiptoed to the door. The basket was filled with mangos, bananas, and bread.

She chose the ripest mango and brushed her lips over its cool, fragrant surface, soothing the tenderness left from Andrew's kisses.

Heaven.

Juice squirted when her thumbs broke the skin, dribbling over her fingers and hands. As she ate, she studied the shadowy interior of Andrew's *choupana,* something she hadn't paid much attention to the night before. Aside from the mattress on the floor, there was a washbasin and a pitcher on a table and a chair carved from a tree log. No pictures adorned the walls. No pretty rugs decorated the hard-packed dirt floor. The curtains were faded and plain. It was like a room in a barracks: stark, functional, and revealing nothing of its occupant's personality. Picturing the inviting coziness of Maria's *choupana,* she compared the two. This was not a home. It was a place to sleep.

She took another bite of the sweet, ripe fruit.

"Are you not going to share?"

Heat coursed through her body at the sound of the sleep-roughened voice. She faced him, wiping her knuckles across her chin.

Andrew lay with his hands folded behind his head, the rumpled sheet twisted around his hips, his eyes

227

glinting wickedly as he surveyed her nude body. His stare held open admiration, and a good deal of longing, making her wonder if this was what Eve felt like in the Garden of Eden. "What makes you think I won't share?"

"Come here." He beckoned with his chin. "And bring your . . . fruit."

Her confidence surged. With a blatant sensuality she never knew she possessed, she swayed her hips and walked toward him. She gave him a sultry smile, then straddled him. His body heat coursed through the sheet, warming the sensitive skin on her inner thighs.

As he watched her, she bit into the mango, chewed slowly, then swallowed. "Did you say you wanted some?"

His eyes darkened. "Foolish woman. Never tease a starving man." He grabbed her wrists and pulled her down to his mouth. His kiss was hard and hungry. In an erotic reminder of their intimacy, she tasted herself on his lips. She kissed him until there was nothing left but the sweetness of the mango, his hot, wet mouth, the rasp of his whiskers.

The half-eaten mango thumped onto his chest and rolled onto the sheet.

" 'Twas delicious," he murmured, dragging his lips along her jaw to nibble her neck and ear.

"I love when you do that," she said on a sigh. "It drives me crazy."

"Does it, now?" He slipped his fingers into the hair at the nape of her neck and kissed the hollow of her throat. "And this?"

"That, too . . ." Her voice sounded as though it

came from someone else, some passion-dazed, love-drugged, wanton woman. "Would you like some more?" she asked dreamily, grabbing the mango before it rolled off the mattress.

"Aye. Much more."

"You're insatiable," she said. "Thank goodness."

They exchanged glances and laughed.

He brought her hand to his mouth, suckled her middle finger, and proceeded to do things with his tongue that made her think of all the wonderful, erotic things he'd done to her the night before. Then he turned his attention to her other hand—the hand that clutched the mango—chasing a glistening rivulet of juice past her wrist and down her arm.

"Prepare to be devoured, milady." With that, he suckled her elbow.

She pulled back, wriggling atop him.

"Carly—" he warned with a sharp intake of breath. She felt him swell and harden further. " 'Tis not yet time for dessert."

"Dessert?" she asked, incredulous. "I don't know about you, but I consider it the main course."

His gaze held hers as he dipped his finger into the mango's moist, yielding flesh. He painted a circle around her left nipple, then wet his finger again and touched the cool stickiness to her other breast, teasing the tight, sensitive tip. She became his canvas as he created a masterpiece with brushstrokes of mango juice on every part of her that yearned for his caress. Heat spiraled out from the places his fingertips touched her and throbbed to life between her thighs. She moaned through her clenched teeth, arching her back. He used her closeness to draw her nipple into his mouth. Convulsively, her hand clamped around the now soggy mango. Juice drizzled onto his chest. They paused, eyeing the glittering drops, then each other.

"Your turn." She pushed him down on the pillow.

His eyes sparked with anticipation.

She drew a sticky heart on his chest. "This is how much I love you," she said, painting the arrow slowly crosswise. "And this is how much I want you." She dragged her open mouth over the contours of his chest, the damp hair, delighting in the feel of him, his scent, the heat of his skin.

His groan ended in a swift intake of breath as she flicked her tongue over the erect tips of his nipples. He pressed his hands to the back of her head and raised his pelvis.

Breathless, she pretended to get up. "Am I too heavy?"

He clamped his hands over her hips. "That's quite far enough." He grabbed her wrists. By the time he was through kissing her, she could barely draw in a breath.

"Put me inside you," he said, his voice harsh and tender at the same time.

She bunched the sheet in her hands and pulled it down, her first glimpse of him in the daylight. He had narrow hips, and his long thighs were powerfully muscled and sprinkled with dark hair. "You're perfect," she whispered, closing her hand around his rigid shaft.

As she caressed him, his eyes grew heavy-lidded. "Now, Carly," he gasped.

Kneeling, she lowered herself onto him, slowly, stretching out the anticipation . . . making it last. She propped herself up with her arms and pushed down the last inch, clenching her inner muscles as she welcomed him fully into her body.

Andrew groaned his pleasure. Gripping her buttocks, he arched upward, half lifting her off the bed.

"Love me, Andrew," she pleaded, panting from the exquisite fullness of having him inside her. "Don't stop."

He didn't.

He claimed her, body and spirit, bestowing the gift of pleasure as no one ever had. By the time she settled back to earth that morning, something magical had happened. She believed that all those wishes she'd made on all those shooting stars were going to come true.

Carly spent the rest of the day on the beach in the shade of a palm, alternately napping and reading and contemplating how good it felt to be back on terra firma.

Emerald Isle was a storybook tropical island, unspoiled and empty of the trappings of modern-day tourism. Though the lagoon and the area between the village and the beach were lovely, they were all she'd seen. She longed to visit the rest. Particularly after a breathless Theo stopped by to tell her about the Boca, a hole in the sea-swept rocks on the rugged northern shore. Each time a wave washed into a cave nearby, water surged out of the hole and sprayed high into the air.

"The best part of all, Carly, is that the water makes a rainbow as it falls."

She hoped to entice Andrew into going for a hike if he returned before sunset. *If* he returned by then. He'd been aboard the *Phoenix* all day, overseeing the crew as they made repairs and unloaded the remainder of the cargo. The men skilled in carpentry were already busy fixing areas damaged by the warship that were now accessible in the calm, shallow waters. Others were cleaning the ship from top to bottom, polishing the wood, scraping barnacles off the hull, patching sails and sewing new ones—a chore Carly had volunteered to help complete. It would take months to finish everything.

She scooped up a handful of warm sand and trickled a stream into her palm. From somewhere inland, the scent of flowers wafted by. Sea birds soared overhead, borne on the afternoon trades, and the cooling breeze lifted her hair, making it weightless around her shoulders.

The agreeable sensations reminded her of the very un-Carlylike decision she'd made after Andrew left that morning. Until she faced having to leave the island, she would live from day to day, enjoying the simplest pleasures, savoring her newfound appreciation of life and the heady sensation of being in love—truly in love—for the first time. A fragile happiness she prayed would not be shattered and taken unexpectedly by events beyond her control.

Carly gathered her things and walked back to the village. Deep laughter and the sound of masculine conversation emanated from the cleared area in front of the *choupanas*. The odor of tobacco and perspiration hung in the humid air. Apparently in the midst of a meeting, the men were gathered around the tables.

"Milady!" Cuddy's call alerted Andrew to her presence.

Feeling a blush creep slowly up her neck, Carly waved and hastened her pace. Her long night of erotic abandon with their captain was too fresh in her mind—and between her thighs—to allow her to face him in front of his crew.

Andrew beckoned to her.

No way.

Her face heated further. Smiling serenely, she gave a friendly wave, walking away as quickly as she could without appearing to run.

She heard the men laugh.

Andrew jogged up behind her and grabbed her arm. "Slow down, Carly."

"Not now," she said through gritted teeth.

"Come. The men want to see you."

"I don't feel social."

"Whyever not?" His eyes sparked wickedly.

She was going to kill him. "You know . . . *why.*"

"Because we made love?"

"Yes," she hissed. "I don't have the kind of face that keeps secrets. And I'd rather not have everyone know we're sleeping together." Glancing behind him to the grinning men, who seemed to be enjoying every nuance of their conversation, she said sullenly, "Though it looks like they already do."

Acting affronted, he snatched her hand and pressed it between his rough palms. "They most certainly do not. I like to think I have a bit of discretion, Miss Callahan. 'Tis a small island, though. They will sort it out before long." He drew her closer and brushed his lips over hers.

She reared back, her face hot. "What do you say we don't give them a head start? I'd rather wait until they know I'm staying here."

"They know."

Her gaze swerved to the men. Cuddy grinned and waved. Gibbons, massive arms crossed over his chest, gave her a fatherly smile.

"What in the world did you tell them?"

"Only that you do not wish to marry the duke," he said. "And that in less than three weeks, at the pre-arranged time, I'll send a party to deliver the happy news to Richard's men."

Speechless, she blinked. The enormity of what Andrew had done, the promise he'd made to her—and kept—meant more to her than he could imagine.

"Come," he coaxed, pulling her to the center of the group.

She inhaled deeply and smoothed her hair off her forehead, offering a weak smile to the familiar faces surrounding her. Booth shot her a chilling look. "Keep'n her will get ya killed, Cap'n." Then he rose to his feet and marched off. Her smile died on her lips.

Before she could contemplate the implications of Booth's overt display of hatred, Andrew announced, "Lady Amanda, who prefers we call her Carly, has chosen not to honor her betrothal to the duke of Westridge."

The men cheered wildly.

"As agreed, I will distribute gold equal to the amount of the ransom."

That brought more applause and a few whistles. Her chagrin faded into relief.

"Will ya stay with us on the island, milady?" Jonesy called out, his question echoed by the others.

"I sure will," she said, propping her hands on her hips. "I prefer your fine company any day to that of the worthless worm Richard. As for your captain"—she sighed theatrically—"I suppose I can endure him if I must."

"Endure me, she shall." Andrew curled one hand behind her head and kissed her soundly on the mouth. As she stood in breathless surprise, he nuzzled the side of her neck. Desire throbbed to life between her legs.

The men whistled their approval.

Andrew gave them a cheery salute. Lacing his fingers with hers, he led her away. Once on the path, he casually draped his arm over her shoulder. He smelled faintly of exertion and tobacco.

"Not everyone's pleased with your change in plans," she said.

"My men? Like hell they aren't. They're getting their gold and they don't have to risk their dirty hides to have it."

"Booth isn't."

" 'Tis simply the way the man acts." He paused by a barrel of rainwater, scooped some into a cup, and handed it to her before helping himself. "Have you eaten?" he asked quietly.

"Not since lunch."

"I'm ravenous."

"I'll find us some fruit and bread," she said. "There's leftover pork, too."

Andrew cupped her chin in his hand. In her earnest desire to please him, she'd missed the point. "I'm not interested in food." He dropped the statement into her lap with a meaningful glance.

"Well, to be honest, neither am I," Carly said with saucy candor. "Particularly after your little performance in front of the men. Nice kiss, by the way."

Chuckling, Andrew trailed one finger down her sun-warmed throat, raising gooseflesh in its wake. "You've bloody well fired up my appetite now," he said, fingering the knot of silk tied above her breasts. " 'Twill take *hours* to satisfy."

Her eyes widened. For once, she was speechless. No swift rejoinders or witty remarks.

Pleased with himself, Andrew clasped her hand and brought her home.

"It is *not* a plump bottom!"

Andrew flipped her onto her stomach, playfully nipping her left cheek. "You have the most deliciously *round* bottom, then. 'Tis as provoking as hell." On all fours, he leaned over her, nibbling his way up her back. Then he rolled to his side, pulling her with him. They lovingly stroked and kissed each other.

With a lazy stretch, she shifted position and winced. "A bath in the spring would sound nice right now. Or better yet, a tub of hot water."

"Easily arranged." Both tenderness and guilt flooded him at the sight of her swollen lips, her cheeks and chin abraded by his whiskers. He should have shaved this afternoon. He shouldn't have taken her so many times since last night, for that matter. Why hadn't he given more thought to how his appetite would affect her?

"You wouldn't mind?" she asked.

He kissed the tip of her freckled nose. " 'Tis no bother, love. You'll have your hot bath. Then we'll sleep."

"Just sleep, huh?"

"Indeed." With mock indignation, he declared, "However irresistible I am to you, you must allow me to rest. I am exhausted." He fell backward on the mattress to prove his point.

She gave a genuine belly laugh. "Nice try, Spencer, but you know and I know, it's me who can't keep up with you. Don't worry, though—" She winked suggestively. "Tomorrow I'll be as good as new."

"If not, there are other ways to give each other pleasure." He brushed his lips over hers. "In fact, I know of one you particularly enjoy."

She sighed into his mouth.

"You know the one, then," he said huskily.

"Oh, yes."

He gave her a gentle, lingering kiss before pulling away. "If you insist on distracting me, you will never have your swim."

Carly giggled as he faked a limp across the dirt floor to where his clothing hung on the opposite wall. She dressed in his oversized shirt while he tugged on his pants. Without a belt, they dipped below his navel. "What a hunk," she murmured, running her gaze over his muscled torso.

He slid a wary glance downward. "A 'hunk'?"

"It's my twenty-first-century way of saying that you're incredibly good-looking."

He scratched his bare chest and grinned. His jaw and chin had that scruffy look she loved. His chestnut-colored hair, streaked from the sun, stuck up in all directions. She tenderly combed it with her fingers, revealing the red spots on his neck where she'd given him love bites. Looking lower, she noticed scratches on his left shoulder. *Scratches?* The love bites she remembered, but the scratches? It must have been another wanton moment . . . but which one? "Everyone's going to know exactly what you've been doing all afternoon, Captain."

"Will they, now?"

"Yep. You look like you've been very thoroughly made love to."

"That I have." Not bothered by his disheveled appearance in the least, he wrapped his arm over her shoulders, holding her close in the twilight as they walked to the beach.

A sudden snapping of sticks and the thud of booted feet interrupted the peaceful sound of crickets, frogs, and surf.

She and Andrew were barefoot.

"Looka here. Now ain't this sweet?"

The raspy voice chilled her soul.

"Think yer one of them bluebloods now, Spencer?"

Andrew stiffened. He moved her to the edge of the path before turning his attention to the dark form behind them. "You've been taken care of, Booth. If it's not to your satisfaction, leave. No one will stop you."

The man's hair was damp and slicked back from his face, revealing narrowed, bloodshot eyes. The evening breeze brought the odor of booze. "You promised me my share of the ransom. And I ain't leavin' without it."

Crap. Her pulse kicked into double time. She should have known the bastard wouldn't give up without a fight.

"Mr. Booth," Andrew warned.

"Yer high an' mighty now that ya got yerself the lady. 'Twasn't so long ago you were rottin' behind bars. Where were yer gentlemen and lady friends then?"

"Go about your business, Booth," Andrew said in a low, ominous tone. "Now."

Booth's gaze veered to her, freezing her with the icy

hatred in their depths. He gave a harsh laugh. "Spencer, yer a bigger fool than I thought. I can't believe yer givin' up a fortune for this titless wench."

Mortified, she inhaled sharply.

Then Andrew lunged for Booth, knocking him to the ground with a horrific scrape along the pebbly sand.

Chapter Seventeen

Carly cupped her hands around her mouth and screamed toward the village. "Help! We need help! At the beach!" Urgently she scanned the ground. She was damned good with a gun; some of that skill had to transfer to sticks and stones.

She heard the revolting thud of a fist hitting flesh, then Andrew's muffled grunt of pain. Both were large men. But what Andrew had in height, Booth made up for with sheer bulk. Guilt swamped her as she chose a fist-sized rock, then discarded it to snatch a larger one. This wouldn't have happened if she hadn't asked for a swim.

But the two men would have come to blows eventually. That was her fault, too. She'd been wrong to keep Booth's assault a secret. It had allowed him to do what he pleased unchecked. Now he'd attacked Andrew.

Adrenaline pumped in her veins; ragged breaths tore at her dry throat. She tested the weight of the rock, raised her shaking arm as the men tumbled past. *Damn it.* They rolled too fast, too unpredictably. She pranced backward, aiming at Booth's head. Then Andrew's shoulder blocked her view. Frustration bit at her insides. If she threw the rock at Booth, she could just as easily hit Andrew. The helplessness and choking fear she'd felt that night alone with Booth came flooding back—this time multiplied a thousandfold.

If Booth killed Andrew, not only would she lose the man she loved, but she'd be left alone on an island in the 1800s with no protection or means.

"Help!" she shouted toward the ocean, desperate now, praying that another couple had opted for a late swim.

Voices sang out from the direction of the village. Her knees nearly buckled with relief. Gasping, she glanced up the hill. Torches burst through the lush jungle, conveyed by what had to be fifty women and men, some in nightshirts, cutlasses drawn. Chickens darted ahead, squawking, while roosters crowed and the flea-bitten black-and-white dog that followed her around hoping for scraps sprinted in frenzied circles to the wails of crying babies.

Gibbons aimed his pistol. "Booth! Leave the captain be or you're a dead man." But the same problem that kept her from hurling the rock prevented him from firing.

Booth slammed Andrew onto his back. Andrew twisted free and locked his arm around Booth's thick neck, wrenching him backward. " 'Tis enough, man!"

Blood sprayed in bursts from Booth's mouth and

battered nose while he struggled in Andrew's stranglehold. His face turned purple; a vein pulsed in each sweaty temple.

Teeth bared, Andrew gave his forearm a savage jerk. Booth gurgled, clawing at his arm. "What'll it be, Booth?"

He shuddered, wheezed his surrender. Andrew released him, and he sagged to his hands and knees, gasping, splattering droplets of blood onto the sand.

Brushing grit from his torn pants, Andrew straightened. Blood streamed from a cut above his right eye; bruises and dirty scrapes marred his shoulders and back. He took the pistol Gibbons handed him and beckoned to her.

She hurried to his side. "You're hurt," she said tightly.

He ignored her remark, his attention trained on Booth. He spoke softly so only she could hear. "Honor is at stake here. Yours, love, and mine. I have to do this." His expression was bleak as he pressed the muzzle to the back of Booth's head.

Carly's heart lurched. Was he going to execute him?

"Now," he began calmly, "what exactly occurred between you and Mr. Booth?"

Hesitant, she eyed Booth, then searched the crowd for Theo. The boy was unaware of the danger her confession might place him in, yet she had to tell the truth. She'd held her silence for too long, and now they were all paying for it. "He assaulted me."

Andrew's eyes turned hard.

"Months ago . . . about the time of the Neptune ceremony. He found me on the deck one night, and he . . ." She took a shuddering breath.

"Speak," Andrew whispered harshly.

"He cornered me, pushed me into an alcove where no one could see us. He took himself out of his pants and—" She averted her eyes from the back of Booth's head. "I thought he was going to rape me."

Andrew's eyes flashed. "Why didn't you tell me?"

"He said he'd hurt Theo." She studied the boy's wan face and lowered her voice. "I couldn't risk that. I figured I'd eventually settle the score. But when things quieted down, I let it go."

"Let it go?" Andrew demanded, aghast. "He humiliated you. He made threats against one of my sailors. You should have told me, Carly. You should have trusted me."

"Trusted you?" She gaped at him. They were still whispering, but they might as well have been shouting at each other. "You didn't believe a word I said at that time. You thought I was mad."

"Whether or not I thought you daft," he said stiffly, "you should have come to me."

"I wanted to. But I wasn't able to trust." She smoothed her hand over his beard-roughened cheek. "I was afraid to rely on anyone."

Was she ready to tell him exactly why?

" 'Twas my duty to protect you then. I failed. It won't happen a second time." He butted the muzzle against Booth's head. "I've heard about all I can stomach."

"Finish what ye started then," Booth muttered in a gravelly taunt.

Andrew's expression was so cold, so foreign to the man she'd come to know, that she braced herself, repelled by the prospect of viewing Booth's imminent demise at such close range. "You freed me from prison, Mr. Booth. 'Tis the reason you are still alive— the only reason. In exchange, I want you to leave.

243

Know this—if you return, for any reason, I'll kill you." He and Booth regarded each other for several almost unbearably tense heartbeats. "Now get the bloody hell off my island. Ryan, Carstens!" he shouted to Booth's cronies. "Take him. He's in no shape to row." Dispatching one of the children, Andrew said, "Find a cask of drinking water—make that two—and bring them to the shore. Make haste!"

Booth spat a bloody glob of saliva onto the dirt, scrutinizing Andrew and Carly in turn as his friends lifted him to his feet. The entire village followed the three men to where the longboats sat on the beach. Andrew kept the pistol aimed at their backs. The crowd magically dispersed, allowing him a clear view of their retreat.

Only after the men shoved one of the small boats into the surf did Andrew lower the pistol. Carly wound her arms around his waist. He drew her to his chest, burying his hand in the hair at the nape of her neck. "He'll not hurt you anymore," he murmured.

"Spencer, you bastard!" The shout interrupted their brief kiss. Booth was balancing himself in the boat, one arm clutched to his belly. "I'll have my gold!" he bellowed, hoarse, defiant. "One way or the other! If not from you, then from Westridge!"

Andrew grabbed Carly's arm and propelled her away from the water, walking so fast that she stumbled. " 'Tis over, ladies and gentlemen," he called briskly. "Go back to bed."

"Crap, Andrew. What if he finds the duke's ship and brings them here?"

"Nay!" Andrew said, overly loud. "An empty threat. He'll not know where to find them. Only Cuddy and I know where the ransom was to be exchanged. 'Tis nowhere near Emerald Isle."

"Then where will he go?"

"The mainland. A full day's sail with the trades."

"What if he tells someone else about us?"

"Who? The Portuguese? The plantation owners? I've traded with them for years. Neither will be interested."

She glanced behind her. The longboat was now a speck in the dark surf.

"Booth's a privateer," Andrew said, his tone gentler. "He's also a wanted man. He'd best find himself another ship and sail out."

"Good riddance," she muttered.

"Aye." Laying his arm protectively over her shoulders, he guided her back to the *choupana*.

Weak from exhaustion, Carly wedged a rolled washcloth between the back of her head and the narrow edge of the metal tub. After they returned, she'd tended Andrew's wounds, then urged him to rest. But he wouldn't hear of it. "I promised you a bath, and you shall have it," he'd said.

Only her knees and head poked above the water as the soothing warmth worked its way into her body—a weary and shaken body. If only Andrew would be quiet, she could slip into oblivion.

"Perhaps if we were to sail to the precise location, on the date and time exactly one year from the date you arrived,'twould work," Andrew reasoned aloud.

Lying on the mattress, hands laced behind his head, he was no doubt working off the lingering adrenaline from the fight by talking incessantly about how he could help her get back to the twenty-first century. Solving the problem of how that might be accomplished presented him with a challenge he couldn't resist.

Carly opened one eye. "If what you're proposing is to reverse what happened, we'd have to get into the air. Not only would we need a storm, we'd need a hot air balloon."

Andrew rolled onto his side, his eyes shining with the same boyish excitement he had when he talked about helicopters.

Exasperated, she blurted, "You're nuts! We'll get ourselves killed. I don't even know how I got here, let alone how to get back."

"You've given up before you've begun," he said irritably.

She couldn't blame him. Had she criticized his creative and unconventional plan to defeat the warship, he would have reacted the same way. Besides, he hadn't offered to come along. He loved her and she loved him, but she couldn't assume that he wanted to spend his life with her. If she'd learned any lesson from her years with Rick, it was that.

She stepped out of the tub and dried off. "Let's go to sleep. I'm tired, and your eye's swelling."

To her dismay, Andrew ignored her attempt to dismiss his newly hatched plan. "What do you remember of the night you came to the *Phoenix*?"

"I woke in your bed. I saw you—"

"Before you came to be in the water."

"We took off from Aviano, an airbase in Italy." As she described the journey to the carrier in detail, frantic, dark images flickered through her mind. "Heavy rain smothered my engines. Kind of like drowning a steam engine with water."

Andrew interrupted her with more questions about

flying. Those questions led to more questions. Although the concept of computers caused him to stumble more than once, overall, it amazed her how much he grasped.

"Even with my protective clothing on," she said, "I doubt I would have lasted more than an hour or two. If you hadn't pulled me from the water, I would have died."

"I've got you."

The disjointed nightmares of the past few months suddenly came together, shaking her very soul. "Oh, my God, the dreams! Andrew, the dreams are the rescue. When I dream, *your* arms come around me. *You're* the one holding me and telling me not to be afraid." She narrowed her eyes. "You have the same dream, don't you?"

Brooding, he frowned at the ceiling.

"You do. I know you do. That's all it is. A memory of you rescuing me."

"In my dreams I cannot hold on to you," he said grimly. " 'Tis not what happened that night."

Clutching the towel to her breasts, she kneeled beside him. "No," she whispered. "That night you saved my life."

He rested one hand on her thigh, gave a sigh that sounded as though it emanated from the depths of his soul. Then he grasped her shoulders, pulling her over him. Her towel fell open, and water dripped from the still-wet ends of her hair onto his bare chest. "I fear your return will be in the same manner as your arrival," he said. "If you must leave me—" He swallowed hard. "Don't leave me, Carly."

Her heart twisted. "How can you think I'd leave you?"

His expressive face clouded over. She felt his stomach muscles clench. Silent, he averted his gaze. For the first time since they'd become intimate, she hadn't a clue as to what he was thinking.

Everything had changed in the space of one day. They had so much to lose—there was so much more at stake now.

Mentally and physically exhausted, she settled next to his warm, comforting nakedness, relieved to feel his arms come around her. Yet, as tired as they both were, sleep was long in coming.

Chapter Eighteen

The deepening twilight held the promise of a mild evening. Hand in hand, Carly and Andrew walked along the water's edge. The sun settled toward the horizon, where towering indigo clouds pulsed with lightning far to the west.

"This is the earliest I've seen you come ashore in days," she said. He'd been working furiously aboard the *Phoenix*. Although they didn't see each other much during the day, they did have the nights together. Nights of passionate lovemaking. And little time for conversation before they fell asleep. "What's wrong with taking a day off?"

"There are too many tasks yet to be done on the *Phoenix*." He looked positively bleak.

Carly's heart wrenched. He wanted so much to protect her, but why wouldn't he confide in her? "This is all because of Booth, isn't it? You think he's angry enough to track down that man-of-war and reveal our location. Or where you plan to rendezvous with Richard's men."

He waved away her concern. "Booth's a wanted man himself. He will not risk it."

Carly refused to accept Andrew's reassurances. Instinct told her that he was deeply worried. She gave his hand a reassuring squeeze and gazed at him. The lump over his right eye had subsided in the days since the fight with Booth, but bluish-yellow smudges remained.

Joyful barking erupted from behind them, scattering her dismal thoughts. The black-and-white dog raced by with three shrieking children in hot pursuit. In their haste, the youngsters splashed Carly and Andrew. She welcomed the spray, grinning at the sight of the youngest child—a skinny-legged girl no more than three, her legs spinning hard to keep up with the older children. "Look how cute," Carly crooned. "Makes me want a dozen of my own."

Andrew grumbled something unintelligible.

She glanced up to find him scowling. Taken aback, Carly asked, "Don't you ever want children?"

He let out an edgy sigh. "We did not take precautions," he said, splaying his hand over her stomach. " 'Twas foolish. What if you are with child?"

She felt uneasy. "What if I am?"

His telling silence sliced through her. With revolting clarity, she recalled the look of distaste she'd seen on Rick's face when she'd told him she was pregnant. He hadn't wanted their child because he hadn't wanted *her*. Her own father hadn't wanted her. Well, she didn't need them, either. And she didn't need Andrew.

Backing away, Carly held her hands high to ward off more of Andrew's lies. She couldn't bear to listen. It would break her heart. "If you just want a sex toy, go find yourself one, because I'm not it. Shouldn't be too tough. I've noticed more than a few women who look willing."

He gazed at her in utter bewilderment. "Carly?"

"Don't say anything!" Her lower lip quivered. "It's over."

"Over?"

"Damned right. If you don't want our baby, you can't have me." She turned and ran as fast as she could.

"Carly!"

She fled blindly, not knowing where, only that she had to get away from the pain and humiliation. She was better off alone. She could get by without anyone's help.

She could take care of herself.

Her legs pumped; her heart hammered wildly. She was fast, but Andrew was faster, and she wasn't surprised to hear the sound of his feet thundering behind her.

"Good God, woman, *stop!*"

He caught her, and they fell, tumbling over the sand. She threw punches until her fists throbbed, fighting back with the frenzied desperation of a wild animal until he crushed her to his chest and encased her in his powerful arms. Stinging fists and sheer exhaustion finally forced her to cease her struggles.

"Carly," he gasped when she stilled, "whatever I have done to hurt you, I am sorry for it."

He tried to meet her gaze, but she turned away. "Y-you don't want a child with me."

His eyes flashed. "I never said that."

"You didn't have to. I could see it in the way you looked at me," she said. "I know that look."

"What you saw was fear. *Fear,* Carly. I dread what I cannot control. Two of my men have run off with Booth, and the meeting with Richard's men is in two weeks. I am wanted for murder, for piracy, and now for kidnapping. If I have gotten you with child, 'twill be another loved one to worry about. I will not rest until I see you both to safety."

Andrew fought the sickening dread that had been dogging him for days. "Look at me," he beseeched her. "I love you, Carly. I would not intentionally hurt you. Or abandon you."

Her wide brown eyes brimmed with anguish and vulnerability. "Yeah, well, it's happened twice. Third time's a charm."

He bristled. "Why do you doubt me?"

Her face contorted, but she did not weep.

"Tell me what happened, love. 'Tis eating you up inside."

She stared at the horizon. "There was a baby," she whispered.

"A baby? Yours?"

"Mine."

Astonishment, possessiveness, and curiosity tumbled end over end, slamming into him and rendering him speechless.

She extricated herself from his embrace and rose to her feet. "I used birth control, but it happened anyway. I was thrilled, and I assumed Rick would be, too. Unfortunately, he wasn't."

Andrew nursed the thought of bloody well planting his fist in the man's teeth.

"He said he'd marry me—if that's what I wanted."
Carly winced. "Some proposal, huh? But I accepted
because I couldn't bear the thought of my child growing up without a father. Like I did."

"Yet you did not marry him."

She clenched her fists, then unclenched them, over
and over. "Rick's parents were wealthy. They convinced him that I wasn't the proper choice for a wife.
His mother even hinted that I was trying to trick him
into marriage." Wrapping one arm around her waist,
she lifted a trembling hand to her mouth. "They pres-
sured me to end the pregnancy." Tears welled in her
eyes. "I was so ashamed," she said hoarsely. "How
could they ask me to do that when they knew my
mother was dying? Rick knew how close I was to her.
That baby was as much a part of my mother as it was
of me. I knew when Mom died it would be the only
family I had left, so I said no." She spread her hands
over her stomach. The protective gesture made his
chest ache. He longed to go to her but sensed she
needed to finish.

"That's when Rick left."

Andrew's nostrils flared. "He left you to face the
worst time of your life alone."

Was there anything that he and this woman did not
share?

"Yes. And it hurt; it hurt like hell." Carly took a
shaky breath. "I promised Mom that if the baby was a
girl, I'd name her Rose. After her. But I never let on
what happened with Rick. She died believing I'd be
getting married, that I'd have all the things she'd
never had." Carly's voice cracked. "I miscarried the
baby two days after her funeral. I was only three
months pregnant, but when I lost that life growing

inside me, it was as though *my* life was swept out, too. After that, I swore I'd never again rely on anyone else. Then I came here and met you and everything changed."

"Then why didn't you believe I'd want your child?"

She dashed away her tears with the heel of her palm. "Because I expected it. And dreaded it." She regarded him. "Deep down I thought what we had was too good to be true."

He walked to her. "To have a child with you—my God, Carly, I could not imagine a greater joy. I love you."

She began to weep. He gathered her into his arms and took her grief inside him as though it was his own. "Know this, love: You'll not be alone anymore. No matter how fast you run, I will catch you. And no matter where you go . . . I will find you."

Kissing the top of her head, he stroked his fingers over her dampened hair. His heartbeats thrummed in time to her pulse. "You did nothing to deserve such cruelty," he said. "The men who hurt you were weak and unworthy of your love. They are the ones to be pitied." He framed her face in his hands. "Not you."

She wanted to believe; he could see it in her eyes.

"Not you," he repeated.

Touching her fingertip to his mouth, she traced his words. "Not . . . *us.*"

"Aye," he whispered gruffly. " 'Twas a hard lesson we learned. One I vow our children will never have to face."

Our children.

Carly's emotions tumbled. She wanted to laugh, to cry. Andrew was drawing the festering grief from her soul as though it were venom from a snakebite. And now his love was pouring into her in its place.

"Wealth, status, power," he said quietly. " 'Tis a seductive trilogy. Once, they were all I sought. They mean nothing to me now. I want a simple life, Carly, happiness. You."

Her heart soared. "If you keep that up, you'll be stuck with me for good."

"I have nothing to offer," he said quickly. "No land, little money, no title. Only a nomad's life."

"You're more than any of that, Andrew. So much more."

He grasped her shoulders and moved her back. "Marry me, Carly Callahan. Make me the happiest man on God's green earth."

"Yes," she sang out. "Yes, yes, yes."

With uncharacteristic abandon, he whooped loudly and lifted her, spinning her around. Laughing, they fell onto the sand. He rolled her onto her back, propped himself over her. "We'll sail as soon as the *Phoenix* is ready."

"Can't we get married here?"

"We have no man of God on the island. No church."

"But you're a sea captain. Doesn't that give you the authority to perform marriages?"

"At sea." He contemplated her words. "As to performing my own marriage, I've never heard of such a thing."

"You never heard of women falling through time, either."

He laughed long and hard.

"So is that a 'yes'? Oh, let's do it, Andrew. I want to be your wife. We can cross the *t*'s and dot the *i*'s later."

He replied with a warm, lingering kiss.

"Where will we sail when the *Phoenix* is ready?"

"Wherever you want, love, save England."

"Definitely not England," she said flatly.

"And be warned—if you wish to return to your home, you'll be bringing your husband along for the ride."

She gave a soft cry and kissed him. "Truth is, the idea of returning home has lost its appeal." Aside from her career, which she loved, nothing awaited her there but loneliness and broken dreams. "The *Phoenix* feels more like home than home ever did."

"Then you won't mind sailing again so soon?"

"Not at all! How about America?"

"I'll admit, I do admire the lot of them."

"Those former colonist upstarts," she said wryly.

"Aye, and I'm taking one on as a wife."

"America," she said on a sigh. "What an adventure. To get to the West Coast, we'll have to sail around the Cape of Good Hope, then across the Pacific, right?"

"With stops in Polynesia and the Sandwich Islands." His enthusiasm equaled her own.

"Theo will want to come."

"I'll disband the crew," Andrew said. "But all those who wish to come along will be welcome."

She clasped her hands together. "We'll go to California. I don't think it's officially part of the country yet, but it will be. You'd love it. It's beautiful along the coast. I happen to know where the best real estate is, too. We'll find some land near Carmel—no, Santa Barbara. It's gorgeous there. The climate's mild year-round."

"I grew up in London. I have never worked the land, though I rather like the idea."

"You wouldn't have to. We could start a shipping business."

"Or build them," he interjected. "I've often entertained the thought."

"We'd need capital, though, for either venture."

"We have the Blue Star of Delhi, and some gold."

"Gold," Carly breathed. The Gold Rush. When was it? In 1849—not for almost three more decades. Her mind raced ahead. "If we run out of money, I know a place near Sacramento, in the Sierras, where we can find some more. Of course we'll have to keep it secret, and we'd only take what we needed."

Andrew pressed his finger to her mouth, interrupting a rather nice daydream of them knee-deep in a river, gold pans in hand.

"One thing at a time," he said. "My head is spinning."

The scruffy black-and-white dog trotted past, kicking up powdery sand in his effort to evade his pint-sized entourage. The pooch bolted one way, but the children veered the other. Giggling, they danced around Carly and Andrew, chattering in a mix of Portuguese, English, and the local dialect.

"Be off with you!" Andrew shooed them away. In a fresh fit of giggles, they ran away. He raised himself on one elbow and smiled down at her. "How was that for a stern fatherly voice?"

She laughed. "How many should we have? Two? Three's a good number."

"Let me see." He stretched his hand across her hips, a calculating gleam in his eyes. "You are small-boned, but you have wide hips—"

"*Wide* hips?" she repeated indignantly.

"Very sexy hips, I might add."

She grinned, satisfied.

"Childbearing hips, nonetheless." He blocked her playful punch. "You will bear me many children." he said smugly, covering her body with his. "Three, you say? Bah! Eight at the very least. A veritable litter of squealing babes." He rocked his hips against her and said, "Each and every one the result of my loyal husbandly duties."

She took his earlobe in her teeth and tugged gently. "That was a very nineteenth-century thing to say."

"I am a very nineteenth-century man."

"Yes, you are," she agreed, sighing as he settled his warm mouth over hers.

"I, Andrew Edward Spencer, take thee, Carly Ann Callahan, to be my lawfully wedded wife. To have and to hold from this day forward. For better or for worse. For richer, for poorer. In sickness and in health. To love and to cherish. I promise to be faithful to you until death do us part."

Carly tucked an errant flower into her hair. Then she tilted her chin up to gaze at Andrew, so handsome in his dark gray suit. His blue eyes glittered with emotion as he recited the vows.

"Do you, Carly Ann Callahan, take me . . . ?" he began.

Tears rolled slowly down her cheeks as the crowd of ex-pirates and villagers, children, dogs, and roosters looked on. The wedding was supposed to have been a symbolic ceremony between just the two of them. But Carly had told Maria about the plans, and it was one secret the woman refused to keep. Now, the entire village was gathered on the beach to watch the ceremony.

". . . In sickness and in health, to love and to cherish, and promise to be faithful until death do us part?"

"I do," she promised in a husky voice.

There was silence as Andrew rooted around in his pocket for the ring—one that had been his mother's—and her mother's before that.

Carly swallowed as he slipped the ring onto her finger. The rose sapphire set on a gold filigree band glinted in the hazy sunshine.

Evidently moved as much as she, Andrew cleared his throat. "I now pronounce us husband and wife."

The crowd roared their approval, which caused the babies, startled by the cheering to wail, setting off the roosters, who had managed to behave themselves during the ceremony.

Willoughby, of all people, bellowed above the chaos, "Go on, kiss the bride!"

Solemnly, Andrew brushed the pads of his fingers along her jaw. She lifted her chin, meeting him halfway, sealing their vows with a kiss of lifelong trust and love.

Applause overrode the cheering. Andrew caught her around the waist and twirled her around, scattering the flowers she'd woven into her hair over the pebbly sand. Her simple, hand-sewn ivory dress fluttered over her bare legs . . . and bare feet.

As they walked through the crowd, shaking hands, hugging, accepting congratulations, the scent of smoke and roasted pig filtered through the grove of palms that sheltered the village from the beach.

When they'd eaten their fill and drunk toasts ranging from simple goodwill to lusty suggestions as to what to do on their wedding night, Andrew took

259

Carly's hand and said, "We will not spend this night in the *choupana.*"

"Where, then?" she asked expectantly. "The beach?"

He shook his head.

"The falls?"

"No—"

Carly gave a quick triumphant laugh. "The lagoon!"

"You're getting warmer," he said, gathering her into his arms. He relished the feel of her slender curves under his palms, molded his hands to her bottom, pressing her to him. His desire grew from a smoldering burn to an aching, heavy heat. He would make love to her as her husband tonight. The thought aroused him like no other.

After a circuitous route to the lagoon, and numerous delays when she'd insisted on a kiss—he had gone on to kiss every part of her that wasn't covered by her white silk dress—he led her over the rise that overlooked the lagoon.

"Close your eyes," he directed.

She squeezed her eyes shut, lifted her chin, and smiled.

Gently, he pushed her in front of him. His heart slammed against his chest; he was as excited as a small boy.

"Open."

Carly's eyes widened. He heard her suck in a breath. "A *choupana*—our *choupana?*"

"Ours, love. Our home for the time we have left here."

She hesitated with her fingers on the door latch. "Actually, you're supposed to carry me inside for good luck."

He swept her into his arms and stepped inside, feeling her delight course through him as she took in the furnishings. Maria and the other women had sewn curtains, a tablecloth, sheets, pillowcases, and a blanket. A carved wooden bowl of ripe mangos and a vase of flowers sat atop the table next to two chairs.

He lowered her to her feet. "Welcome home."

"It's lovely," she whispered fervently. "A real home."

The next thing he knew, she was wiping her eyes. His heart swelled with love. It seemed she had been crying on and off for a week—the same woman who'd shed nary a tear for an entire voyage.

"You brought the furniture from the *Phoenix*. The bed, the desk, and your blue robe," she said with a sly smile, glancing at one of the chairs. She sat on the edge of the mattress, bouncing a bit, her eyes sparkling in open invitation. "Just think of the things we can do in a real bed."

He moved her thighs aside and stepped between them. "Not think, wife. Do." Slipping his thumbs inside the neckline of her dress, he eased it off her shoulders.

He bent down to kiss her, showing her without words how he meant to take her body.

Breathless, she pushed him away. "The robe, Andrew. The *robe.*"

"The robe?" Bewildered, he followed her gaze to where his brocade robe lay tossed over the back of the chair.

She wrapped his collar around her knuckles. "Take off your clothes and put on the robe." She gave him an impatient shake. "You don't know how many times and how many ways I've fantasized about taking that

261

robe off you, and the things I've imagined doing to you once it was off—"

"Enough, woman," he said huskily, stopping her erotic recitation with his mouth. "I'll retrieve the bloody robe."

A wave slammed him up against metal. His back, his arm, on fire. Agony erupted in a cry of pain through his clenched teeth. Blindly, he swept his arms back and forth, feeling for something, anything, to help him find her.

"I've got you!" He held her as though he'd never let her go. She was so cold. "Don't sleep! Don't leave me!" His gasps turned to pants. He fought to control the pain so he could stay conscious. He didn't dare loosen his grip on her for a moment. He was what was keeping her alive.

But something pulled her from his arms. He struggled in vain to reach her.

"I don't want to lose you! Carly!"

"Andrew, sweetheart. It's okay. It's only a dream."

Carly's soft, sleep-thickened voice seeped into his consciousness, chasing away the last tortured traces of the nightmare.

"Bloody hell." He hauled her to him, holding her as he could not in the dream. The room was dark, silent but for his ragged breathing and the faint, steady breaths of his wife. In the four days since moving into the new *choupana*, he hadn't once had the nightmare. But the respite was over.

A breeze sailed through the window as Carly soothed him. She caressed his back, combed her slender fingers through his hair. In that moment, her love for him became a tangible thing, surging into him with profound power.

Rolling her onto her back, he sought the completion of that love. He parted her lips with his, cupped her warm breasts in his hands. She welcomed him with a soft moan as he slipped inside her. They made love with a hot, silent passion, their fingers laced together. When she climaxed, her hands squeezed his almost to the point of pain, and he reached his release with the same soundless intensity.

He held her until the gray light of dawn suffused the room. She'd fallen back asleep. Andrew kissed her lips softly so she would not wake. Soon they would leave the island and he'd see her safely to America. Tenderly, he lay his palm over her warm belly and closed his eyes. If they had made a child tonight, the baby would be born in safety.

The breeze coming through the window strengthened. The hair on the back of his neck prickled. Then a resounding explosion tore through the early morning calm.

Andrew flew out of bed and had his pants half on before Carly had come fully awake.

Another explosion followed the first, and was met with a shrieking protest by the island's monkeys.

Carly stumbled out of bed and snatched her dress from the chair, clutching the bunched silk to her breasts. "What is it?"

He shoved his pistol and a bag of black powder into the waistband of his trousers. "We're under attack."

Chapter Nineteen

Cold fear plunged into Carly's stomach. She knotted the dress around her as she bumped into chairs, the corner of the bed, frantically searching the room. "The gun. Where's the gun?"

Andrew swiped for her hand and missed. "Make haste, Carly."

She ran to the trunk and rooted through the clothing stored inside. "Andrew," she gasped, staggering backward. "My gun's not here. It's aboard the *Phoenix*! In your safe, with the sapphire and the gold."

The savings for their new life.

A series of sharp detonations drowned out a distant explosion. "Carly, now!" Andrew seized her hand and yanked her out the door.

Stumbling in tow, she struggled to match Andrew's long strides. They raced into the jungle. Darkness enveloped them, the cool, humid air muffling the sound of another explosion and magnifying their harsh gasps.

"Who do you think it is?" she asked breathlessly.

"Don't know—" He veered onto a path that led down a grassy hill. " 'Tis cannon fire, though."

His palm was sweaty, his skin pale against his dark whiskers. He was afraid. Fear settled a little bit deeper inside her.

Emerging into the sunshine, they sprinted toward the village. Pebbles brutally pricked the raw skin on the soles of her feet, cut when she'd stepped on the vegetation covering the jungle floor. Andrew didn't slow until he pulled her through the grove of palms between the village and the small harbor where the *Phoenix* sat unprotected. The air was thick with the acrid odor of gunpowder and the scent of burning wood.

"Holy Mother of God," Andrew exclaimed. The *Phoenix* was sinking. Swollen clouds of black smoke floated into the sky from her burning masts and sails. Silent, he watched his ship burn, and his dreams with it.

Overseeing the destruction was a familiar warship.

"The *Longreach,*" he said bitterly. "I would not have thought it possible."

Carly pressed her knuckles to her mouth. She reeled with the full impact of the hatred Andrew had struggled with in the years before he met her. It clogged her throat, choked and sickened her. The duke of Westridge would not rest until he had shattered Andrew's soul.

"They'll be coming ashore, Carly. We don't have much time. We've a small fortification in the interior, built for a situation such as this. Food, water, everything we need. Nearly impossible to find unless one knows the way."

"Jungle warfare . . . unconventional tactics." She grasped at the prospect of surviving, of evading their pursuers. "We can hide for months if we have to, pick them off one by one if they come looking for us."

"Aye, spitfire," he said admiringly, taking her hand. "That we will."

Cuddy and Gibbons met them halfway to the village. The men quickly exchanged ideas, agreeing that the best course of action was indeed a prolonged stay in the hidden fort.

Andrew and his officers supervised the hasty gathering of supplies, ensuring that one man was present with each group that assembled and disappeared into the jungle. The efficiency of the evacuation amazed her. They must have practiced this many times before.

When the village emptied, Cuddy led their small party into the forest. Carly trailed Gibbons and his family. Theo walked at her side. Pistol drawn, Andrew brought up the rear. They hiked inland and uphill, jogging at times, until the path narrowed to shoulder width, slowing their pace. Perspiration from exertion and anxiety dampened her dress. She swished past leafy vines and shrubs. Some scratched her bare arms; others sprouted sticky blossoms that left a residue on her skin. The hum of millions of insects muffled the sound of her labored breathing.

Every few minutes she glanced over her shoulder at her husband. *We're going to get away,* she told him with her eyes.

The humidity climbed and her strength flagged. But

hope kept her going. Just as she allowed herself to believe that they were really going to make it, all hell broke loose.

From behind . . . shouting and unfamiliar voices.

She spun around just as Andrew disappeared into the underbrush. Her stomach squeezed into a knot. "Where's he going?" she asked Cuddy. "Why isn't he coming?"

"They're overtaking us. He'll hold them off."

"Alone?" Her gun was locked in a chest on the *Phoenix*. If only she could will it into her hand. "Why?"

" 'Tis what he ordered should this occur." He snatched her elbow, urging her along. "He'll return once we've gained some distance. Don't ya worry, lass. They won't track him. The man knows his way through the jungle like no other."

The crack of a pistol obliterated the sound of chirping insects. A projectile whooshed past her ear, and a girl's high-pitched voice cried out in surprise. Cuddy shoved Carly to the ground. "Leila's hit," she heard Gibbons say.

Breathless, they regrouped around the girl, who swayed on her feet, her face screwed up in pain. Theo crouched in front of her. " 'Tis but a flesh wound," he said gently, prying her hand from her upper arm. Where the bullet had grazed Leila's skin, a furrow was rapidly filling with blood.

Circumspect, his hand moving in soothing circles over Maria's back, Gibbons allowed Theo to care for his stepdaughter.

Theo shrugged off his shirt, fastened a torn sleeve around Leila's thin arm, and scooped her into his arms. Then Gibbons led the shaken party into the shadows, veering off the path that Andrew guarded. In hopes of confusing their pursuers, Carly surmised, if they sneaked past Andrew.

Or killed him.

Last in line now, she glanced over her shoulder. The jungle was dark, quiet. Disturbingly so. No voices, no shots.

Something was wrong.

A premonition of dread pierced her insides, and her steps faltered. She was running blindly and alone, doing as she was told. And it was wrong.

She belonged with her husband.

What was the point of being safe if she didn't have Andrew with her? *Life will mean nothing without him.*

She caught up to Theo. "I'm going after him," she whispered urgently. "Don't follow. I—I don't know what will happen."

His eyes widened.

Before he could speak, pistol fire exploded.

"I have to go." It was her only chance. The disorder left in the wake of the shooting allowed her a chance to bolt. *Before* Cuddy and Gibbons discovered she was missing. She offered a smile to Leila, let her hand slide down Theo's arm. "I love you, kiddo." Her throat constricted. "I'm so proud of you," she whispered.

Then she ran.

She raced through the unrelenting foliage for all she was worth, plunging downhill until her lungs were ready to burst.

Whither thou goest . . .

On the path, she stumbled over a vine.

I will go.

Gritting her teeth against the pain, she regained her footing and pushed herself faster, harder.

Where thou lodgest . . . I will lodge.

"Andrew!"

He whirled to face her. "No, Carly—go back."

"I won't."

His incredulity darkened to fury.

"We're married," she implored. "For better or for worse; you said it yourself. We'll figure this out together."

"Drop your weapons, sir!" someone called from behind the trees.

Carly swore under her breath.

Fifty paces away, two burly young officers appeared, aiming their pistols at Andrew. Behind the hard-eyed thugs stood a dozen sweaty seamen in ragged clothes, none of them armed.

"Drop your weapons," the officer repeated.

Andrew let his pistol and dagger fall.

Carly crushed her hands into fists. The wedding ring pinched her skin, but she welcomed the pain. "It's better this way," she said in a fierce whisper, knowing Andrew was furious that she had returned.

"Carly . . ." His mouth twisted ruefully.

"Do you think I'd be safer without you?" she said in hushed tones as the group closed in on them. "Alone in a century I wasn't born in? On a tiny island in the middle of nowhere? Jesus, Andrew. You'd never know what happened to me. You'd always wonder."

Andrew expelled a ragged breath.

The second officer, the one with burn scars marring the left side of his face, retrieved Andrew's weapons and roughly frisked him. "Are you Andrew Spencer?"

Andrew squared his shoulders. "Aye."

"By order of the king, you are under arrest." He thrust the muzzle of his pistol at Andrew's back. "Move." The other officer indicated with a sweep of his hand that Carly was to walk beside him. She furtively switched her wedding ring from her left hand to the pinkie finger on her right, adjusting the gold band so that it would stay snug.

The path ended where the beach began. Her battered feet welcomed the silky sand, only to sting again when they hit salt water.

They waded out to one of two waiting longboats. As they rowed past the smoldering remains of the *Phoenix,* Andrew's eyes narrowed. With his mouth set in a determined line, he had the look of intense concentration he wore whenever he formulated a battle plan. Their very lives depended on his solution.

And on her ability to convince the crew that she was Lady Amanda.

Perspiration shone on his face. He would not look at her, nor would he talk to her. Uneasiness thrummed between them as the rhythmic slash of the oars brought them closer and closer.

Amazing how quickly life could change. Only hours ago, Andrew had made love to her in the peacefulness of dawn. She'd given herself completely, given until there was nothing left of her that wasn't his, too. Now he sat in gloomy silence, locked in his own thoughts.

"Stop looking like you're going to your death," she whispered harshly, reasonably certain their captors were engrossed in a private conversation. "The charges against you will never hold up in court. You were blackmailed. Anyone can see that."

He gave her a look one might give an innocent child. " 'Twill not matter."

"We'll find a good lawyer, witnesses who can vouch for your whereabouts the night the earl's daughter was murdered."

"I will not be permitted to testify, nor will my barrister be allowed to cross-examine witnesses brought in on my behalf. The trial will be swift, the outcome set in stone."

"That's crazy. A trial like this will last for months."

"In your time, perhaps," he said bleakly. "Here I've known of but one trial that lasted beyond a day."

Contemplating his words, she stared blankly at the warship ahead. It sounded like the British justice system was ripe for a little influence peddling, a little twenty-first-century-style scandal. Somehow, she'd find a way to bring the duke down and free Andrew in the process.

"You must accept the possibility that I will be hanged," Andrew said, gauging her reaction. One of the officers glanced his way, but he continued. "At Newgate, or perhaps Tilbury Point for the piracy."

She shivered. It would not happen that way. She would not allow him to be hanged.

The seamen stored the oars on the bottom of the longboat. As it coasted up to the glistening wooden hull of the *Longreach,* Andrew regarded her with the blue-eyed gaze that had stolen her heart months ago.

I love you, she mouthed.

"Send the lady up first," someone called down from the great ship.

Carly worked at staying calm. As she climbed aboard, a tall, impeccably dressed man offered her his hand, helping her up to the deck. He wore civilian garb, not a uniform. With his sandy-haired good looks and elegant features, he struck her as the archetype of British aristocracy.

Detached, his expression vaguely repulsed, he scrutinized her from head to toe. Feeling naked in the wet silk that clung to her bare skin, she folded her arms over her chest.

"You'll want to change," he said dispassionately. "Ensign?"

"Yes, sir."

She glanced behind him to an officer who looked to be her age. The man pushed his glasses higher on his narrow nose and nodded curtly. "Ensign Rudolph Bern, milady. Ship's doctor."

"Bern will escort you to your quarters," the chilly-eyed gentleman said. "Once he sees to your good health, you may exchange . . . that"—he gestured to her wrap—"for a more suitable gown."

A commotion announced Andrew's arrival.

The nobleman lifted his gaze. Finally, true emotion suffused his face. But it was hatred, deep and unmistakable. Cheeks flushed and eyes bright—almost maniacal, Carly thought with trepidation—the man called out, "Why, if it isn't the slippery rogue himself, the unwanted bastard of my uncle's whore."

Andrew's struggle to compose himself was not lost on Carly. Calmly, he replied, "So, you traded the drawing rooms of London for months at sea to hunt me down, 'slippery rogue' that I am. Bloody commendable—"

"Whatever it takes to protect my investment."

Andrew snorted. "Either way, you're the last man I expected to see, Westridge."

Westridge? Carly's head snapped back to the duke.

"Richard!" She hurled herself into his arms, plastering her cold, wet body to his pristine white lawn shirt. "You saved me. Thank you, thank you."

Sickened, Andrew watched the cur who had murdered his family hold his wife, the woman he loved more than life itself. He feared for her as never before. But he could no more keep her from harm than he was able to save his mother and brother. When would he stop paying for the mistake he had made? Seeking his cousin's title with a young man's blind arrogance?

"I could not bear the thought of another day with those horrid pirates," Carly wailed. "I prayed you would come for me, and you did." Pointedly, she glanced Andrew's way.

The apprehension in her eyes hit him hard. She was terrified, yet she was playing her game with airy aplomb. Her sheer courage stunned him, and his last shreds of anger dissolved into pride.

Westridge peeled Carly's arms from his shoulders one at a time. She sniffled, gazing at him with honey-brown eyes brimming with tears and trust. "Oh, you are everything I'd hoped you would be."

In answer, he unfolded a linen handkerchief and dabbed at water droplets marring his gleaming boots.

Carly fought the evil urge to shake herself like a wet puppy. "How did you ever find me?" As long as Richard was convinced that she was his betrothed, she had a chance at saving Andrew's life.

"I found you after receiving some unexpected help," Richard said. "A rather disheveled fellow, looking to trade information for gold. I believe his name was Barts . . . or Bellows."

"Booth," Ensign Bern supplied.

Dread clogged Carly's throat. If Booth was onboard—

"Of course, gold is not what we gave the man." Richard exchanged amused glances with the two goons who had seized Andrew. "I do not tolerate beggars onboard this ship. No, indeed."

Bern, the doctor, winced and averted his eyes.

Richard folded his handkerchief. "Secure the prisoner."

Carly braced herself as a sailor hoisted a heavy, rusted set of shackles. A flurry of emotions flickered over Andrew's face with the cold metallic click of the handcuffs locking into place.

"Display him on the quarterdeck, for now," The duke said out the corner of his mouth. "Perhaps this miserable tropical sun or the lack of water will do him in. Barring that, what say you we stow him in the hold?"

Shaken by a mental image of Andrew in a dank cell, alone, chained, lying in his own filth, she gulped several deep breaths.

"If that doesn't do it," he droned on, seemingly enamored with the sound of his own voice, "perhaps a flogging will. Shall I allow you the pleasure of the first stroke, dear Amanda, or would you prefer the last?"

Appalled, she dropped her gaze. The monster expected her to be impressed by his overt cruelty.

Richard summoned Bern. "It's time. Escort the lady to her quarters."

"Yes, Your Grace," the doctor said briskly.

Carly followed the ensign belowdecks into a narrow, darkened passageway. Bern led her into a tiny but luxuriously appointed cabin, locking the door behind him.

He leaned against it, facing her. "I've been sent to determine whether you are a virgin."

She felt the blood drain from her face. Then a heated blush surged back with equal force. "You insult my betrothed with your doubts."

"It is His Grace who is concerned that his bride has been soiled."

Mortified, Carly gaped at him.

Bern removed his glasses and regarded her with intelligent, dark brown eyes. "We will not do the examination," he said wearily. "Are you or are you not a virgin? Tell me the answer to give the duke. I've patients to attend to."

For once in her life she was speechless.

"So be it, milady. You are a virgin." He returned to the door and added quietly, "There are ways to pretend."

Stunned by his unexpected kindness, she held his searching gaze. She couldn't read enough in his dark eyes to tell if he was willing to risk helping her free Andrew, but he had saved her with the virginity business, so there was a chance she could persuade him to cooperate.

He grasped the doorknob, twisted it. Her heart raced. *Think fast.* What would Lady Amanda do? "Wait, ensign!"

He released the knob.

"Do you know who my father is?"

"Of course."

"You know, then, that he is a very wealthy man, do you not?"

The doctor appeared bewildered. "I do."

"On the other hand, the duke has property, but

hardly a penny, er, a shilling to his name, which is why, I suppose, he wanted to marry me so badly," she said, fabricating the story as she went, trying her damnedest to recall what Andrew had told her, while praying her ruse would work. She cupped her hand around her mouth as though revealing the utmost of confidences. " 'Tell Richard yes,' I told my father. I rather liked the idea of being a duchess. Which brings me to my point. If I'm happy, Papa's happy. And he is most generous with his appreciation, for whomever might . . . help me," she concluded pointedly.

His dark brows lifted. "You're offering me money."

Her apprehension skyrocketed. She was bartering for Andrew's life with funds she didn't have. "That depends on your cooperation."

"I see." He replaced his glasses. Studied her. Then he shook his head and stepped into the corridor, easing the door closed behind him.

Hell. If this were a dogfight, she'd be dead. She'd miscalculated. The doctor was loyal to his master.

But instead of conceding defeat, she hardened with resolve. She'd figure out something, find someone else to help her and Andrew. Meanwhile, she'd play the duke's game.

She cleaned her face, her scratched and filthy hands and feet, using the washbasin in the cabin, then turned her attention to an enormous, dusty trunk. Beneath its heavy lid were gowns and undergarments and shoes. She sorted through the beautiful hand-sewn, beaded, and embroidered garments, searching for a gown she could don without help. With an ease that startled her, she layered her body with vintage underwear—chemise, corset, petticoats, and stockings. As though she'd dressed this way all her life, she buttoned a pale blue gown decorated with too many frivolous white bows, then wedged her feet into slipperlike pumps.

Exhausted, she fell to her knees in front of the open trunk. The glint of something gold caught her eye, a hand-sized oval frame tied with red ribbon to an envelope.

Decorated with a wax seal. The Paxton crest.

She tore it open and read the enclosed note.

Something to ease your homesickness, sugarplum. Hurry home. All my love, Papa.

Barely breathing now, she lifted the gilt-edged frame and brought it closer. It was a tiny, old-fashioned painting of a man and two young women. A family, maybe. The white-haired gentleman was robust, red-cheeked, and she felt herself inexplicably drawn to his friendly face. He stood behind a pretty girl with curly black hair. She reminded Carly of someone, but for the life of her, she couldn't remember whom.

Carly followed the man's hand to where it rested on the other woman's shoulder. She had a pale heart-shaped face and wide eyes. Brown eyes. Her blond hair was swept up in an old-fashioned style, framing her face with silvery tendrils. Although she wore an expression of impish innocence, she appeared somewhat sad.

Carly's chest squeezed tight. Hands shaking, she lifted the portrait to her eyes. Good Lord, *this* woman was more than familiar. This woman was *her*.

Chapter Twenty

Clutching the framed miniature in her hand, Carly lifted the heavy skirts of her old-fashioned dress higher and hurried toward the quarterdeck. Upon seeing her husband, she felt a rush of emotion so profound that she could hardly breathe. Her chest tightened, and black spots danced before her eyes, eyes that threatened to flood with tears if she didn't get hold of herself quickly.

Slowing, she approached Andrew. He was shackled, displayed like a trophy aft of the main mast. Perspiring in the ferocious sun, he lifted the ends of his mouth in the barest hint of a smile when he spied her. But the officer with the scarred face sat nearby, in the shade of a tarp, eyeing her with suspicion as she approached, so she immediately launched into her best imitation of Lady Amanda, spoiled heiress.

"You horrid pirate!" she shrieked at Andrew. "How could you steal me the way you did? I was so frightened. I'll never be able to forgive you."

Dozens of sailors watched her performance but averted their eyes submissively when she looked their way. An undercurrent of fear permeated the crew; a former officer herself, she could sense it. She'd bet her bottom dollar that they'd suffered at the hands of the duke, and unless she figured out something soon, her husband would, too.

Shakily, she raised her voice and thrust the frame at Andrew. "These are the people you took me from! My family, look! Lord Paxton, my sister, and—and—" She grappled with the words. "And me . . ."

He watched her intently for several heartbeats. Then his gaze lowered to the little portrait and he grew pale.

"You see, don't you!" She edged closer, knowing it was a risk but not caring. It was critical that Andrew understand what she'd discovered. Body heat and desperate yearning thrummed between them. He smelled like sweat and damp wool, but she'd sell her soul to hold him close, to feel his strength. "I look so much like her that," her voice dropped lower, "I think I *am* her."

Andrew choked. "How, Carly?" he asked in a raw whisper.

"I'm not sure. The instant the shock wore off, I tried to piece together the puzzle. That meant exploring every possibility, no matter how bizarre. I never gave much thought to the plausibility of reincarnation, but look at the coincidences here. They're too strong to ignore. What if I *am* Amanda? Say, one or two lives farther along? There was a cosmic mix-up when I was hurt in the crash. I ended up back here, instead of where I'm supposed to be."

Andrew groaned. "I'm still sorting out your journey through time. Now this."

"Amanda!" Richard bellowed from some distance.

She swallowed, glancing wildly around the deck. "Paxton loves her very much. He said so, in a letter. He wouldn't want to cause her pain. And putting you to death would. That's the key, Andrew, the key to keeping you out of Newgate."

Andrew's breath rushed out, and he squeezed his eyes shut. When he opened them, they were moist. " 'Tis a blessing. God must have his reasons."

"I think so, too."

"What in the blazes are you doing, woman?" Richard demanded almost possessively as he sauntered up to them.

His presence meant her precious visit with Andrew was over. Infuriated, she snapped, "Taunting him, I suppose. Showing him my family who misses me, hoping I'd spur something resembling an apology. But no-oo." She gathered her skirts. "You're despicable," she hissed, aiming words meant for the duke at Andrew. "You make me sick. And you haven't an ounce of shame in your beastly body." Unwanted tears welling, she marched off.

The duke caught up to her. "I miss my family," she told him, sniffling, unable to come up with anything better to explain her tears.

"I see." His face was impassive, and his cold gray eyes lacked anything resembling human emotion. So much for conjuring sympathy, she thought bleakly.

Silent, he escorted her belowdecks.

"I'll lock you inside," he informed her once inside

the cabin. Before she could protest, he held up one hand. "It's for your own good. The men have been without female companionship for months. Wouldn't do for you to be harmed before we reach England." His gaze settled on her breasts, snugly outlined by her bodice, but he perused her in a detached way, as one might examine a possession.

"I wanted your sister, you know," he said quietly. "Sweet, virginal Augusta." His mouth dipped in a sneer. "The audacity of Paxton to have misled me into thinking I was to marry his youngest daughter. How dare he change his bloody mind, deciding instead to saddle me with a rumored-to-be-lunatic, seven-and-twenty-year-old woman? Though you appear far younger with your slight build, wide brown eyes, and pale hair"—he brushed her cheek in a fleeting caress—"you are a hideous departure from what I prefer."

The flickering lamplight played over his patrician features as he looked skyward. "The humiliation you have caused this family goes on, Uncle," he said, apparently blaming Andrew's dead father. "You left the duchess childless because you squandered your seed on a whore who sullied the Spencer name by producing one nuisance bastard after another. It's taken me years to get rid of them all. But now I have. Yet, it appears I have no choice but to take Paxton's presumably mad and positively past-her-prime daughter as a wife." He seemed perplexed for a moment, almost childlike, like a lost little boy. "It's not fair."

Carly whistled softly when the door slammed.

The man was deranged.

Unstable and unpredictable.

Combined with his malice and obvious intelligence, it chilled her to the core.

* * *

That evening someone rapped on the door. "Come in."

She heard the tinkle of keys, and then Ensign Bern stepped inside with a tray of steaming, fatty boiled meat, pudding, and potatoes.

She thanked him, and put the tray aside.

"Lieutenant Spencer is in the hold for the night. I gave him water and treated his sunburn."

Did you feed him? she yearned to ask. *Did you remove his shackles?*

But she remained silent. She'd revealed too much to the doctor already. She could only assume that Andrew was doing his part, gaining the doctor's trust and sympathy, or maybe working on other sailors, whose loyalty to the duke was weaker.

"I've been with my patients in sick bay," Bern explained, "or I'd have come sooner."

Her heart skipped a beat. She had been vaccinated, but Andrew could catch something, particularly if he was in a weakened condition. "Disease?" she asked uneasily.

Anger shadowed his drawn face. "Not what is typically found in men's bodies, nay. What I treat is the animalistic result of one man's diseased mind."

Carly's breath caught in her throat.

He hated Richard!

She wrung her hands, again seeing in the doctor the prospect of an ally, but afraid to hope this time, afraid to lose such a precious opportunity. "It's all right," she ventured hesitantly. "You can say what you want to me."

Bern frowned and clasped his hands behind his back, gazing at the candle by her bedside. "Many times, too many times, the duke has issued rather sadistic punishments when perhaps a verbal reprimand would have sufficed. When I spoke to him about the vicious floggings, he explained that the crew needed to be toughened before they engaged Spencer and his pirates in battle. Of course, you already know about the towing accomplished when we engaged Spencer in the doldrums. We lost a dozen men to the heat."

Bern exhaled, sounding wearied beyond his years. "While we docked on the mainland seeing to repairs, the first lieutenant and I asked that he cease the madness. Such barbarism may be common practice on some ships, but we wanted no part of it."

"But he didn't stop," Carly murmured.

"And he won't. He flogged the first lieutenant to death that day. But he let me live, because I'm the only man who can keep alive the poor souls he needs to work this ship." His mouth twisted. "The few healthy men left are his minions."

He gestured to her untouched dinner. "Please, don't let me keep you from your meal."

"Actually, this situation is not conducive to my appetite."

He considered her, then nodded. "The *Longreach* is paralleling the coastline, and it will through the night." He hesitated, as though mulling something over.

Puzzled, she said, "Go on."

"If . . . if I were to say to you, milady, that the opportunity exists, this very night, to take advantage of that proximity . . . might you?"

She froze. Was he talking mutiny? Jumping ship?

She clamped down on her surge of excitement. She wasn't leaving without Andrew.

Her heart thudded in her throat as she carefully chose her words. "If I were to say to *you*, ensign, that true love comes first . . . might you understand why I cannot go?"

Bern's countenance softened. He withdrew a ring of large, old-fashioned keys from his pocket. "Take these." He pressed them into her hand. "You'll know why when morning comes," he said softly, then backed out the door.

Richard burst into her cabin. "Get up!"

Having slept fully clothed, she glowered at him from a cot littered with mangled white bows that had come loose from her gown.

"Come on," he snapped, snatching her upper arm in a painful grip.

Carly hurried to keep up. The warship's timbers creaked on the swells. But there was no one to work the sails. Except for the man at the wheel, the deck was deserted. Yesterday, six longboats trailed the stern on ropes. Now only one remained.

"Where is everyone?" she asked innocently.

In his most pronounced display of emotion toward her to date, he growled, "They've mutinied! Deserters, the lot of them! I'm going after them, however. I'll find where the bounders have ferreted themselves away." He plowed one hand through his hair. "Now I'll have to speed up our friend Spencer's demise, as if I didn't have enough things to worry about."

Carly's stomach twisted. Richard had never intended for Andrew to stand trial. He meant to kill him first, and that made their dilemma far more desperate.

"I'll be in the wardroom with my officers, discussing the situation. Serve us breakfast there." He deposited her into a large cabin that was as hot as a furnace.

"You want me to *cook?*"

"Yes, I want you to cook. And don't tell me you never learned how. You've half a brain—use it!" He slammed the door.

Gasping, she leaned against a wide wooden table riddled with slashes. Daylight seeped through the smoke vent in the ceiling, making it difficult to see more than a few feet in front of her. She ignited a rush from the galley stove, which was thankfully still burning, and lit a few stubby candles.

She sat for awhile, trying to collect her wits. On the downside, she had no weapons, and all the good guys who might have gotten her some had jumped ship. On the positive side, very few sailors were probably left onboard, and they'd be overburdened and distracted trying to sail and navigate a warship, while placating an angry lunatic.

Her hand closed over the bulge in her skirt. Bern's keys were hidden in her dress. There were five. He said he treated prisoners. One key must be for the hold, and another for shackles. Andrew's shackles, she prayed.

She busied herself with the mundane chore of preparing breakfast as she struggled to take advantage of the new situation. She scrounged around the galley, looking for biscuits, oatmeal, and sugar. Her dress pasted itself to her sweaty skin and her hair hung in dreadlocks. Better not to tidy up, she thought, in case the duke or his thugs were contemplating using her for sustenance beyond food. With that in mind, she rubbed ashes on her cheek and sprinkled some in her hair.

The galley grew dimmer as she worked. The cheap, foul-smelling candles had already burned down to pools of hissing, melted tallow. She was sloppy in replacing them, not bothered, for once, by splattering hot tallow on a wooden floor and table. The duke and his entire ship could go up in flames, for all she cared. Heck, why not throw a few candles in the powder room for some added excitement?

A candle in the powder room.

"Whoa." Her heart stopped, then restarted with a thunderous beat. Could she? Blow the ship to smithereens, the duke and his murderers with it?

Squeezing her eyes shut she concentrated, remembering the sketch of the warship Andrew had used the day they formulated their plan to destroy its rudder. The powder magazine was located well below the waterline, three or four companionways below the topmost deck. The room was small, with a hatch only the gunner could unlock, something hardly ever done at sea—no one wanted to chance a stray spark getting inside.

She stopped herself in the middle of loading silverware onto the cart. If she were to set off an explosion in the powder magazine while she and Andrew were still aboard, they'd die with the duke.

They'd have to escape first.

But how? How did one blast apart a ship after the fact?

Leave a candle burning in the powder room.

She'd learned that during battle, boys known as powder monkeys squeezed through small windows in the powder room walls, hunkering down inside to shuttle powder out to the men operating the cannons. She was petite, too. Well, except for her butt. Certainly she could squeeze into the magazine like a powder monkey.

286

Once inside, she'd set a candle on the powder bags she knew were stored next to wooden barrels of the stuff.

She wheeled a rickety wooden cart of food to the wardroom, while her mind percolated with hatching plans. A burning candle was a ticking clock. She'd have to free Andrew, swim to the longboat, and row away in the finite minutes it gave them.

How much time would a candle give them? An hour? Two? They burned at different rates depending on thickness and quality. The beeswax candles in her quarters were cleaner and slower burning than the tallow ones in the galley. . . .

The whole thing was awfully dicey.

She paused in front of the wardroom door, listening to the voices of the duke and his men. Her gaze drifted to the horizon, where warm rain obscured the craggy African coastline. As the shower passed overhead, droplets softened the edges of the half-dozen huts in what she guessed was a village.

Why not just free Andrew, get into the longboat, and escape?

No. Richard was relentless—she'd already learned that. Left alive, he'd hunt them down and kill them. If not her and Andrew, then Bern and the others.

Exploding the ship with him in it was her only option.

Again, she gazed at the beach. If she did anything at all, it would have to be tonight. Who knew how much longer they'd follow the coast? In a longboat without a compass or water, she and Andrew wouldn't last long on the open sea, though she made a mental note to bring a bag of supplies with her later . . . just in case.

Forcing a pleasant smile on her face, she opened the

door and breezed inside. Time to feed the demons their breakfast.

"Andrew," she whispered against the solid wooden door, glancing nervously behind her into the darkness of the hold. No one had followed her. "Andrew, can you hear me?"

"Carly!" The familiar deep voice sounded hoarse.

"There's been a mutiny," she quickly told him. "Almost everyone jumped ship last night."

"Who is left?" His voice sounded nearer now, and more alert.

"Richard's here. And those two jerks who captured you." Again she peered into the dank, lantern-lit hold. "And the little troll who usually guards your cell. Except, at the moment, he's too busy sailing and steering."

"Four? Are you telling me that only four men are left?"

"Yes. And they're all so preoccupied by the mutiny that they left me alone to cook their meals." She'd attended them charmingly and docilely all day, keeping them well stuffed. "They ignore me, so I listen to them talk, and they talk a lot. They intend to patrol the coast. They're going to use a cannon to terrorize villages and other ships until they track down the sailors. I can see the coastline, but I don't know how much longer we'll follow it without enough men to work the sails."

"We have to act tonight."

"That's what I think, too."

Something scrabbled down the companionway. Carly gasped. A tiny shadow scurried past. A rat. Relieved, she shut her eyes. "I told them I had to clean the galley and make dinner, so they don't know I'm here. I have a plan to run by you before I search out the powder room."

Silence.

"And I have keys, Andrew. Bern left me keys. I can get you out!"

"Not until after dark," he said briskly. "And only if you're certain the guard is occupied elsewhere. We've no weapons."

"I know," she murmured. "I'll come at midnight. Are you shackled?"

"Aye."

She flattened her hands on the door, pressed her cheek to the rough wood. How she ached to hold him again.

"You mentioned the powder magazine, Carly. Why?"

"This is my plan: I'll light a candle in the powder room and we'll escape before the ship blows."

"Woman, do you have any idea how risky such an operation is? Candles throw sparks. Hot tallow drips."

She clenched her hands into fists. "Richard said he'd kill you before we got to England. Because of the mutiny, I think it might be sooner rather than later. So, yes, I think it's risky, and, yes, I stand the chance of destroying us all, but I'm sure you'll agree that possible death beats certain death any day."

She heard his deep sigh. "If it costs me my life to see you safe," he said, "so be it."

"But I won't be safe," she shot back. "The duke already said he wants to marry my sister, so I don't have high hopes for surviving this voyage, either."

More silence.

Meaning he was now considering the possibilities, the risks, the consequences of her crazy plan.

"Do you remember everything you learned about the magazine?" he asked finally.

She breathed silent thanks. "Yes, most of it."

He quickly reviewed the dangers and the setup of the room, nonetheless.

"I've been researching candles, too," she said. Each time she returned to the sweltering galley, she lit them, her chest tight with anxiety. Afraid to risk jotting down figures, she struggled to keep the results clear in her head. "I'm studying how they burn, Andrew, the individual characteristics. Tallow versus beeswax, fat versus thin. By the time I'm through, I'll know exactly the length of wax we need."

"Two hours," he said. "I'll want two hours."

She exhaled. "Okay."

"If you haven't already, determine how many minutes a knuckle's length of wax gives us. Then five knuckle lengths."

"I will."

"Then multiply and divide, snuff out candles, and start new ones. Break off bottoms and try different wicks."

"Yes, I'll do all that."

"And then, my little spitfire, I want you to get down on your knees and pray for all you're worth."

A prolonged roll of thunder rumbled in the distance as Carly left the cabin. By midnight, wind had transformed the sea into a seething sheet of foam. With most of its sails wrapped, the warship plunged and rose on the swells.

Except for the sounds of the rising gale, the decks

were deathly still and deserted. Complacent, Richard hadn't posted a single lookout. Cruel dictators made such sloppy leaders.

It didn't surprise her to see Andrew's warden asleep in his hammock, clutching to his chest the bottle she'd just happened to leave near the wheel after dinner. For a typical seaman, brandy was rare and precious, an unexpected treat she knew would put him under for the night.

The stage was set.

Now all she had to do was perform.

The lantern she carried scarcely lit the length of her shadow. The duke had locked her in when he retired for the night, but as she'd discovered that morning, Bern's keys worked from the inside, as well as the exterior.

The ship yawed, and she staggered to a stop outside the powder room. The storm was getting worse. She'd have to wedge each candle even deeper between bags of powder to keep them from tipping. That would leave them less than two hours, but how much less, she didn't know.

She withdrew one of two identical, long, thin beeswax candles from the folds of her dress. Hands shaking as much from apprehension as excitement, she lit one wick with the lantern flame, then fastened the lamp on a hook on an exterior wall made for that purpose. Powder rooms weren't lit from within; too dangerous. Instead, lanterns were hung outside double-glazed portholes, allowing illumination—but not sparks—inside.

She stripped to her chemise. Then, feet first, holding the candle straight out in front of her, she shimmied backward through a tiny hatchway barely wide enough for her thighs and hips. She grunted, pushed herself with her hands until her rear end cleared, then eased down to a crouch between the wooden barrels inside the powder room.

She stayed like that for a long moment, unable to move, her breaths hissing in and out. She was actually sitting in her underwear, holding a lit candle in a room stacked from floor to ceiling with gunpowder.

Swallowing hard, she stretched her arms outside the hatch and lit the second candle from the first, insurance in case one burned out. Then, working swiftly and carefully, she jammed the candles between cylindrical linen bags of powder—deeper than she'd wanted to, but the heavy seas left her no choice.

The warship lurched, then rolled.

Not breathing, she stared at the candles. The flames danced, but the stems stayed upright.

Thank you.

She scrambled out, dressed, and snatched the lantern.

The clock was ticking . . .

Her insides felt watery as she dashed to Andrew's cell. Leaking barrels blocked her way. Stumbling, she flew forward, scraping her palms over the rough floor and jamming splinters into her knees. On her feet again, she ran through the darkness, crunching over filth left by a crew that didn't care about the state of their ship. She lifted her skirts higher. They were heavier than she was used to and slowed her down. Startled, rats scampered by, bumped into her, scraping her shins with their sharp little claws.

She halted by Andrew's door. "Andrew!" She fought to catch her breath while she sorted through the keys. "It's done. I had to push them in pretty far because of the swells. I don't know how much time is left."

"Open the bloody door!"

"I have to find the key first."

In her haste she dropped the key ring. She aimed the lantern at the floor, groping blindly.

The clock ticked. . . .

Her fingers closed around cold metal. She scooped them up, her hands shaking as she tried each old-fashioned key in turn.

She shoved the second to last key into the opening, and the lock turned with a heavy metallic click. She flew into Andrew's arms. Wrapping her fingers in his hair, she met his desperate, hungry kiss.

He pulled away, breathless. "Come on, love. There's little time." She unlocked his shackles.

They raced up the companionways and out to the deck. A line of thunderstorms was fast approaching. The ship pitched on the waves, its helm unmanned, its sails useless. Andrew gripped her tightly, guiding her to the stern, where a single longboat bounced in the wake. She could hear his ragged breathing above the booming of the surf and her pulse.

Using a pulley, he towed the boat closer. "Jump!" he shouted, never letting go of her hand.

Cold seawater gushed up her nose. Andrew was a powerful swimmer, and he dragged her upward to the surface, then propelled her through the swells to the boat.

They fell onto its bottom, panting. Then he cut the line and they spun free. "Hold on!" Andrew grabbed the oars. "I'm going to row like hell."

Rain came down in cold, slanting spikes. She sat, facing her husband, her teeth chattering. Andrew gasped with the strain of his efforts. The current and the winds were working against them.

The clock ticked. . . .

Behind Andrew loomed the warship. She kept her eyes trained on the deck, scanning for signs of the duke or his men. But not one of the cowardly murderers ventured on deck. Even so, knowing what was about to happen to them nauseated her. She shivered uncontrollably now, unable to pull her gaze from the *Longreach,* looking so lost without its crew. Driven by the gale, it slowly listed to one side.

Oh, Lord, the candles.

Carly's voice was flat, guttural. "Andrew . . . row . . . faster."

He saw the fear in her face and turned to glance over his shoulder. An earsplitting crack tore through the rain. Then the ship rolled sharply. "Bloody hell."

The *Longreach* blew up.

A fireball shot into the air, a half-mile high or more.

For an instant they were bathed in a flickering sunset, then the roar of the explosion plowed into their bodies like a physical blow.

Andrew dove for her, sending her sprawling onto her back.

It grew quieter, just wind, rain, and the crackling of burning timbers. Clearly alarmed, and intent on escaping a threat she didn't see, Andrew righted himself and began rowing, harder and faster than she'd thought was humanly possible.

A freight train–like rumble came out of nowhere.

The sea dropped out beneath the little boat.

"Oh, Carly," he said sorrowfully, releasing the oars. "Oh, my love."

Her fingers clamped tight over edge of the hull. "What! What is it?"

Desperation etching his shadowy face, he seized her in his arms and squeezed the breath from her. "I've got you," he said. "Hold me. Hold me tight."

The stars winked out one by one as something unimaginably huge arced over them. Then, falling slowly, ever so slowly, the wave descended.

Her skull exploded in white-hot pain. Seawater roared in over their heads and wrenched Andrew's hands from her waist to her hips. They flipped over. His fingers raked down her hips to her thighs. Then he was gone.

"No!"

So dark . . . can't breathe.

"Jolly Roger One, this is Jolly Roger Four."

Lightning flashed, intense and painful.

"Mayday. Mayday," she called to the other aircraft. *No one can hear me. Fifteen thousand feet and dropping. The storm wrenched and kicked. Her fingers slipped off the throttles.* Start, start, start, please start.

One thousand, eight hundred . . .

She squeezed her eyes shut and bailed out.

So cold . . .

A vibration built above the thunder until the very air drummed with the beat. Rain slashed across searchlights. She yearned to clasp the hands that reached for her.

"I've got you."

Blessed warmth. But it was taken away so quickly. Metal shrieked, a hideous howl, then scraping, a chop,

chop, chop of blades striking the sea. The deep voice was no longer with her.

"Where are you?" she cried out, groping blindly.

Rain and the frigid wind battered her. She was too heavy, too exhausted. Arms came around her this time.

"Come on, stay with me. Don't sleep!"

She tried. Oh, God, she tried, but she couldn't keep her eyes from closing. . . .

Chapter Twenty-one

Carly became aware of a fuzzy white light, then a faint, steady beeping. She couldn't fathom where she was. The white light grew brighter if she tried to open her eyes, dimmer if she rolled them back. She gave up after a while and let the warm, familiar nothingness engulf her.

Consciousness tiptoed in. The white light was still behind her eyelids, the beeping ceaseless. There was music. Familiar, somehow . . .

It was the unmistakable theme song of *The Price Is Right*.

The world roared back. Carly plunged into awareness. Moaning, she draped her arm over her face.

"Welcome home, honey."

Carly peered over her arm. A smiling woman stood

over her, her enormous bosom straining against a crisp
tan uniform. Calm, efficient, she adjusted a tube running into Carly's arm before she tucked a blanket
around her waist.

Carly's gaze dropped. A row of faded blue letters
adorned the sheet's starched border.

USS *Dwight D. Eisenhower*.

Carly grabbed hold of the bedsheet. No wedding
ring adorned her left hand.

*"Know this, love. You'll not be alone anymore. No
matter how fast you run, I will catch you. And no matter where you go, I will find you."*

Utter desolation choked her. "Where's Andrew?"

"Easy, Lieutenant." The woman's kind, dark eyes
belied her stern tone as she sat at the edge of the bed.
"You can call your Andrew on the phone as soon as you
feel up to it. Aw, smile, honey. You're fine. No broken
bones. You'll be back in your jet before you know it."

Your jet.

Carly took in the details of the room. Dividers surrounded her bed, affording some privacy from the rest
of the bustling infirmary, but not much. Just outside
the hatch stood a group of sailors. One young seaman
wore a Walkman, his lips moving in time to the music.

Carly winced. Shiny silver fixtures blinded her;
everywhere lights blinked on and off. She swerved her
gaze back to the television, where a woman caressed a
shiny new car before a cheering crowd. The modernity
of her surroundings was overwhelming—the light too
white and crisp, the bulkheads too clean, too sterile,
the sounds too sharp.

"What's happened?" Carly blinked rapidly. "This is
the twenty-first century."

The medic chuckled. "You'd think it was the caveman days, judging by the men on this ship."

Carly stared. The woman frowned. Then she pressed a button by the bed. "Do you know your name, honey?"

"Yes, ma'am. Carly Callahan."

"Good morning, Lieutenant Callahan," a male voice sang out. "Hope you've enjoyed your leave. Time to get back to work."

A grinning man strode past the partition. He had blond hair, a sunburned nose, and flight surgeon insignia on his uniform. As he aimed a penlight into Carly's eyes, the medic adjusted the IVs. She picked up a clipboard and copied information from a monitor by the bed.

"You were out for three days," the doctor said. "Due to medication, for the most part."

Carly's hopes plunged. *Three days.* "Felt longer," she replied glumly.

"Usually does," he said cheerily. "No damage to the noggin, though. I'll clear you to fly when I get the thumbs up from the chief surgeon and Commander Martinez."

She squeezed her eyes shut. How could six months have happened in three days?

Her husband was dead.

Her throat tightened. Oh, God, how could she accept the fact that Andrew wasn't real? That her life with him had been nothing more than a hallucination? A delusion that had run its course.

Coming awake slowly, Carly flexed her left arm. Tubes tugged on the inside of her elbow. The plastic led to an IV stand, where an upside-down can of Coors

Light was crudely taped to the top rack, sprouting a tube that appeared to wind down to her arm. "What the—?"

"Mornin', Carly."

Commander Martinez was ensconced in the chair by the bed, his feet propped on the blanket. "So," he said, grinning, "I give you the keys to a jet, and you throw it in the goddamned pond. Think they grow on trees?"

She stifled a resigned sigh. Here she was, back in her old life, like nothing had ever happened. It made her sick. "Hey, Skipper. Who put the beer can up there?"

His eyes shone. "Guess."

She managed a smile. "Where are they?"

"On their way down. They miss ya." He smoothed one hand over his black crewcut. "How do you feel? You weren't in the best shape when they hauled you in here."

She shrugged stiffly. "Sore. My neck hurts."

And my heart has been shattered into a million pieces.

He crossed one black flight boot over the other. "Have they told you everything yet?"

"Like what?"

"Ah—" He pushed at the inside of his cheek with his tongue. "What do you remember?"

Her squadron mates burst past the partition, startling her with their rowdy energy. She used to think nothing of their noise and perpetual motion, but now she felt overwhelmed as they fired off one remark after another.

"We missed you, squirt."

"You'll do anything to sleep in."

"You look like shi—I mean doggy-doo."

"They give you them funny pills? The good stuff? Have any extra?"

Despite her heavy heart, she laughed. "It's good to see you again, guys."

Her wingman, Hojo, tossed a rumpled bouquet of flowers on the bed.

"Thanks." She gestured toward the beer can. "By the way, nice touch."

"I'll have your hides if you boys try that again." The medic stood by the partition, scowling, her fists propped on her wide hips. Pushing past the men, smirking and shaking her head, she yanked off the sticky tape holding the beer can. "And get your feet off the bed, Commander."

Sheepish, the skipper scooted up to a sitting position.

"So, Squirt," Hojo said, grinning at her, "I guess your number wasn't up."

"She doesn't remember," the skipper said.

"She doesn't? Oh, man, wait 'til you hear. A civilian helicopter picked you up. English dudes."

An English rescuer? What a sick coincidence.

"Ten minutes later, they crashed. Massive rotor failure. No one made it out alive, 'cept you and the pilot."

"He's okay, then?"

"He has a busted arm," the skipper replied. "Bumps, bruises, fractured vertebrae."

Suddenly her problems seemed insignificant. "His back? Is he paralyzed?"

The skipper shook his head. "They've done all the tests and he checked out okay."

Carly exhaled slowly. "Sounds like I got the better end of the deal."

"The Brit got the better deal if you ask me." Hojo grinned wolfishly.

The men guffawed.

Her cheeks grew hot. Uneasy, she eyed Commander Martinez. "What's the joke, Skipper?"

"You had hypothermia by the time he rescued you. When the chopper crashed, you were exposed to the cold all over again. You were pretty much out of it, so the Brit had to lift you into a life raft. Dead weight. No one knows how he did it with his injuries." His Adam's apple bobbed. "You guys were out there for hours before you got picked up."

"Bet he wished it was longer," said Brad, another squadron pal. "Because he stripped off all your clothes. His, too. Then he found a blanket and snuggled."

The blood drained from her face. She glanced from grinning face to face, mortified.

The skipper's dark brows drew together. "Okay, guys, enough." He balanced his elbows on his knees. "Carly, listen. As bashed up as that chopper pilot was, he thought of you first. He saved your life, squirt. Kept you alive with his body heat. He's a goddamned hero, if you ask me."

Her squadron mates echoed him with hearty enthusiasm.

Carly went rigid. It was worse than she'd thought. Not only was Andrew a fantasy, she'd conjured him while lying naked with a stranger. "Did I say anything? Did I do anything stupid?" To her horror, a tear made its way down her cheek. "This is so embarrassing."

The skipper jerked his thumb at the divider. "Guys, why don't you take off for awhile?"

Her squadron mates backed away, shaken. They had never seen her cry.

"I feel awful, squirt," Hojo said. "I'm really sorry we brought this up."

"You'll feel better if you see him," Brad urged. "He's a real nice guy—for a Brit." He forced a laugh. "You know, stiff upper lip and all."

Carly dropped her face into her hands.

When the men left, the skipper leaned toward her, his dark brown eyes searching hers. He'd been married for twenty years and had five daughters. Unlike the other men she worked with, he always understood when she was upset. "He's driving the medics crazy. He wants to see you, but he can't get out of bed, and the flight surgeon said not to disturb you with a phone call. The weather's cleared, so they're gonna airlift him out to a civilian hospital. Before you lose the chance, I'd go see the guy. I know he'd appreciate a few words of thanks."

Carly recoiled. "No way!"

"He saved your life. Don't discount that."

She bit her lip and sullenly played with the hem of the blanket.

"Okay," he said tiredly, rising to his feet. "Listen, you didn't do or say anything dumb. You were out cold, if that makes you feel any better."

It didn't. She stared straight ahead.

"He's not the kind of guy who'd embarrass you," he persisted.

Silence.

"Okay, I can see I'm not getting through right now. I'll drop by later."

When he disappeared behind the bulkhead, she twisted around and slammed her fist into the pillow.

303

* * *

"You're doing nothing but moping," the medic accused that afternoon. "They're not gonna put you back on flying status unless you perk up. Outside the sunshine's streaming. Finally. A sparkling Mediterranean day. I'd like to be sittin' on the Riviera, instead of this oversized tin can, wouldn't you?"

Carly stared at her burger and fries and aimlessly pushed the food around her plate.

"Aw, honey." She sat on the edge of the mattress. "Whatever it is, it can't be that bad."

Carly gave her a long look.

The big woman sighed. "Listen, why don't you visit that nice English fellow?"

"I don't think so."

"All the females on duty think he's adorable. But"—she sighed wistfully—"he's only interested in you."

Carly pinched the bridge of her nose. But her snub had no effect. The woman kept right on talking.

"He has a real title, lord or sir or something like that."

Carly dropped her hand. *"Sir?"*

She looked like she'd just scored a jackpot. "He's an aviation artist, too. Well known, they say. On top of that, he owns a helicopter company. They do salvage—treasure hunting. Isn't that exciting, honey? They were on their way home from a job when they heard your distress call."

The medic drummed her fingers on the bedside table. "What . . . is . . . his . . . name? Ah! Drew Spencer. *Lord* Drew Spencer. His father's a real English duke. Imagine that."

Carly choked. "What did you say his name was?"

"Drew. Drew Spencer."

Carly's heart slammed against her chest. She gulped a deep breath, then another. Hope sparked to life, despite her effort to remain detached. Before it grew into a fire and burned her, she'd better do something to extinguish it. And the only way she could do that was to prove to herself that Andrew wasn't in that other room.

Carly set aside her tray. "I'll go see him."

"Atta girl! You'll make his day."

She helped Carly out of bed and into an aqua hospital robe. Wobbly, Carly wrapped her fingers around the IV pole and used it for support.

"Good luck, honey," the woman said.

Carly groaned. "I'll need it."

She crept past the other beds, all empty. Then she shuffled along the bulkhead, past the pharmacy and the clinic. The walk down the short corridor separating the two areas was the longest of her life.

One of the medics saw her coming and motioned to a partition. "Go on in, Lieutenant," he said, grinning from ear to ear.

The wheels on her IV stand rudely squealed her arrival.

But the patient was sleeping.

She watched him warily. A head of disheveled, wavy chestnut-brown hair was half hidden beneath the sheet. He was lying on his back, one arm thrown carelessly over his head, the other immobilized in a cast. She began to pant. Her fingertips felt cold.

This was a bad idea. She'd better leave.

No, get it over with.

She craned her neck. He had dimples, the barest trace of whiskers above a sensual mouth. Her heart skidded to a stop.

He was the image of Andrew.

Her heart did a flip. She backed away, tripping over her IV stand and clumsily righting herself. The clattering of tubes and bottles and metal clips woke the man. Vivid blue eyes followed the sound. When he focused on her, his gaze softened.

In their depths was the soul of the man she loved.

"Andrew," she said on a soft breath.

Part of her wanted to panic, to flee and never return. The other part desperately wanted to believe, to cling to the plausibility of wishes-come-true, of destiny.

"Hello, love." He held his good arm toward her.

Her mouth tightened. "Impossible."

Unable to think, unable to speak, hoping against all hope, she inched toward him. His warm fingers closed over her left hand. After a moment of resistance, she let him open her clenched fist.

Gently, he said, "It seems the ring didn't make it back with us."

Her eyes misted with tears. "It *is* you."

He held open his arms, and she hurled herself into them. Then she remembered his injured back and eased her fall at the last minute. Impatient with her gentleness, he crushed her to his chest in a fierce embrace. Her IV stand tangled with his and crashed onto the bed, unplugging his heart monitor and setting off an alarm.

Medical staff rushed in. Andrew called over her head, "We'd like a few moments alone, if you don't mind." Then he pulled her down to his mouth.

And kissed her senseless.

Joy unfurled in her heart. Molding herself to him, she shuddered with the raw emotion in his fierce, passionate embrace. He clamped her head in one big hand and groaned. The sound vibrated in her chest.

When they moved apart, she narrowed her eyes. "You're from here, from now? The twenty-first century?

"Same as you. Except I couldn't recall my present life *then*. I do now . . . some of it, anyway." Winding her hair around his fingers, he said, "Memories are coming back bit by bit. The doctors said the rest will come in time."

Before she could reply, he coaxed her into another long and hungry kiss to assuage the nightmare they'd survived.

Breathless, Carly lifted her head. "Do you think we really knew each other in the past?"

"I know we did." Andrew dragged his fingertips over her lips. "We fell in love against the odds, but it ended in tragedy. I suppose it must have plucked an angel's heartstrings, because here we are. Against the odds again."

"A second chance," Carly whispered as the revelation sank in.

"We'll make it legal this time." He fingered the place where she'd worn the ring. "As soon as I can walk."

The thought hit her all at once. "You said you couldn't remember much. What if you're married?"

He pressed her hand to his lips. "My father has telephoned several times. He assures me there are no wives. There was a fiancée several years ago, but she's history."

She laughed with the odd sound of his modern speech.

"You'll be a duchess someday. Are you up to that? I know how you feel about aristocrats."

"Anything, Andrew. Anywhere. As long as I can be with you."

His dimples deepened. "I promised you forever, Carly."

Her lips caught his words. She shuddered with the passion in his kiss, losing herself in the magic, the miracle, the mystery of it all. Somehow, between life and death, between heaven and earth, she'd found a love transcending time itself.

Epilogue

Carly leaned forward as Chris Eaton, Spencer Aviation's chief pilot, rolled the helicopter into a bank for one last sweeping pass over the island.

"There he is!" Carly sang out, drawing the children close. "There's Daddy. See him? He's coming out of the water now."

The children wriggled out of their seat belts and scrambled onto her lap. Their soft, fragrant hair brushed Carly's cheek as the three of them pressed their faces to the Plexiglas.

Andrew had thrown off his scuba gear and was jogging toward the landing site, waving vigorously at the helicopter. He'd sounded positively triumphant when he'd telephoned her at dawn the day before.

Almost to the point of obsession, he'd been searching for the wreck of the *Phoenix* for years, determined to find it. Now, he hoped, he had.

"I see him now!" squealed five-year-old Amanda.

Clearly perturbed that his little sister—who was an entire year younger—had spotted his father first, Theo demanded, "Mandy, where?"

"There."

Theo's Spencer-blue eyes lit up. "I see him!"

Except for a sprinkling of freckles on their noses, all three of Carly and Andrew's children resembled their father. After their youngest, eighteen-month-old Rose, had been born, yet another replica of Andrew, Carly told her husband that his Spencer genes had employed bully tactics to remain dominant, marching over her DNA and clubbing her Callahan genes into submission.

"I bet Daddy missed you a whole lot," Carly said. " 'Cause we missed him, right?"

"Yes!" they chorused.

Carly deftly deflected their bony knees and elbows. Five months into her pregnancy, her stomach was still on the tender side. She hadn't been showing last month when Andrew headed to western Africa from his family's estate, where they were spending the summer. But she sure was now.

"Seen enough, Carly? Ready to go on in?" Chris asked from the front seat. With his prematurely gray hair and easy grin, Carly figured he had to be one of Cuddy Egan's descendants.

"Ready." She gave him a thumbs-up. She was on maternity leave from her part-time flying job in the Navy Reserve, and it felt great getting back in the air, even if it was only as a passenger.

She lifted Amanda off her lap and buckled her in. "You, too, Theo. Strap in."

Carly leaned back against the leather headrest as the helicopter descended. The brief flyby of the tropical island had brought back many memories. Memories that only she and Andrew shared—a past life and love that would forever remain their secret.

Gusts from the blades whirled up a cloud of sand. The humid air was turbulent, but the children giggled in delight. They seemed unaffected by two exhausting days of travel—an airline flight from Heathrow to Athens, a charter to an overnight in São Tomé, and then one of the company helicopters to the island.

With a solid thunk, they landed. The blades slowed with a gradually decreasing whine. Chris slid his sunglasses into his hair and proceeded to shut the helicopter down.

Carly tossed an assortment of toys, empty containers of apple juice, and a paperback into her voluminous straw bag. Slipping off her strappy sandals, she dropped them in, too. "Okay, kiddos. Let's go see Daddy."

The children burst past the door and sprinted toward Andrew. Sunlight flashed off their coltish limbs and their wavy chestnut-colored hair.

Wearing only a pair of baggy cutoff khakis and an enviable suntan, Andrew propped his fists on his hips and waited for the children to reach him.

"Daddy! Daddy!"

He scooped up Amanda and spun her around. "How are you, beautiful? I missed you!" Grabbing Theo on the second pass, Andrew hugged them close. "I missed you, too, little man."

Carly walked over the pebbly sand to her husband. The trades ruffled her shoulder-length layered hair, and her tomato-red sundress stretched deliciously tight across her expanding bosom. Granted, she and Andrew loved children, but graduating into a B-cup-size bra by the time Rose was born had Carly longing for at least a half dozen more.

The children scampered off to watch the divers working near the turquoise water. Andrew hurried toward her, a look of boyish excitement on his face. It looked as though he hadn't bothered to shave in days, and his hair, which had grown longer than he usually wore it, curled defiantly at the back of his neck. Except for the fine lines etched around his mouth and eyes, and a hint of gray at his temples, he looked exactly as he had on the *Phoenix*.

One hundred and eighty years ago.

Andrew tucked her into his embrace and kissed her. "Hello, love," he said in his deep, rich voice.

Carly twined her arms over his sun-warmed shoulders and inhaled deeply. "Missed you."

"It was a long trip," he said, smoothing one hand over her belly. "Feel all right?"

"A bit tired. São Tomé is beautiful."

"How's my baby Rose?"

"She's great. Your parents are busy spoiling her."

"The usual," he said.

Carly laughed. "Rosie misses you. We all did."

A tender brush of his lips over hers told her he'd felt the same. "We raised the chest yesterday," he said. "It's intact."

Her heart skipped a beat. "When can we open it?"

"Now." He took her by the hand, leading her to the water's edge, where Theo and Amanda were romping over the sand on a caffeine high fueled by the Cokes the divers had given them.

Grabbing them both by the waistbands of their shorts, Andrew plucked them off their feet. "Come on, you two. Treasure time."

They squealed and pedaled their legs faster. Andrew dumped them on a blanket spread over the cool, shady sand under a tarp. Yet unopened, the rusted chest was propped on a platform, surrounded by the various tools that had been used to unlock it.

Theo's eyes widened. "Is it really a treasure chest, Daddy?"

"It certainly is."

"Did a pirate man leave it here a long time ago?" asked Amanda. Popping her thumb back into her mouth, she contemplated her father with a gaze that seemed to hold wisdom far beyond her years.

Andrew winked at Carly. "Aye. Once, a pirate and his fair maiden left it here long ago."

Carly gave a soft laugh. He hadn't used that word in years.

Taking her hand in his, he asked, "Ready, love?"

Her heart thundered, and her skin felt flushed. "I'm so nervous. I think this is it."

"I do, too."

Bits of rust floated like snowflakes as he lifted the lid. Fingers twined, they leaned forward.

Carly gasped.

Andrew breathed words of astonishment.

Nestled in a nest of age-blackened gold coins was a sapphire the size of a small egg. And next to the jewel sat the most amazing thing of all. A Glock 26 handgun.

* * *

That evening, Carly crouched between Theo and Amanda in one of the two tents Andrew had erected on the beach. "Isn't this exciting? We're camping next to the lagoon. First thing in the morning, we'll go swimming."

Amanda's eyes were already closed, and Theo's were halfway there. Carly kissed them on their soft little mouths, then their silky heads. "Love you. If you need me or Daddy in the night, remember we're right next door."

They nodded drowsily. She tucked the quilt over their legs and backed out of the tent. In the moonlit darkness, she felt Andrew's arms come around her from behind.

She leaned into him. "Hi, sweetheart." He smelled faintly of beer and cigars, having shared briefly in the divers' celebration before returning to the tents.

Pressing his lips to the side of her throat, he caressed her stomach with his palms, so tenderly, the way he'd done when she'd carried Theo, Amanda, and Rose.

A meteorite arced across the indigo sky, trailing a frothy tail of stardust in its wake.

"A shooting star," they chorused in hushed voices.

"Make a wish," Andrew said.

Carly squeezed her eyes shut then said, "Your turn."

"I already have." He turned her to face him, holding her close. "The same one over and over."

The moon rose higher. The sea hissed with the ebbing tide as night birds flitted overhead. Cradling their unborn child between them, they clung to each other as the moment lingered, stretched out, the wheels of time grinding inexorably forward to the future they both welcomed.

"I love you," she whispered, goose bumps prickling her arms. "I've always loved you."

Andrew settled his mouth over hers, kissing her with an intoxicating mix of passion and familiarity, a longtime lover's kiss, a kiss that spoke of respect, of trust.

Of destiny.

Exhaling slowly, he drew back and fingered the top button of her dress. She smiled knowingly, then put her hand in his.

"Come, Aphrodite," he said, leading her toward the lagoon. "I want to see you in the moonlight."

Prince Of Thieves

Saranne Dawson

Lord Roderic Hode, the former Earl of Varley, is Maryana's king's sworn enemy and now leads a rogue band of thieves who steals from the rich and gives to the poor. But when she looks into Roderic's blazing eyes, she sees his passion for life, for his people, for her. Deep in the forest, he takes her to the peak of ecstasy and joins their souls with a desire sanctioned only by love. Torn between her heritage and a love that knows no bounds, Maryana will gladly renounce her people if only she can forever remain in the strong arms of her prince of thieves.

___52288-8 $5.50 US/$6.50 CAN

Dorchester Publishing Co., Inc.
P.O. Box 6640
Wayne, PA 19087-8640

Please add $1.75 for shipping and handling for the first book and $.50 for each book thereafter. NY, NYC, and PA residents, please add appropriate sales tax. No cash, stamps, or C.O.D.s. All orders shipped within 6 weeks via postal service book rate. Canadian orders require $2.00 extra postage and must be paid in U.S. dollars through a U.S. banking facility.

Name_____

Address_____

City_____ State_____ Zip_____

I have enclosed $_____ in payment for the checked book(s).

Payment <u>must</u> accompany all orders. ❑ Please send a free catalog.

DEBRA DIER

SHADOW OF THE STORM

He is her dashing childhood hero, the man to whom she will willingly surrender her innocence in a night of blazing ecstasy. But when Ian Tremayne cruelly abandons her after a bitter misunderstanding, Sabrina O'Neill vows to have revenge on the handsome Yankee. But the virile Tremayne is more than ready for the challenge. Together, they will enter a high-stakes game of deadly illusion and sizzling desire that will shatter Sabrina's well-crafted facade.

___4397-1 $5.99 US/$6.99 CAN

Masquerade

Katherine Deauxpille, Elaine Fox, Linda Jones, & Sharon Pisacreta

In the whirling decadence of Carnival, all forms of desire are unveiled. Amidst the crush of those attending the balls, filling the waterways, and traveling in the gondolas of post-Napoleonic Venice, nothing is unavailable—should one know where to look. Amongst the throngs are artists and seducers, nobles and thieves, and not all of them are what they appear. But in that frantic congress of people lurks something more than animal passion, something more than a paradise of the flesh. Love, should one seek it out, can be found within this shadowy communion of people—and as four beauties learn, all one need do is unmask it.

___4577-X $5.99 US/$6.99 CAN

She arrives at Darkstone Manor without friends or fortune, welcomed only by the hiss of the sea in the midnight hush. Lily Trehearne was born a lady, but now she resigns herself to a life of backbreaking drudgery, inescapable poverty and unquestioning obedience to the lord of the manor. Tormented and brooding, Devon Darkwell threatens Lily's safety almost as much as he thrills her senses. From the moment he catches her swimming nude in the moonlight, his compelling masculinity holds her spellbound. But each step he takes toward claiming her body brings him closer to learning the terrible secrets of her soul.

___4497-8 $5.99 US/$6.99 CAN

Dorchester Publishing Co., Inc.
P.O. Box 6640
Wayne, PA 19087-8640

Please add $1.75 for shipping and handling for the first book and $.50 for each book thereafter. NY, NYC, and PA residents, please add appropriate sales tax. No cash, stamps, or C.O.D.s. All orders shipped within 6 weeks via postal service book rate. Canadian orders require $2.00 extra postage and must be paid in U.S. dollars through a U.S. banking facility.

Name_____
Address_____
City_____ State_____ Zip_____
I have enclosed $_____ in payment for the checked book(s).
Payment <u>must</u> accompany all orders. ☐ Please send a free catalog.
    CHECK OUT OUR WEBSITE! www.dorchesterpub.com